PRAISE

A Very Bavarian Christmas

"If you're looking for a holiday-themed read that will warm your heart but also make you think, *A Very Bavarian Christmas* is the perfect pick! The storyline and characters draw you in from the get-go and you'll find yourself relating to their struggles, cheering for their victories, and being reminded that everyone needs grace and kindness, because we never know what it's been like to walk in their shoes."

—**CRYSTAL PAINE**, New York Times bestselling author, podcaster, and founder of MoneySavingMom.com

"Just in time to remind us all of the hope still waiting at the end of a hard year, comes Katie Reid's *A Very Bavarian Christmas*. Let her reluctant ornament decorator, Holly, remind you why home is a beacon, healing a gift, and how love, like hot chocolate and the meaning of Christmas, can warm you from the inside."

—**LISA-JO BAKER**, bestselling author of *Never Unfriended* and podcast co-host of Out of the Ordinary

"Bavarian Falls is the capital city of Christmas, and Holly Noel is its most reluctant citizen. Sparkling with humor and radiating with warmth, *A Very Bavarian Christmas* is a heartwarming tale in which Christmas spirit is abundant, but not without strings attached. Fans of Hallmark's 'Countdown to Christmas' will be swept away by this powerful journey of healing, reconciliation, and the second chances we must allow ourselves to take."

—**BETHANY TURNER**, award-winning author of *The Secret Life of Sarah Hollenbeck* and *Hadley Beckett's Next Dish*

"Author Katie Reid shares an honest, true-to-life story of love and loss, acceptance and forgiveness. As heartwarming as a cup of hot cocoa and filled with authentic, memorable characters, *A Very Bavarian Christmas* will transport you to a world where romance and real life, heartache and promise converge, all generously sprinkled with Christmas magic."

—**KATE BATTISTELLI**, author of *The God Dare*

"I am not exaggerating when I tell you I literally could not put this book down. I read it in one sitting. The plot took me right into the holiday-loving town. I could picture the scenes as if they were my favorite Hallmark Movie. Happy holiday feels filled my heart as the plot and excellent character development drew me right in."

—**JENNIFER HAND**,
Executive Director of Coming Alive Ministries

"*A Very Bavarian Christmas* is the perfect cozy read. As a perfectionist who fears failure and the dreaded 'not living up to my potential' more than anything, I identified so much with the main character of this book. And as a self-proclaimed holiday movie superfan, I adored the setting of a Christmas store in a Christmas town during the Christmas season! For anyone who struggles with a life that doesn't meet her hopes and expectations or anyone who loves sweet romantic comedies with a holiday twist, this book is a gift for every season!"

—**MARY CARVER**, host of The Couch podcast
and co-author of *Fake Snow & Real Faith*

"*A Very Bavarian Christmas* is everything you want in a story to delight you over the holidays! I hope this is the first of many novels from Katie Reid!"

—**AMBER LIA**, bestselling co-author of
Triggers and *Marriage Triggers*

A Very Bavarian Christmas

Katie M. Reid © 2020
A Very Bavarian Christmas
First edition, September 2020

Editing: Janyre Tromp
Cover Design & Illustration: Jami Amerine, sacredgroundstickyfloors.com
Interior Formatting: Melinda Martin, melindamartin.me
Author Photo: Molly Bea Photography

This is a work of fiction. Names, characters, businesses, places, events, locales, and incidents are either the products of the author's imagination or used in a fictitious manner. Any resemblance to actual persons, living or dead, or actual events is purely coincidental.

ISBN: 978-1-7354685-0-1 paperback
        978-1-7354685-1-8 epub
        978-1-7354685-2-5 hardback

A Very Bavarian Christmas

A NOVEL

KATIE M. REID

Dedication

To the real Holly Noel:

You are the Christmas Queen, my friend!
Grateful for you and your Holly-day cheer.

**To Bethany Turner, Robin Jones Gunn,
and Annie F. Downs:**

You played a big part in inspiring me to write this.

To the 30-something who can relate:
I see you and He does, too.

Contents

CHAPTER 1

Behold, She Will Be Called

HOLLY COULDN'T BELIEVE THIS WAS HER ACTUAL LIFE. She begrudgingly tied on her red apron and plastered on a forced, albeit festive, smile as she pushed through the swinging doors that led from the break room to the sprawling showroom of Neumann's, otherwise known as the mile-long Christmas store. Every hour, on the hour, a message rang throughout the store: "Willkommen to Neumann's—a mile of Christmas joy for every girl and boy. Whether you're one or a hundred and two, we've got something special just for you. Happy shopping!"

As she made her way to her work station Holly wondered why on earth she let her mother talk her into working at Neumann's. "It's the Most Wonderful Time of the Year" swelled from the rafters, but a "Bah humbug!" anthem retorted in Holly's heart.

This was never the plan.

Holly sighed and tightened her messy bun before taking her position behind the ornament personalization counter. Moving back to her hometown of Bavarian Falls to regroup as a thirty-something had not been part of Holly's life goals. But here she was, on her fifth day of work, applying her art degree to fragile ornaments.

"Hey, Holly. Ready to make someone's holiday brighter?" teased her co-worker, Andy.

"I'll do my darnedest, but truthfully, Christmas and I aren't the best pairing."

"Your secret is safe with me, Holly-girl," Andy assured her.

Although they hadn't known each other long, Andy reminded Holly of her older brother, Gabe, particularly because teasing was his preferred method of communication.

Holly flashed him a genuine smile as she picked up her clipboard with the printed spreadsheet of custom orders for the day.

"I don't understand why we can't use a computer instead of this clipboard."

"But that would be out of place now, wouldn't it?" chuckled Andy, gesturing to the time capsule of Christmas nostalgia that surrounded them—all 5,280 feet of it.

"Hulllllooo! Holly! I've got some good news to deliver," sang the store manager, Ms. Betty Jo Wilson.

If ever there was a woman who embodied Christmas cheer, she was it. With her rosy cheeks, blinking necklace that lit up brighter than Rudolph's nose and had a setting that could induce a seizure, and obnoxious socks that jingled as she walked, Betty Jo was one-of-a-kind.

"Special delivery for Miss Holly Noel! Your beloved name tag has arrived, and now you are...official. An official member of the Neumann family," cooed the store manager.

"Um...thanks, Betty Jo. Wow, my first *and* middle names, huh? I haven't been called by both names since...."

"I just couldn't resist. I mean...is there not a more perfect name for a Neumann's employee than Holly Noel? It made my day!"

"Why...um, thank you."

"Now there's one thing left to do before I'm off to straighten up Station 10."

Betty Jo explained in a very loud whisper, "The angel ornaments end up in such disarray after the preschool groups visit. Those little cherubs act like little devils sometimes."

At this heretical admission, Betty Jo snort-laughed before continuing, "But I digress...the matter at hand, or should I say, in my hand...is to present you with this name tag, Neumann's style."

Andy tried to muffle his laughter as Holly fought to maintain her composure.

"We have a tradition here, Miss Holly Noel, that you probably aren't aware of. When a new employee has been here for a week with satisfactory results, I pin on their name tag. Disclaimer, I've only poked two employees to the point of shedding blood."

Holly's eyes widened as Betty Jo repeated her snort-laugh.

"It was just a dab of blood, dear, that's all. I promise. I had you a tad worried, didn't I?"

One last snort-laugh for good measure.

"As I was saying, I will pin this name tag on your cute self as our theme music plays. Any employee who is within reasonable walking distance will join in singing, as we willkommen you to the Neumann's family."

Andy's knowing smile met Holly's "You knew about this?" glare, as Betty Jo busted out her walkie-talkie to let the higher-up know it was time to cue the music.

N is for Nativity…that celebrates the Savior's birth.
E is for Emmanuel…Christmas is with us every day.
U is for the Unique ways…we spread this yuletide cheer.
M is for…."

Betty Jo, Andy, and a handful of employees—who'd hustled over from their stations as soon as they heard the opening notes of the theme song—jubilantly sang their hearts out. Andy was loudest of all. After N-E-U-M-A-N-N-S was spelled out and the final chord resounded, Holly's official name tag was pinned on her apron by Betty Jo.

Spoiler alert: no blood shed.

After the loyal entourage dispersed, Holly and Andy turned their attention back to the custom orders. Holly bit the right side of her lip as she concentrated on her first ornament of the day. As she carefully rotated the silver ornament to add a flourish, the reflection of her name tag caught her eye and led her down memory lane.

"And behold, she shall be called, Holly Noel Brigham."

Holly wasn't there when her name was first declared, but every December 24th, when a birthday candle was added to her cake, Holly's beloved Grandpa Dale recounted the moment.

"Your mama was as big as a barn that Thanksgiving Day—ready to pop like a turkey." Grandpa paused the infamous account here to briefly brush Holly's cheek with his weathered hand.

"Now, where was I?"

"The turkey," offered Holly.

"Ah, yes…the turkey. You see, your mama and dad could not agree on a name for you. They tossed around names like Winter, Mary, Jeannette, and Isabella, but they couldn't come to a consensus for their second born, who was due around Jesus' birthday."

He continued, "Dinner was getting cold, and I had a hankering for some stuffing, so I interrupted their debate with my own idea for a name that would be worthy of my granddaughter."

Holly joined in, as she and Grandpa Dale repeated his well-worn words, first spoken over her mom's bulging belly circa 1987: "And behold, she shall be called, Holly Noel Brigham."

And the rest is history.

"Holly…Holly…." Andy waved his hands in front of his co-worker as she stared off in the direction of the Precious Moments display.

"Earth to Holly."

"Gosh, so sorry. What do you need? I mean, how can I help you?"

"Just because you have your official name tag now, Holly-girl, doesn't mean you are entitled to head off to La La Land. Look, here comes our favorite customer."

Holly tried to focus on the task before her—pleasing Mrs. Rasmussen. It was going to be a long day for sure.

"Are all four ornaments ready this time? I'm late for a

lunch date with Dr. Rasmussen, but I dashed over here after my hair appointment to make sure they are ready and perfecto for my little darlings."

Holly swallowed hard, unable to think of anything nice to say. Donna Rasmussen was one of Neumann's most frequent customers, but she was not the easiest to get along with. This much Holly knew, after only a week on the job. Donna's bright white teeth were contrasted by her out-of-season tan— the result of a recent Caribbean cruise with her husband. She flashed a wide smile in Andy's direction as she continued.

"You know, Henry doesn't understand why I get my darlings new ornaments every year, but since they already have monogrammed stockings, I don't see any reason why I shouldn't get them annual ornaments, too."

"These are definitely collectibles. They're imported from Italy. You have great taste, ma'am."

"Oh, Andy, always the charmer. Thanks for being on my side."

Holly carefully retrieved the delicate ornaments from behind the counter for Mrs. Rasmussen to inspect, *again*. Earlier in the week, Holly had been tasked with her first ornament personalization order. In the process, she had accidentally misspelled a few of Mrs. Rasmussen's grandchildren's names. Let's just say the blunder had not been well received. As badly as Holly felt, she couldn't help but wonder what the adult children of Dr. and Mrs. Rasmussen were like, since they'd been given such off-the-wall names by their parents.

"Let me take a closer look," said Donna, relying on her turquoise-rimmed bifocals to bring clarity to her thorough inspection.

"Hmmm, okay…let's see…."

Donna inspected each stroke of Holly's hand lettering on the fancy ornaments. The seconds seemed to crawl through molasses as Donna continued to evaluate Holly's handiwork.

Holly's jaw clenched. She was sure she had gotten it right this time. In fact, it had taken her a whole hour to redo Hildebrandt. Try hand lettering that on a glass ornament that is only four inches in diameter.

"Hmmm…okay…and…we're done!"

Holly hadn't realized she was holding her breath, until an exhale of relief emerged sharply.

"I am sorry to report that you two won't see me again until next week, because Holly, you've passed the test. I won't need you to redo any of them—these are just right for my little darlings."

Mrs. Rasmussen was satisfied. It was a Christmas miracle. Well, technically, it was a November 6th miracle, according to the life-sized countdown-to-Christmas calendar adjacent to Station 8.

"I promised Henry I wouldn't buy any more decorations—well, this week, anyway. I'll pay for these gems today, but I promise I'll be back on Monday for the new additions to my Christmas village. Can't wait to add to my collection. Henry turned his pool table over to me because my Christmas village keeps growing. I told him we might have to buy another pool table so my village can continue to expand."

Suddenly a distorted version of Robert Palmer's "Bad Case of Loving You" blared over the holiday carols, interrupting Donna's pool-table-turned-Christmas-village narrative. She fumbled to retrieve her phone before the ringtone reached the chorus.

"It's Henry," she hurriedly explained. "Gotta run to the checkout. I'm late!" Donna turned on a sugary greeting for her husband. "Hi, Hunky. I'm on my way! So sorry but I had to make a quick stop." She flashed her pearly whites as she whispered, "Can one of you carry the ornaments over to the checkout while I finish this call?"

"Sure thing." Andy volunteered as tribute, much to Holly's relief. He carefully put the lid on the box of fragile ornaments and made his way to the checkout, with Donna in tow.

"Yes, of course, I'll be there in ten...mwah!"

Before she and Andy were out of range, Donna called over her shoulder to Holly, "You know what, I'll take a picture of my darlings' faces when I present these beauties to them... then you'll understand why I can't resist spoiling them."

"Sounds good," Holly said with an obligatory wave. She added the German greeting for "bye" for good measure. "Auf Wiedersehen, Mrs. Rasmussen."

Whew. Glad that's over with. Now, back to the custom orders on my clipboard.

Ten minutes passed, and Andy still had not returned. Holly assumed Mrs. R. had convinced him to load her custom ornaments into her BMW, and maybe even serve as chauffeur to her lunch date with Hunky—err, Dr. Rasmussen.

Crash.

Jingle.

Clank.

Jingle.

Thud.

"Ugh."

Had the "ugh" been an octave higher, Holly might have suspected that Betty Jo had tripped over the wedding ornament display, due to the jingles and all. But no, it wasn't the manager that ruined Holly's concentration, causing her to turn a "J" into a "U" on her latest ornament project. The "ugh" originated from someone else.

This "someone else" was lean and towering, with a boyish face and trendy-rimmed glasses (that had 100% been ordered from a popular eyeglass website). Holly estimated he was in his mid-twenties. He was quite a spectacle, all legs and wedding ornaments, tangled in a clumsy contortion. He quickly stood up, his blushing cheeks matching his red Neumann's vest as he tried to reassemble the disrupted display.

Holly's frustration dissipated as she realized how embarrassed this guy was. She set down her now-ruined ornament and hurried over to help.

"Oh man, I'm, I'm really sorry about the racket…" he stammered, as he met Holly's brown eyes with his baby blues.

Holly diverted her attention to a stray ornament that had rolled out of reach—a result of the crash between the lanky human and the wedding display. She moved to retrieve it, when the tall glass of water himself grabbed her forearm.

"No, wait, please. You don't have to do that. I mean…I appreciate it and all. But you shouldn't have to clean up my mess."

Holly met his eager eyes again.

"I'm Frank," he announced as he untangled and stood to shake her hand.

"Frank from the Falls? That's unfortunate," Holly sucked in a breath, wishing she could pull the idiotic words back into her mouth that floated in the air between them. It wasn't the first time she found herself saying out loud what she should have kept to herself.

"I know, right?" Frank laughed freely at Holly's teasing comment. "I'm surprised we haven't met before. You must be new here?"

"Not new to Bavarian Falls—but new to Frank from the Falls."

Insert foot in mouth.

Frank crossed his arms in apparent amusement, as if settling into a front row seat to Holly's awkwardness.

"And new to working here. It's my first week, so, yeah, I got pinned today…I mean, uh, you know, got my official name tag." She didn't want to be rude, so she quickly shook his waiting hand.

"Holly Noel. Wow, looks who's talking—that's quite the perfect name for this place, now, isn't it?

"So I've been told," Holly offered, glancing back at her work station.

Where was Andy?

"Well, it's a pleasure to meet you," Frank said, bowing in a gesture of welcome.

"Uh, thanks. Hey, well, if you have this under control, I need to get back to work. I don't think the customer who was expecting 'Jeremiah' on an ornament will appreciate 'Ueremiah' instead."

"Huh?

"Never mind…nice to meet you, Frank." Holly turned on her heels faster than she could spell "Ueremiah."

She darted behind the counter and spotted Andy heading

her way.

"What took you so long?" Holly pressed.

"Don't ask."

"Ugh."

It was Frank again, giving a sheepish expression and shrug in Holly's and Andy's direction, after hearing a final *crunch* beneath his feet.

Holly blew a stray hair from her forehead as she began another ornament for J-e-r-e-m-i-a-h. The aptness of "Christmas in a Small Town" playing over the speakers as she worked was not lost on her.

No further run-ins with Betty Jo, Mrs. Rasmussen, or flailing Frank allowed Holly to complete sixteen hand-painted ornaments before five o'clock chimed inside the store. Finally, she was free from the arena of holiday hubbub…at least until Monday morning.

CHAPTER 2

Reality Check

A HARSH GUST OF WIND GREETED HOLLY AS THE automatic doors at the west exit opened. She pulled her fur-lined collar up around her neck to ward off the bite in the November air. The gray Midwestern sky matched her mood. She pulled out her car keys and walked swiftly to her blue Prius. The dent in its front bumper mirrored the dent in her bank account and her heart.

Once in the driver's seat, Holly rubbed her ice-cold hands together, willing the circulation to improve as she waited for her car to warm up. She decided against turning the radio on. Her ears needed a reprieve from the constant stream of Christmas music played at N-E-U-M-A-N-N-S.

In the biting silence, Holly let out a sigh, taking stock of her present situation.

Moving back to my hometown for the holidays...a seasonal

job that is all about the holiday that hurts my heart…and to top it off, I'm living at home again, at the ripe old age of thirty-two. Is this some sort of cliché Christmas movie?

Holly could almost picture it: Heartbroken single girl moves home to sort out her disappointing life. She and the most eligible bachelor in town—who predictably resembles a modern Mr. Darcy—run into each other in the baking section of the local grocery store. Within a week, heartbroken girl decides her hometown isn't so bad after all.

But there is one dilemma: How will she ever fund her dream of opening a bakery?

Holly's imagination fills in the solution: After a few minutes of mental anguish, a homing pigeon lands on said girl's windowsill with a tiny scroll affixed to its neck, tied with a scarlet thread and a sprig of holly for good measure. Girl unrolls the scroll (making sure the animal is not harmed in the process) and finds a familiar address written on it in tiny calligraphy. Girl throws on her down coat, but doesn't waste time zipping it. She arrives at her destination, lungs burning from the winter chill.

Could it be true?

Yes, of course! The charming movie bachelor has secretly funded her childhood dream of opening a bakery downtown in the brick building she had her eye on—because he's loaded, naturally.

Fast forward to the grand opening of the gifted bakery, aptly named Heart-Breakery—a nod to the owner's once bitter heart turned sweet.

Her most popular item on the menu? Bottomless break-up fro-yo (half the calories to ensure you don't have two things to cry about). If that's not sugary enough, the couple finally kisses outside the bakery, seconds before the closing credits roll. Cue the idyllic snowflakes that appear as a magical backdrop for their newfound, delicious (and predictable) love.

Bzzzt. Bzzzt.

An incoming text snapped Holly from her glucose-saturated holiday cynicism.

Have u escaped the snow globe yet?

Holly smiled, responding to her childhood friend, Elaine:

Just barely! Weird day. When are you done at the Inn?

In an hour. C U at 7, right?

Holly confirmed with a thumbs up before she began the drive home.

Exiting the parking lot, she sped past the Stille Nacht Sanctuary, trying to avoid eye contact with the gleaming monument.

Reason number 122.

Holly kept an unofficial tally of the reasons why she was fed up with Christmas. Silent Night just made the list. Often it's the last carol sung at Christmas Eve services, while drippy candle wax burns hands and the wonder of the season warms heart. But Silent Night held bittersweet memories for the beloved daughter of Carl Brigham.

✳ ✳ ✳

For the first seven years of her life, Holly loved the fact that her birthday was on Christmas Eve. Her parents made a point of picking out an extra special birthday gift for her to open after the Christmas Eve service. Grandpa Dale and Grandma Bea, her mother's parents, came over to help celebrate as they all enjoyed a lavish spread of appetizers, ranging from German cheeses with crackers, to Buckeye cookies, to shrimp cocktail.

Holly's older brother by three years teased her endlessly about her name and the date on which her birthday fell.

"You should have been born on October 31st, li'l sis, then you would've been guaranteed as much candy as you wanted, instead of just candy canes. And then we could call you Hollyween, instead of Holly Noel," guffawed Gabe.

"Ha, ha! Maybe you should have been born on Christmas, Gabe-riel, since you announced Jesus' birth to Mary all those years ago."

"Hardy, har, har...." Gabe rolled his eyes as he walked out of the living room.

While Grandma Bea helped Holly's mom put the finishing touches on her birthday cake and Grandpa Dale went to locate Gabe, Holly and her dad were left in the living room, accompanied by the colored lights on the piney-fresh tree. Dad insisted on getting a real Christmas tree each year, much to the protest of mom's allergies. Only a Balsam fir would do.

"It's quite a special night, isn't it, Holly Noel?

"Yeah, I guess. But I'm not sure I like my birthday being so close to Christmas anymore. Maybe Gabe is right. It'd be nice to have my birthday at a different time of year. Gabe gets presents in June, and a pool party, and he gets to go to Sugar Shock for ice cream, and…."

"Oh, sweet girl. *You* are the lucky one. Your birthday is closest to Jesus' birth. And He must have known you'd be exceptional at spreading Holly-day cheer, too," he chuckled at his corny pun.

"Oh, Dad." Holly's lip started quivering.

"What is it, honey? Did I upset you with my teasing?"

"It's not that. It's just…well, this year is different because you'll be gone soon. Y'know?"

"Yes, I know."

A salty tear escaped from her brown eyes, paired with an involuntary sniffle. Holly fiddled with the hem of her velvety dress, avoiding eye contact with her dad. She didn't know why she was crying. It wasn't like her father hadn't been deployed before, but this time was different somehow. He moved closer to her on the sofa, placing his hand on hers.

"I know it's hard that I'm leaving soon. But I'm asking you to be brave. Braver than ever before. It reminds me of something I read once: 'We each carry our own brand of courage… yours in the letting go, mine in the holding on.'"

The almost seven-year-old crinkled her nose, "Huh? Can you say that in English, please?"

Dad tried again. "Let's see. How about this? When you're brave, it helps me be strong."

"But I don't *feel* brave, Daddy. What if you don't come back?" More tears fell, temporarily staining her velvet dress.

Dad reached into his pocket to retrieve his white handkerchief.

Holly wadded the cloth in her hands, the softness as familiar and comfortable as her father's soothing voice. She didn't know anybody else who used a handkerchief, except for the fancy one, edged with scallops and dainty yellow flowers that Grandma Bea displayed in a shadow box in her guest room.

"There, there, sweet girl. You know what? It's no accident that you live on Kühn's Way. Kühn is a German word for brave. So the place where you live is the way of the brave."

"Okay, Dad...I'll try to remember that."

"That's my girl." He squeezed her shoulder before adding, "Just think, this time next year, your dear old dad should be back. Let's count on it, shall we?"

"How high do we have to count?" blinked Holly, absentmindedly wiping her sniffles with the back of her hand, instead of on Dad's handkerchief that was still in her lap.

She never did get an answer as to how high she should count. At that moment, an operatic version of "Happy Birthday" filled the room, as Grandma Bea and Mother rounded the corner with a cake shaped like her favorite Beanie Baby, Chilly the Polar Bear.

Her reluctant brother entered the room, followed by Grandpa Dale with camera in hand.

"Chilly!" cried Holly.

"Should I turn up the heat?" Dad asked.

Mother shook her head, pointing to the cake. Dad gave her a knowing smile. He added his rich baritone voice to the mix, "Happy birthday, dear Holly No-el. Happy birthday to you!"

Holly's tears were temporarily forgotten at the sight of her surprise Chilly Bear cake.

The vibrato of Grandma Bea's last note lingered in the air as Holly prepared to blow out all seven candles at once.

She inhaled deeply, puffing her chest with determination, before releasing a big puff of air (and a bit of accidental spit) on the glowing candles. Her birthday wish in 1994—besides wanting a June birthday like Gabe's—was to be brave, so that Daddy would be strong.

A lot of good being brave had done that little seven-year-old girl. The thirty-two-year-old version of her was back home shopping at Greta's Grocery for her mother just like she had in high school—of course, this time she carefully avoided the baking aisle, in case a Mr. Darcy look-alike was lurking nearby. She waited extra long to get the thick cut salami, even though she preferred the thin, in an effort to honor her mom's specifications. Holly's car stuttered to a stop in the driveway of 725 Kühn's Way, Bavarian Falls. 12253 is the zip code, if you plan on sending your annual "my family is better than yours" Christmas card.

Holly threw her keys on the counter and shoved her mom's very precise "check the list twice before you leave" grocery items into the fridge.

"Oh, there you are." Anna Brigham, outfitted in coordinating workout gear, entered the kitchen with a stack of clean kitchen towels in hand. She smiled at her daughter as she snuggled the pile into a basket in the cupboard, squaring the corner of the top towel before patting the stack as if the towels were obedient children. A characteristic Holly did not seem to embody. "Did you—"

"Yep. I got what you wanted: Roy's famous Rye bread, a pound of *thick cut* salami, and a slab of Spundekäs cheese. It's all there."

Anna opened the fridge to discreetly inspect the contents of the grocery bag.

"You could at least wait to check the bag until I leave the room…I'm not twelve anymore, you know. I think I can—"

"Oh dear," Anna interrupted. "I did say Rauchkäse cheese, not Spundekäs cheese. There really is a big difference between the two. Do you think you could go b—"

"You know what? I've had a looonnng day at the most Christmasy place on Earth and don't really feel like going back out."

"Really. If you're not going to do something right…."

Holly heard the mantra throughout her entire childhood. She couldn't do anything right.

"It's cheese, Mom. Cheese."

"Holly, don't you think you're overreacting a bit?"

"Overreacting?! Don't you think it's humiliating enough to be sleeping in my old bedroom, with my Beanie Babies hanging precariously in a hammock over my head, and now, my mom is voicemailing me a grocery list—instead of texting like a normal person—to pick up her precious items, and *then* she reminds me how incompetent I am for not getting her darn list right?!"

"Oh dear. I'm sorry." Holly's mom swiped at an imaginary stain on the countertop. "I…well…I don't want this to come across the wrong way, but is it your special time of the month? You know, I have some dark chocolate hidden away. You're welcome to it."

Holly spun without a word and stormed out of the room, not willing to give the one and only Anna Brigham the satisfaction of being right.

Holly slammed her bedroom door and slid down to the cornflower blue carpet. The carpet her Dad had splurged on because it reminded his daughter of the color of Anne of Green Gables' puff-sleeved dress in her favorite movie. Just like when Anne (with an "e") cracked her slate over Gilbert's head, Holly had acted like a child. She let her head rest against the wall. Something about being home brought out her once angsty teenage self.

The least she should have done was let her mom share her secret chocolate stash. Then she could go back to it the next time Holly and her mom fought…which seemed to happen all too often.

Holly knew she shouldn't let it get the best of her, but it was as if her mom was holding a victory flag above her own daughter's defeat. Not that her mom had wanted her to fail, but she was the one who had made it clear to Holly that her dreams of a community art space in the city needed a reality check—that they were "all wings and no roots" and "pie-in-the-sky instead of money in the bank."

As much as it pained her to admit it, her mom had been right. Holly's depleted bank account and deflated spirit were proof. Her temporary detour home felt more like a dead end.

Holly traced her finger on the carpet, wondering where

to find joy again, like the joy she had when she first moved to Chicago and everything felt like Christmas Eve used too—full of expectant hope and endless possibilities.

The booming chorus of "Rolling in the Deep" jolted Holly from her melancholy musing, reminding her she had plans for the evening.

Holly grabbed her phone from her back pocket. It was time to pull herself together and go live a little, even within the parameters of her hometown.

Thank goodness for Elaine. The reconnection with her childhood friend had been a silver lining over the last month. She also proved to be a reputable karaoke companion, so Holly could keep up her weekend tradition of singing her heart out to Whitney, Carrie, or Adele…whichever powerhouse fit her mood.

Holly untied her red apron and hung it on the back of her door, leaving her name tag safely pinned to it. She touched up her make-up, refreshed her messy bun, and headed for the door.

As she passed the den she slowed, spotting her dad sitting in his recliner, watching a game show.

"Hi, Dad." Holly put her arm on his shoulder.

He muted the TV and turned slowly toward her.

"Huh-hi. How was your day?" His once soothing voice had been exchanged for a stuttering, more laborious version after he returned from overseas.

"It was interesting, that's for sure. I'll have to tell you about it later. I'm headed over to meet Elaine at the Inn."

Later. That word was like a broken-in backpack for Holly, used in an effort to stuff down and transport her pain away from the present moment. *Later* was a diversion to avoid the messy unpacking of her big feelings.

Gone were the days when she and her dad conversed with ease. Now, lengthy conversations were too taxing on him. Holly kept things more surface level in an effort to be gentler on them both. But in actuality, the short, simplified exchanges felt like an abrasion of steel wool upon the heart of a daughter who missed her dad's relational availability.

One of her favorite things they used to do when Dad's body and mind were still strong and sound, was Saturday Workshop. Her mom packed them a sack lunch to enjoy while they tinkered in the garage. Dad blasted big band music from the stereo as he tackled fix-it projects at his work bench. Holly sat at her makeshift art station nearby, painting in time to the music. Carefree chatter and laughter splattered onto the drop cloth between them as father and daughter attended to their hobbies.

Presently, from the confines of his recliner, Holly's dad searched her eyes, as if trying to read her at a deeper level but not being able to break through.

The familiar ache burned in Holly's throat. Her dad's words surfaced again from the past: *Be brave, child. I need you to be brave.*

She swallowed hard.

"I love you, Holl-y-ee."

With a quick kiss on the cheek, Holly answered, "I love you too, Dad. More than you know."

Holly turned toward the door before the rebel tear escaped down her freshly done face and made itself known to her father. Even though she was the child and he was the parent, she resolved to be strong for him, as they once again repeated their awkward dance of letting go and holding on.

CHAPTER 3

Hometown Famous

THE EDELWEISS INN PARKING LOT WAS ALMOST FULL, AS expected. Unlike the Canada geese that fly south in winter, gaggles of tourists flock to Bavarian Falls when the weather turns colder. Holly was grateful to find a parking spot, even though it was near the back of the restaurant.

The *beep beep* of her car doors locking was followed by an audible stomach rumble. Holly was ready for the Inn's famous club sandwich.

She could have entered through the staff entrance like she had the Friday before, but Holly opted for the longer, more frigid walk around so she could take in the ornate beauty of the impressive front entrance. It was quite a sight with its snow-white pillars crowned with pine garland. Like a Thomas Kinkade painting, the golden glow from the chandeliers beckoned onlookers to come closer. But the showstopper was the tantalizing aroma of home-cooked cuisine wafting from the iconic restaurant.

So much history represented. So many meals served and guests welcomed. It was kind of like stepping into a different time and place, reminding Holly of her family's vacation to Mackinac Island when she was in middle school.

When the Brigham family had disembarked the ferry, Holly felt transported to another era as horse and carriages replaced horse engines on the island. The porch of the Grand Hotel was flooded with 1912 period attire, as tourists gathered for a Titanic-themed weekend.

Grandpa Dale and Grandma Bea were still living then, but Dad seemed an ocean away. Mom did her best to plan the perfect getaway, trying to schedule every minute of the trip, from the ferry arrival to the old-fashioned photos to lunch on the lawn in front of the hotel. But she stressed herself and her kids with her tendency to micromanage fun.

Thankfully Grandpa Dale served as a needed diversion. He made room for his fifteen-year-old grandson and twelve-year-old granddaughter to get into a healthy dose of mischief and experience the vacation of a lifetime. Gabe and Holly ate their weight in fudge samples, as they mooched from store to store.

The enchanting kaleidoscope of yesteryear afforded a temporary reprieve from the claustrophobic environment of home. Navigating puberty under the watchful eye of her overbearing mother while experiencing the emotional distance of her disabled dad was no picnic. The wind off the lake blew Holly's hair out of place as she jumped into the whimsical landscape with both sneakered feet. It was a needed escape from Holly's fractured childhood—from the tear that had taken place five years prior, when dad came home broken.

The memory of the Mackinac Island vacation ushered in the familiar yet unsettling blend of pain and joy so intermixed they couldn't be readily or neatly separated.

God, You've certainly "blessed me with big emotions," like Grandma Bea used to say. But right now, I could use a break from all the feelings. Is that too much to ask?

Determined to keep the heartache at bay, Holly steadied herself on the handrail as she made her way up the steps to the grand entrance of the Edelweiss Inn.

Couples were everywhere, cuddling in the brisk night as they waited for their names to be called. Holly felt invisible as she meandered her way through the crowd. The cozy displays of affection surrounding her were a stark contrast to her date-less reality. Her hometown continually reminded her of what she didn't have.

"Herzlich Willkommen bei uns! Kommen Sie rein!" Ms. Claire Weber, decked in a floor-length black dress with an eyelet collar, greeted Holly as she entered the Inn.

"Danke schön," Holly responded, thankful for Ms. Claire's welcoming countenance.

Prior to retirement, Ms. Claire had been the high school guidance counselor. When Holly's mom had been skeptical about Holly pursuing art as a career, Ms. Claire had encouraged her to stay the course. She had secured her place as advocate in Holly's book. Now Ms. Claire spent most evenings as head hostess at the Inn, as she wanted to stay busy and in touch with the heartbeat of the community. Instead of advising students on class schedules and career paths, she advised restaurant patrons on where to head—booth or table—regarding their next culinary experience.

"Grabbing a bite before the main event?" smiled Ms. Claire.

"Yes, ma'am."

Elaine, dressed in her Colonial-style uniform with puffed sleeves and white pinafore apron, her curls tucked into a braid, hurried over to where Ms. Claire and Holly were conversing.

"I've got to cash out two tables and then I'm outta here," explained Elaine.

"Sounds good, and so does the world-famous club sandwich," confessed Holly.

"You got that right!" agreed Elaine.

"I'd be happy to place that order now, to speed up your wait time," offered the hostess.

"Vielen Dank," curtsied Holly, as her stomach applauded with anticipation.

✳ ✳ ✳

After Elaine's shift was over and they'd devoured the twin club sandwiches, the two friends returned to Elaine's apartment so she could get ready for their night on the town.

"You sure you don't want to wear your stylish uniform for karaoke?" teased Holly.

"Yeah, right! This getup is no guy magnet, that's for sure!"

Elaine turned on the TV before retrieving her out-on-the-town outfit from her closet—form-fitting black leggings and a square-neck, long-sleeved top.

"I know it's still November, but whatcha think, green

or red?"

"Hmm. Which one makes you feel more alive?"

"You're a weird one, Brigham. I'm alive either way."

"Green then. 'Cause the Grinch likes it."

"Naturally," Elaine rolled her eyes with a smile. "Hope the fellas don't think my heart is missing in this one."

"Not a chance. Your heart is bigger than Texas."

"I'm going to take that as a compliment."

"Good!"

Holly laughed easily around Elaine. There were no pretenses. No need to impress or flatter. Quirks and hang-ups weren't deal breakers. Decades of friendship, even though there were some fits and starts through middle school, provided solid ground beneath their feet.

Elaine got ready in the bathroom while Holly picked up a design magazine from the pallet coffee table.

The smell of jasmine filtered from the bathroom as Elaine spruced up.

"What is this?" asked Holly, gesturing to the show on TV.

"This is one of my new favorite Christmas movies."

"Oh, brother. The plots in those are so cookie cutter. I bet I can tell you what happens before it ends."

"Doubt it! This one has a big twist," boasted Elaine.

"I'll bet. What's it called?" asked Holly.

"Pepper's Mint Twist."

"Come again?"

"Pepper's Mint Twist. The main girl, Pepper, is a broke college student, studying law in an effort to defend small businesses against corporate takeovers. She cares for an elderly woman as a side job. Between studying and her job, Pepper barely has a social life. Surprisingly, when the elderly woman passes away, she leaves her fortune, a.k.a. her 'mint,' to poor Pepper. But the twist is that in order for her to access the money, she has to date the woman's grandson for one month and give him a chance to win her heart. The grandson works for a big company that is trying to buy out a locally-owned bakery. Needless to say, sparks fly in the form of heated arguments. But near the end of their required dating period, different sparks fly as Pepper and the guy lock lips under the mistletoe after finding a way to move forward together and save the bakery."

"Please tell me the bakery is not called Heart-Breakery?" groaned Holly.

"Um, no. But clever."

"And there aren't any homing pigeons in the movie, are there?" asked Holly, wondering if she should give up her art ambitions to write formulaic screenplays instead.

"What are you talkin' about?"

"Never mind."

"This one's different, I'm tellin' ya. You should give it a chance."

"Elaine, you are the Christmas Queen, aren't you? It's amazing we're friends after all these years. It's not my favorite, ya know?"

"I know," Elaine said softly.

Holly realized she had been too much in her head for weeks. It was time to think about something other than her woes and wounds. It was time to cut loose and release her inner pop star downtown at Klingemann's Tavern. "How about some karaoke?!"

Elaine clicked off the movie and was out of her bedroom

before Holly could blink twice. The two friends flung on their winter coats and headed down the stairs. No car keys needed, since Elaine's loft apartment was located only a few blocks from Klingemann's Tavern: home to German beer, a colorful array of locals mixed with a handful of tourists, and, most importantly, Friday night karaoke.

"Elaine, please reassure me that I'm not living out the lyrics to a country song," pleaded Holly, her breath leaving white puffs in the air from the cold.

"Ha! You don't mean that one about the brown-eyed girl with big dreams who wanted to make it in the city, but eventually realizes that all she's ever wanted is found in her hometown, where she's famous in the eyes of the locals?"

"My worst fear is living a clichéd life that everyone can predict before I see it coming. Geez, is there really a song like that?"

"Sure is. It's called 'Hometown Famous,' and I just wrote it."

Holly's gloved hand punched Elaine's arm.

"Ouch!"

They rounded the corner and took in the festive display. No matter how many times Holly walked these streets, the twinkling lights overhead stirred up a childlike wonder within her. You'd have to be a Scrooge not to be moved by this picturesque town. Even though the holidays were a source of sadness for Holly, she was determined to put the ghosts of the past behind her—at least for tonight. Rousing music served as the soundtrack as bundled townies and tourists partook of the nightlife in Bavarian Falls. The iconic scene begged to be entered into and enjoyed.

"Holly, my friend, tonight isn't about what was or what may be. It's about your right-now life. Look around. You've got a friend who is glad you're here, great music to boost your mood, and who knows, an eligible bachelor may have broken up with his girlfriend, and is looking to meet a nice girl like you. Right now looks pretty good if you ask me."

"Oh Elaine, you're the best. Thank you."

"What are you waiting for?" Elaine returned a glove punch of her own before darting toward the castle style doors. "Let's go!"

Holly smiled, determined to let go of her Eeyore-like mindset, as she willingly followed Tigger into the tavern.

Klingemann's was hopping with local flavor, as Elaine beelined toward an open high-top table. Holly joined her, ready to welcome the weekend by taking in the savory flavors, malted smell, and the crescendo of rich voices.

Holly scanned the growing crowd for hometown regulars, wondering what kind of friendly competition she'd be up against tonight. Midway through her scan, she spotted someone who stood taller than most.

"Frank?" she whispered to herself.

Frank was surrounded by a co-ed group that seemed to be close to his age. Holly tried not to stare but a magnetic force radiated from Frank, demanding her attention. It wasn't a chemical reaction; more like curious anticipation of what might happen next.

What happened next was that Frank, mid-laugh, turned his head and made eye contact before Holly could look away.

Her center of gravity a bit off-kilter, Holly steadied herself on Elaine's shoulder, diverting her gaze from Frank—trying to play it cool even though her sweater felt unbearably stuffy all of a sudden.

"You okay?" asked Elaine.

Holly tried to channel untapped ventriloquist skills as she mouthed, "Guy from work is here. Trying to avoid a run-in."

As soon as the words were out of her mouth, Holly wondered if they were true. Was she trying to avoid Frank, or just avoid him noticing that she'd been watching him?

"I got your six," Elaine reassured her. "This is a place to escape work stressors, not face them."

Holly cautiously stole a glance in Mr. Magnetic's direction. He was still there, but no longer looking her way. It appeared he was telling a compelling account to his captive audience. He was definitely cute in his own sort of way. But he was also younger than her and lived in Bavarian Falls. He was everything she was trying to avoid—stuck in what her life had been a decade ago.

Holly shook off her conflicting feelings and pivoted her attention to her song selection for the evening.

"Oh look, there's Lena and Shayla!" Elaine waved them over.

Holly tried to be open-minded about their party of two becoming a party of four. It was just that one of the plus two headed their way was the size 2, Miss Congeniality-sashed local who ran a successful nonprofit. Lena Albrecht, with her oval face and almond-shaped eyes, was one of the nicest human beings ever, which made it hard to not like her. But next to her, Holly felt like a flop.

"Hey girls!" Shayla bear-hugged Elaine and Holly.

"Happening place, per usual," Lena courteously side-hugged the others.

"Who's ready for a sing off?" Elaine waggled her eyebrows, egging on the other three.

"Lena will have to pass tonight," teased Shayla. "She's got a big date with you-know-who."

Lena blushed, smoothing her sleek raven hair with her dainty palm.

Holly had no idea who you-know-who was. She and Lena hadn't exactly been hanging out much since Holly's walk of shame, from failed city conquest to hometown seasonal employment. But Holly guessed he was probably tall, dark-haired, and practically perfect in every way.

"Spill it, girl. Are you Facebook official?"

"Oh, Elaine. The only time I'm on social media is for work. I don't put much of my personal life out there."

Thankfully, Lena did not own a bakery or a breakery. But she had founded Music Keys, a nonprofit that existed to help individuals with disabilities unlock their potential through music therapy, lessons, and performances.

"Hey, Lena, speaking of social media. Did you see that young man wow the judges on Hidden Talent, with his soulful rendition of 'Music for Us All'?"

"Yes, I did. Wasn't it amazing? That's why we do what we do at Music Keys."

"It was incredible! We were a puddle of tears over at the Inn when Ms. Claire showed it to us."

Shayla's eyes lit up, turning toward Lena. "Speaking of Ms. Claire—"

The exchange was interrupted by a screech of feedback from a mic.

All eyes turned toward the owner of Klingemann's, Klaus (rhymes with house, not Claus).

"So sorry about that, folks. Just testing the system. About ready for your favorite pastime to get under way?"

"Woohoo!" hollered Holly. Her enthusiastic response wasn't just because karaoke was about to start, but because it was bringing an end to Miss Congeniality's glowing success report.

"Gimme five minutes, and we'll be good to go," nodded Klaus.

"Let's get a few apps before the fun starts, shall we?" asked Shayla as her piano-playing fingers tapped the menu in a syncopated rhythm.

"Girl, I can't eat one more thing. Holly and I each had the club at the Inn."

"I gotcha," Shayla smiled, knowingly. "That goodness will keep you full for a week."

"Remind me to tell you about the new initiative we're starting at the studio. It'd be great if you two would like to get involved," added Lena, as Shayla dragged her off to order their appetizers.

Stay down, Eeyore. Believe the best. You don't need to look like her or be like her. She's just a beautiful, successful hometown girl, that's all. Lena's not the enemy. You're good enough, smart enough, and doggone it...

The conclusion of Holly's Stuart Smalley-ish pep talk was cut short by the main event.

"Who's first, ladies?" bellowed Klaus.

Maybe it should have been Claus instead, because at the moment, Klaus was Santa incarnate, delivering cheer to

Holly—wrapped in a mic chord.

"Hit me with your best shot, Mr. K.!" volunteered Elaine.

"I've got next," shouted Holly.

"I'm after Holly," added Shayla, returning with a glass that sported a tiny umbrella.

"You fourth, Lena?" asked Elaine, looking around for Shayla's companion. "Hey, where'd she go?"

"She went to fetch Mr. Dreamy. He texted while we were in line. He thought they were meeting at the touristy bar. He hasn't lived here long. Rookie mistake," explained Shayla.

"Elaine, you're up!" boomed Klaus.

"Ladies, watch out! I'm going to show y'all up!"

The rest of the evening was filled with music, dancing, and fun.

Lena never resurfaced with her boyfriend, but Frank showed up and showed off with a charismatic version of ABBA's "Take a Chance on Me." Holly's mom was a big *Mamma Mia* fan, so Holly was very familiar with the song. The crowd ate up Frank's antics as he sang both the male and female vocals. He locked eyes with Holly several times during the song.

She reached for her beverage, trying to send the "I'm not as impressed as the rest of the crowd" message to him.

As the song ended, Frank shot a finger gun pose in Holly's direction, with a wink.

Gulp.

Shayla whistled over the applauding crowd, "Way to go, Frank! That's what I'm talking about!

"That was impressive," Elaine turned to Holly, "Did he wink at us? What a character!"

"Umm, yeah, something like that."

Holly wasn't sure what to make of Frank's playfulness, but karaoke at Klingemann's was just what the doctor had ordered. Although she wasn't sure what the next few months held, her right-now life, with a mic in hand, felt like a gift.

She unwrapped it with vigor, and a smashing rendition of "Stronger" by Kelly Clarkson.

CHAPTER 4

Released from Leavenworth

HOLLY HAD SPENT THE PAST DECADE OF HER LIFE TRY-
ing to get away from what had been, trying to start anew…
yet there was a comforting familiarity to the hard-backed pew
she occupied at the 9:30am service at St. Schäfer's Lutheran
Church. She had grown up in this congregation. Her physical
growth was marked, year after year, by the distance between
her dangling feet and the evergreen carpet, until that gap eventually closed. But her spiritual growth continued long past the
day her feet finally reached the floor.

The second Sunday of the month, St. Schäfer's hosted a
German service at 11:00am, which Holly attended on occasion. But today, she attended the traditional service with her
parents. The hymns "Now Thank We All Our God," and "We
Gather Together" aptly marked the coming Thanksgiving
holiday. The pipe organ rang out with depth and vibrato as

congregants sang the final line of the latter, "Thy name be ever praised! O Lord, make us free!"

Holly's silent prayer escaped to the rafters of the iconic sanctuary. *Dear God: Help my Dad experience freedom on this side of eternity.*

Her Dad's job in the military had been to usher in freedom for others, yet through an unexpected turn of events, his freedom has been taken in many ways. Well, that wasn't entirely true. Before his job involved preserving freedom, he transported military prisoners to Fort Leavenworth in Kansas—to remove freedom from those who had abused it.

Dad was eventually transferred from Leavenworth to work at the U.S. Army Department office located about half an hour from Bavarian Falls. So they moved back to the Falls, since the commute wasn't long and it was close to Mom's parents. It was a good thing, too. They'd needed her grandparents nearby when Holly's dad was deployed as part of the peace-keeping efforts in Bosnia.

They had said a tearful goodbye to him shortly after Christmas. Holly was freshly seven years old and Gabe was ten. Dad hugged her so tight she could barely breathe. She couldn't stop the tears, but she bit her lip so she wouldn't demand he stay. Grandpa Dale and Grandma Bea looked on as the family of four clung to one another. Dad's wisdom thumped around in Holly's mind as her tears splattered onto his boots: "The place where you live is called courage."

Dad came home almost a year later, but he wasn't the same. During a routine supply transport, he'd suffered a brain aneurysm.

Holly once overheard her mom talking to Grandma Bea

about the irony of Dad coming home wounded, not from combat, but from the time bomb that had been ticking inside his brain, unbeknownst to anyone, until its explosion. Dad had been treated overseas until he was stable enough to return home on medical discharge. He was fortunate to have made it through. Holly's dad was still loving, determined, and strong, but his speech was slow, his memories disjointed at times, and his mobility limited—as evidenced by the cane he used to stabilize himself, as he shuffled from his in-home hospital bed to the recliner. Sometimes his anger flared at seemingly small things—a closed door, the television volume being too low or too high, his cane not being where he thought it was. Instead of laughing and talking with her dad like she used to, Holly often tiptoed around him, never knowing when he might explode.

Since the year-end goodbye in 1995, Christmas marked the fault line between what life used to be like and what it was now like after Dad's aneurysm. Her mom attended to Dad like Florence Nightingale, making him as comfortable as possible, carting him to doctor's appointments and physical therapy sessions. A woman of her word, she lived out the vows she had promised Carl, under a weeping willow, in June of 1984. Anna tried to juggle her new responsibilities well, but her children fumbled to find their footing in the aftermath of the aneurysm earthquake.

Hollow footsteps on the church platform yanked Holly back to the present. "This morning's reading is from Philippians 4:6." Pastor Meyer opened his Bible and set it on the pulpit. "Please read along with me. 'Do not be anxious about anything, but in everything by prayer and supplication with thanksgiving let your requests be made known to God.'"

Nothing like having the Pastor's morning selection point out your painful navel gazing.

Holly had a few words with God, trying to let her request be made known. In many ways it had been easier to stay away from home. But she realized that she needed the Big Guy's help to face what she'd rather avoid.

God? Hey there. It's me, Holly. So, the thing is, I'm tired of feeling like I'm half here. I'm tired of living fragmented. It feels like a part of me is missing. I need a breakthrough. Will You help me out?

No answer floated down from the cathedral-style ceiling, but Holly felt a little better, and a tad bit braver as she resolved to not let her sadness have the final say.

After the service, the Brighams made their way into the fellowship hall for coffee. Many of the 11:00 attendees were there as well, rubbing shoulders with the early risers before they entered the sanctuary.

Holly was thankful for the coffee and the chance to delay the uncomfortable Sunday meal that would likely ensue, with her well-meaning but hovering mother and her disabled father. Holly couldn't wait until Gabe, his wife Monica, and their sweet daughter Claudia arrived in a few weeks to celebrate Thanksgiving. Although she knew Gabe would tease her endlessly about anything and everything, she would appreciate the parental attention not solely being on her.

Her mom was engaged in conversation with the pastor's wife while dad sat nearby, sipping his coffee. His longtime buddy, Walt, sat next to him, shooting the breeze about the latest sporting event.

"Sorry to interrupt, but I'm going to go pull the car around to the side entrance for you," announced Holly.

Carl Brigham smiled at his one and only daughter, and nodded.

"Can you let Chatty Cathy know?" she teased, pointing at her mother, who, from the sound of it, was knee-deep in a debate about what shade of paint would best match the new carpet in the fellowship hall.

"Ya-yew got it. We'll be up soon...*I, I think.*" Carl's eyes twinkled with a bit of mischief.

"Thanks, Dad." Holly headed toward the door that led to the parking lot.

"Oh, there you are, Holly!" called Ms. Claire, dressed in a plum-paisley blouse and tan slacks—quite the change from her traditional hostess uniform at Edelweiss Inn.

"Here I am." Holly smiled.

"I want to introduce you to my nephew, Nik Beckenbauer. I'm trying to make the rounds during fellowship hour to connect him with the younger crowd, so he feels more at home here."

At that moment, a dark-haired, steely-blue-eyed man put his arm around Ms. Claire, as a genuine smile made its way from his mouth to his eyes.

Holly, taken aback by the attractiveness of said nephew, managed to say, "Hi there, willkommen." She stretched out her hand, trying to appear calm, cool, and collected.

Nik responded with a firm handshake, "Good morning, Holly. Nice to meet you."

In that moment, the hot coffee cup in Holly's other hand misbehaved, splashing onto her Sunday best, Ms. Claire's tan slacks, and the carpet.

"Oh no! I'm so sorry, Ms. Claire," gushed Holly, suddenly aware she hadn't let go of Nik's hand through the spill.

"Let me help," Nik offered, releasing Holly's hand to retrieve napkins from a nearby table.

"Are you okay?" Holly asked Claire.

"Oh yes, I'm fine. Nothing that a little laundry magic can't fix."

"I'm afraid I didn't make a good first impression," Holly said sheepishly.

"More like a big splash," chortled Ms. Claire.

Her light-hearted response put Holly at ease.

Just then easy-on-the-eyes Nik returned with a handful of napkins.

He handed some of the them to Holly and his aunt for their coffee-stained clothes as he attended to the floor.

"Let me do that, it was my fault," insisted Holly.

That felt like déjà vu. Didn't Frank say something similar to me when I tried to help him clean up his ornament spill? Almost like Groundhog's Day, except new guy and slightly different circumstances.

"I got this, it's no problem. Besides, I think my committed handshake played into this mess, too." Nik smirked at Holly before returning his attention to the clean-up.

"Our hero," exclaimed Claire. "You know, he's such a help to me around the house, too. I keep trying to shoo him out, but he insists on completing my home repair list first."

Nik acted like he didn't hear his aunt's accolades.

Holly definitely heard the praise Ms. Claire was showering upon him, elevating him to knight-like status. She also noticed that said knight, in the pale blue Oxford shirt, was stooping down to clean up the spill at her feet. If only she had a pair of glass slippers, the scene would have been the stuff of fairy tales—minus the coffee stains on the new carpet.

"Thank you again, I—"

"I don't understand why they put carpet in here in the first place," clucked the pastor's wife, who had rushed over to help Nik.

"They thought long and hard about different flooring, but the noise decibel would have been much louder without carpet," explained Holly's mom, who had accompanied her at the scene of the spill.

Holly wanted to fade into the outdated wallpaper in the Fellowship Hall as the pastor's wife and her mom's banter brought more attention to her ungraceful introduction.

While the women engaged in their lively debate, they didn't seem to notice first-time attender, Nik, who stood up with a handful of hazelnut coffee-stained paper towels in his hand. Though Holly had just met him, Nik's blend of steadiness and mystery, in addition to his good looks, drew her in like an Arthur Hughes painting. She couldn't look away.

Something about Nik made Holly feel like she already knew him.

Bavarian Falls is not where you are going to stay. You're just passing through, remember? Move these thoughts along before this newly relocated man displaces your vision board.

The flooring debate continued, with a lament from Pastor Meyer's wife. "There are ways to soundproof, you know. In fact, Donna Rasmussen was telling me they did something like that over at Blessed Epiphany. But alas, I guess it's too late to change things now."

Ms. Claire, probably not wanting to be roped into the decorating committee's conversation, led Nik over to the trash cans as she mouthed to Holly, "Don't worry about it."

"Thank you," she whispered back.

Holly's mom, oblivious to her daughter's exchange, continued the spontaneous committee meeting near the damp carpet. "You're right, it's too late for a flooring change, but it's not too late to pick out just the right color for these walls. Now, as I was saying, I prefer the Ethereal White over the Nebulous White."

Anna Brigham had a knack for stating her opinion as fact.

"The Ethereal has a bit more of a tan tint than gray, I see what you mean."

Anna smiled, anticipating victory. She'd never been a fan of gray.

A brief pause in the rapid-fire conversation made room for Holly to interject. "I'll go pull the car around."

"Well, that is sweet of you. Are you okay? You usually linger at coffee hour."

"Ma-maybe she's just ha-ha-hungry. I am!" exclaimed Holly's dad, a little too loudly.

"I hear you, dear. Let's get you up and moving," agreed Anna before turning back to the pastor's wife. "Let's chat more this week so we can send the rest of the committee our paint color recommendation before Sunday."

"Sounds good. Chat soon."

"Now, Mr. Brigham, let's get you to your feet." Anna and Holly worked together to assist him.

Midway through Carl's slow shuffle to the door, relying

on his cane and his wife's arm to steady himself and with Holly leading the way, Nik rushed ahead of them to open the door.

"Thank you so much," gushed Anna.

"Always the gentleman," Lena joined him by the door, stating the obvious.

Lena knows Nik?

"Well, hi, Lena," Anna greeted. "How are you doing? I'm hearing great things about Music Keys. We're all so proud of you."

"Thank you, Mrs. Brigham. We're overwhelmed by the community's support. Oh, excuse my manners, have you met Nik?"

"Why, no, we haven't. Hi, Nik. Nice to meet you. I'm Anna Brigham and this is my husband, Carl." Nik shook her hand. When he went to shake Carl's hand, he wasn't sure which hand to reach for—the one steadied by the cane or by Anna's arm. Instead, he patted Carl's arm like a teammate would do to another after a successful play, but with more gentleness.

"Nice to meet you, Mr. and Mrs. Brigham."

"You too, Nik. Now, please, call us Anna and Carl."

"And this is our daughter, Hol—"

"So nice to meet you. Holly, was it?" Nik played along as if they hadn't yet met, offering a slightly less committed handshake than before. "Coffee?" he teased.

"Oh, no thank you, we're headed out," intercepted Anna.

"Nik is Claire Weber's nephew. He recently moved to town from out of state," Lena added.

"And Lena's boyfriend," Nik clarified, wrapping his arm around Lena's petite waist.

Glass slipper shattered before it was worn.

Holly tried to shield her disappointment. Miss Perfect had one-upped her…again.

"Well, that was fast," observed Anna, letting her thoughts spill out unfiltered and then instantly regretting her abruptness.

"Oh, no! Wow, I see how you could think that. See, I don't usually do this sort of thing. But let's just say that Nik and I connected long distance about six months ago. Then an unexpected turn of events allowed for him to move in with his aunt, so he relocated here, and…well, I'm not sad about it," smiled Lena as she looked up at Nik.

"That's great, Lena. Willkommen to Bavarian Falls, Nik. We're glad you're here. Now, I apologize, but we've got to scoot."

"I'm sorry I had to leave karaoke early," Lena tagged on before Holly walked through the arched doorway.

"That was my fault," Nik confessed. "I got mixed up and ended up at New Castle instead of Klingemann's."

"R-r-rookie move," teased Carl.

"Indeed, it was! Place was packed with out-of-towners, like me," laughed Nik.

"Well, it doesn't sound like you're an out-of-towner any-more, with Lena by your side," observed Anna.

"Enjoy your Sunday."

"We will, thanks Mrs. Brig—"

"Anna. Please, call me Anna."

"Ah, heck, I left my phone at the t-t-table. Darn it! Walt was sh-show—"

"Oh dear," Anna stated, as more of an apology about her husband's outburst than concern about his misplaced phone.

"I'll go get it while you make your way to the parking lot," announced Holly.

"Thank you, sweetie. And so nice to meet you, Nik."

Holly headed to retrieve her dad's phone and quickly located it under the table.

"I'm so glad I caught you before you left," called Ms. Claire.

"Oh, please let me know if you can't get that stain out. I'd be happy to replace your pants. Truly."

"I'm not worried about that at all, but I do want to tell you something about my nephew." She lowered her voice.

"Since you've recently relocated here too due to an unexpected turn of events, I thought you, more than anyone, would understand what Nik is feeling, and could be trusted with this sensitive information about him."

For a split second, Holly's imagination ran wild in a swirl of assumptions. Did he just receive a difficult medical diagnosis? No, he looked too healthy and strong for that. Maybe he was a part of a witness protection program? No, that sounded incredibly far-fetched. Maybe he….

"He was recently released."

"Oh, that's too bad. Where was he?"

"He was in Leavenworth," Claire stated emphatically.

Holly's eye widened and her jaw dropped. "Whoa."

"I know, it's shocking. Like I said, he doesn't want people to know. He's trying to start over with a clean slate. Pray for him as he starts over, please?"

"Uh, wow. I mean, yeah, Ms. Claire, I definitely will."

"Thank you, dear. I feel better knowing I've got a prayer partner to help share the load on this one. Nik is a great guy and it's just so upsetting that he got tangled up with the wrong sort of endeavor. I'm glad he's here now."

"Um, yeah, totally," fumbled Holly.

The wrong sort of endeavor? Being incarcerated in Leavenworth was not exactly the result of an endeavor, but a crime! Holly wondered if Pastor Meyer knew that a freshly released prisoner was freely roaming the church halls.

"Of course, he had some other motivations for moving to Bavarian Falls, besides li'l ole me living here," smiled Ms. Claire.

Other motivations indeed! Like robbing a bank perhaps? Or maybe something a little more discreet, like swindling money from unassuming folks at the assisted living facility? And why is Ms. Claire smiling? Holly thought Nik seemed like a nice guy... and wow, those steely blues weren't hard to look at. But maybe that's how he got away with whatever it was that landed him in Leavenworth—his good looks and firm handshake.

Flustered and more than a little bothered, Holly politely excused herself and darted to the parking lot.

Once she was buckled in, her mom dove right in. "Claire's nephew was quite the gentleman."

"You mean the criminal?" Holly's voice escalated.

"Holly! What are you talking about?"

"Oh man, Ms. Claire, probably didn't tell you, did she? Promise me you won't tell any of the other busybodies."

"Holly, watch your mouth."

"What?"

"How about you speak a little kinder about my friends?"

"Fine. Listen…keep this between you and Dad, but Ms. Claire just told me that Nik was recently released from prison."

"That can't be right! Nik was a delight."

"That's probably his tactic, Mom. Charm his way into the hearts of unassuming hometown residents, and *bam*! Your TV is missing…or your life savings!"

"Now, Holly."

"He was in Leavenworth."

Her dad's eyes flickered at the mention of the familiar place where he used to transport military prisoners.

"His build and manners should have tipped me off that he was military. But prison? Carl, what do you think he did to land himself in Leavenworth?"

"Could b-be a na-na-number of things. Are you sure, Holly-ee?"

"Have you known Ms. Claire to be a liar?" challenged Holly.

"Heavens, no," replied Mom.

"Let's get out of here, shall we? I'm starved. And I'd rather not wait around to see the con again."

"Does Lena know?" pressed her mom.

"I can't imagine she does. I mean, why would she willingly date a criminal? Unless she's in on it with him. But that can't be right. Lena's squeaky clean."

"Wouldn't Claire warn her, though?" demanded Anna.

"I'd think so…except when Lena puts her mind to something, there's no stopping her."

CHAPTER 5

Reason 123

BESIDES THE STRANGE ENCOUNTER WITH THE CRIMINAL at church, the rest of the weekend proved uneventful. The bank wasn't open on Sunday, so no robbery to report—yet.

On Monday morning Holly was back at Christmas Wonderland, red apron, name tag, and messy bun in place.

"Well, hello, Sunshine. Ready to roll?" Andy presented his signature snicker before presenting Holly with an ooey, gooey cinnamon roll from Neumann's own Stocking Stuffers' Eatery.

"Ha! Nice Dad-joke. I see what you did there…roll and roll."

"You got me!"

"How was your weekend?" Holly deflected so she wouldn't be tempted to break her word and disclose about Ms. Claire's scandalous nephew. She was determined to keep her lips sealed and prove herself more mature than her mother's friends.

"It was fantastic! I had Oliver this weekend. River isn't frozen yet so we couldn't ice fish. But we took a road trip to the city to watch the Snow Birds play. My ex-wife's boyfriend, Bill, offered us the hockey tickets last minute, because he couldn't go. Normally I wouldn't give him the pleasure of one-upping me, but they were Birds tickets."

"Lucky! Don't blame you a bit. Did Oliver love it?"

"You know it. He talked nonstop and convinced me to spend an arm and a leg for one of those souvenir cups. I swore him to secrecy so he wouldn't tell his mom it'd been filled with enough soda to fill the Danfield River twice over."

"What a special memory."

"It was memorable, alright. We had to stop about fifteen times on the way home for him to use the bathroom after all that liquid sugar."

"I'll bet!"

"You know the crazy thing? Oliver tried to convince me to let him pee in the souvenir cup instead of stopping to use the bathroom. He said that Bill told him that when he was growing up, his mom would let him pee in an empty juice container that she kept in the car so she didn't have to stop so much."

"That's disgusting."

"Right?! Wouldn't want to confuse the pee jar for lemonade."

"Gross," shuddered Holly.

They heard the jingle jangle of Betty Jo's Christmas socks just before she magically appeared in front of the ornament customization station.

"How are my favorite Station 8 employees?" sang the manager.

"Thirsty," offered Holly.

Andy tried to restrain his laughter.

"Well, you know, you can get a complimentary beverage at Stocking Stuffers'. The hot cocoa is divine."

"Thanks, I'll keep that in mind. But right now, I need to get to these orders or I'll never finish on time."

"You're doing great work, Holly Noel. Mrs. Rasmussen made a point of telling me that on Friday—and compliments don't usually free fall from her lips."

"Now, Andy, will you show Holly how to curl the ribbons to our standards today, please?"

"You got it, ma'am."

And with that, the jingles headed off to another section.

"There are ribbon standards?" whispered Holly.

"But of course. Don't worry, you'll get the hang of it."

"Reason 123."

"What was that?" asked Andy.

"Oh nothing, I'm just counting the reasons why I'm not a fan of Christmas."

"Hey watch it, you don't want the boss man or Betty Jo overhearing that. It's pretty much blasphemy around here not to adore Christmas."

"Naturally."

"Now, let's get your ribbon curling tutorial underway."

Holly swallowed, trying not to let Andy see her shaking fingers.

Truth be told, this wasn't her first ribbon tutorial. Her inaugural lesson had taken place right after her Norman Rockwell childhood was overshadowed by a Pablo Picasso abstract.

Dad had been transported home a few days after Thanksgiving in 1996. After his arrival, Grandpa Dale had taken Gabe bowling and Grandma Bea had picked up Holly for some early Christmas shopping. They wanted to keep their grandchildren busy while their daughter tended to their brain-injured son-in-law. They did their best to be strong for the Brigham children. Grandma Bea kept wiping her eyes when she thought Holly wasn't looking.

She helped Holly pick out a holiday coffee mug for mom, the latest Hootie & the Blowfish album for Gabe, and a large print Tom Clancy novel for dad. Afterwards they went back home to Grandma's house to wrap the presents.

All the shiny paper and Christmas lights would normally ensure Holly was in the holiday mood. But the lump in her throat and ache in her tummy felt like she'd swallowed the holly instead of placing the prickly leaves on the mantle. She was glad her dad was home, but sad about the circumstances that had brought him back. She was told that something bad happened to his brain and he was trying to get better. Daddy looked the same except for the wormlike scar on his head. But he didn't act the same. He seemed far away. Holly hoped he'd be all better by Christmas, and that he'd like the book she was wrapping.

Once upon a time, Grandma Bea had worked at a fancy department store, so she took great care in showing Holly how to carefully wrap each package. The apple didn't fall too far from the tree between Holly's grandma and her daughter, as there was a right way to wrap packages. Holly thought it was silly to spend so much time measuring and fussing over the wrapping paper, when the gifts would be opened so quickly.

Well, except for Dad's present. Maybe she should put his in a bag instead, in case he had trouble managing the tape and wrapping paper.

"Here's how you make the curliest ribbons on this side of the Mississippi. Watch carefully."

Holly closely observed as Grandma Bea worked her magic. Long pieces of shiny crimson ribbon became a perfectly formed nest of festive curls.

"Please hand me the tape."

After Grandma Bea's impressive demonstration, it was Holly's turn.

"Be careful. I don't want you to cut yourself with the scissors."

Holly crinkled her nose and tightened her bottom lip as she concentrated on the task. She tried to emulate Grandma's technique with the shiny ribbon, but Holly's best attempt resulted in uneven curls.

"This looks terrible." Holly hurled the ribbons in the direction of the wicker wastebasket.

"Don't give up. Keep trying, and before you know it, you'll be making ribbons so curly that even Shirley Temple will be jealous."

Holly didn't just want to give up the ribbon curling—she wanted to give up her new normal, with a disabled dad and preoccupied mom. She wanted to return to family laughter around the dinner table and watching the Lions play football on Thanksgiving Day. This year, instead of watching the game, Grandpa Dale had taken Gabe and Holly to the community Thanksgiving meal hosted in St. Schäfer's fellowship hall, while Grandma Bea and her mom readied the Brigham home for Carl's arrival.

The previous day, a hospital bed had been delivered to 725 Kühn's Way. Since her dad was experiencing headaches and compromised mobility, the hospital bed would allow him to sleep in a slightly elevated position and would make it easier for him to get out of bed.

Instead of slaving in the kitchen over turkey and dressing or joining the community church dinner, Holly's mom and grandma rearranged the home so there would be a clear path for her dad to walk.

The meal at St. Schäfer's was designed to serve anyone who didn't have family nearby. Grandpa Dale had plenty of friends to talk with, but Gabe and Holly stuck out among the tables filled with seasoned attendees. The fragrance of sage and thyme wafted through the air, but it didn't sit well with Holly's upset stomach. She picked at her food. After two refills of bright red fruit punch, Gabe ripped tiny parts from his Styrofoam cup until there was nothing left but a pile of broken pieces.

"You gonna eat that?" Andy interrupted Holly's flashback as he pointed to the untouched cinnamon roll.

"Definitely. I'll eat while you teach?" bargained Holly.

Andy flashed a mischievous smile. "Confession time." He looked around to make sure Betty Jo hadn't returned unexpectedly. "I'm terrible at the ribbon thing. So I convinced Teresa over at Station 3 to do them for me."

"You're awful! Poor Teresa." Holly closed her eyes as she bit into the tantalizing treat.

"Hey, don't feel too bad for her. We arranged a trade. Teresa curls my ribbons and I warm up her car about ten minutes before she leaves work. That way she doesn't have to get into a cold vehicle."

Holly's eye flew open as she swallowed quickly. "What century are we living in? The dark ages? Where men can't curl ribbons and women are too fragile for winter?"

"Hey, watch it! For starters, I tried to curl the ribbons to standard, but my sausage thumbs don't allow for it. And before you jump to conclusions, you should probably know that Teresa struggles with rheumatoid arthritis and the cold aggravates her symptoms."

"Insert foot. Although not until I finish this pastry. But seriously, I feel terrible. I had no idea." Holly wiped her sticky fingers on a Neumann's branded napkin.

"I know."

"Isn't Teresa around your age?"

"Yes, early forties. Only a few years younger than me," he explained.

"That must be difficult. Does the ribbon curling trigger her arthritis too?" Holly asked gingerly.

"She assured me it didn't."

"Well, you're in luck. My Grandma Bea was a ribbon curling professional, so I think I can manage. I'll go double check my work with Teresa though, just to be sure."

"Hey, I'll come with you," offered Andy, a little too eagerly.

"Oh, I see what's going on here."

"What do you mean, Holly girl?"

"You know, Andy, I'm only a dozen years younger than you…that hardly makes me a girl."

"Well, Holly lady just doesn't have the same ring as Holly

girl, now, does it?"

"Oh, brother."

"Shall we?"

"As fun as it would be to have a field trip to Teresa's station, someone has to stay here in case customers arrive, right?"

Andy tried to camouflage his disappointment—unsuccessfully.

"How about this? I'll send you over with the curled ribbon, and you can have your lady friend check my work. If it's not up to par, you can negotiate some other deal with her. Maybe a dinner date this weekend?" teased Holly.

"I don't know about that, but I'll take one for the team and go solo to the field trip."

"Very generous of you," laughed Holly.

After serving several customers and no sight of Andy returning, Holly retrieved her clipboard with the day's custom orders.

"I'm back!"

Holly spun around, startled by Mrs. Rasmussen.

"Hello! How can I help you today?"

"I'm actually here for the big reveal of the latest installments to the Christmas village. But I wanted to swing by to show you a picture of my darlings. You worked so hard on their ornaments, so I wanted you to see just how adorable they are."

Mrs. Rasmussen unlocked her shiny smart phone and rapidly retrieved the picture of her darlings. Holly fully expected to see Hildebrandt, Bo-Bo the Third, Elora, and Huffy-Jack decked out in their Sunday best, the boys in bow ties and the girls in smocked dresses, posed in front of an enormous fireplace. But instead, she saw a picture of four fancy dogs decked in Christmas hats, posed in front of a massive white brick fireplace with monogrammed silk stockings hanging from the mantle behind them.

"Excuse me, Mrs. Rasmussen, but where are your grandchildren?"

"My grandchildren? Wait, do you know something I don't?" The color drained from Donna's very tan face.

"I don't think so. Is this the wrong picture?'

"Nope. These *are* my little darlings. My doggies. I can't wait to give them the ornaments you made them."

Holly was speechless.

"I do have to keep an eye on Huffy-Jack. He tried to eat last year's ornament. It was probably my fault, because I picked out dog bone ornaments last year."

Just then Andy returned.

"Hi there, Mrs. Rasmussen. Whatcha got there?"

"Just showing Holly a picture of my darlings."

"How is Hilde doing? Man, she's a pretty breed. Think you'll enter her into the show this year?"

"I just might. It depends on whether she can keep the weight on. I've been hand feeding her, just to make sure she gets it all down."

Holly still had no words to offer and no bone to throw the eccentric dentist's wife. Andy didn't miss a beat.

"Well, I'm sure she'll be good as new in no time."

"Thank you."

"Are you headed over to the big reveal of the new Christmas village pieces?

"Indeed! I'm going to go chat with Betty Jo first and then

I'll head over. Ba-bye."

"Bye," Holly managed.

"Her little darlings are dogs?!" Holly whispered in amazement.

"You didn't know?" chuckled Andy.

"How would I know? Who gets hand-painted glass ornaments for their pets?"

"Mrs. R., of course."

"But of course."

Andy greeted a new customer while Holly returned to her checklist. About five minutes into her set-up, she was interrupted. It was going to be a long day.

"How is my favorite Station 8 employee?" asked Frank.

He stood before Holly with a goofy grin, holding a box stamped, "Fragile."

"Hi, Frank."

"These are for you and Andy. Don't worry, no leg lamp inside this 'fra-gee-lay' box."

Holly resisted an eye roll at his reference to The Christmas Story movie. "What a relief!"

"But it does contain new customizable ornaments. Can I put them on the shelf for you?"

"That'd be great, thanks."

"Oh, the pleasure is all mine." He waggled his eyebrows and leaned across her worktable.

Uh-oh. Warning, warning.

Holly blushed, trying to avoid contact with overeager Frank. He shelved the ornaments in the prep room before returning to Holly's work counter.

"So I hear there's a great new band coming into town this

weekend."

"Oh yeah? Hadn't heard." Holly tried her best to keep her tone steady and casual.

"I realize you don't know me from Adam, but um, what do ya say about checking it out with me?"

Holly had never been good at masking her emotions, and Frank's inquiry induced feelings of watercolors trying to mix with oil-based paint. The thought of dating a hometown boy went against her plans to get out of Dodge after the holidays. But Frank made her laugh, and if anyone could use a few laughs, it was Holly.

"Huh, well, gosh…" sputtered Holly, struggling to offer a burnished response.

"Oh, sorry, do you already have plans?"

"Not exactly, it's just that…"

"Stupid me, you probably have a boyfriend, don't you?"

"No—definitely not." Holly scrambled for a response that might put some space between them. "But um, my friend Elaine and I usually hang on the weekends." It was technically true and would buy her some time to figure out how she felt about Frank and boyfriend in the same sentence.

"Oh cool. Elaine Lewis, who was with you at karaoke, right? She can totally come with us."

Come with? As in a third wheel or just as friends or… "Hey, how do you know her last name?"

"This *is* the town where almost everyone knows your name. Elaine and I played on the same team a handful of times during pick-up basketball at the community center."

"She never mentioned that."

Elaine and I are going to dish about this later and she can tell me what to do.

"Why don't you ask her? It'd be fun. Maybe Andy wants to come too?"

Now Holly was entirely confused. Did Frank want to go on a date or invite the entire store to the concert?

"Oh hey, Frank. How are you, man?"

"Doing good. I'll be even better if you join Holly, her friend, and me for the concert downtown on Saturday."

"I wish I could, but I'm already booked."

"Too bad for you. My Grandad can get us front row seats."

"Oh man, maybe next time. Keep me posted."

"Will do."

"So, how 'bout I pick you and Elaine up at 7:00 on Saturday? Just need your address."

"You know, Frank. I don't..."

"Holly, you should go," prodded Andy.

Holly paused for a beat to collect her thoughts, like she did before attempting her first stroke on a canvas. She didn't want to lead Frank on, but maybe he was just looking for friends to hang out with. As Frank and Andy waited for her response, she felt like a piece of plastic fruit on display, ready to be sketched by curious onlookers.

Make a decision already. It's not a marriage proposal, just a casual outing with a coworker. Stop overthinking it!

"Look, I'm sorry. I shouldn't have been so direct. It's just that I thought you'd enjoy some weekend fun in the 'ole town. And who better to take you than Frank from the Falls?" He offered a smile that was equal parts silly and endearing.

"Well, I'd need to check with Elaine."

"Of course. Just swing by my office on Wednesday and

let me know what you decide. Really no pressure, but think about it."

"Will do," resolved Holly.

And with that Frank exited, this time without a crash or jingle.

Holly turned to confront her coworker. "Thanks for nothing. I thought you had my back."

"Frank's a great guy."

"Wait—office? Frank has an office?"

"You don't know, do you?" Andy asked, looking rather amused.

"Spill it!"

"I'll give you three guesses."

"Oh, come on, we've got work to do. I don't have time for games."

"It'll be fun. Promise."

"All right. Let's see…Frank is an oversized elf from the North Pole who's here to reconnect with his biological father."

"Seriously. His name is Frank, remember, not Buddy the Elf."

"There's not a sequel yet?" joked Holly, referring to one of the only Christmas movies she didn't mind.

"You have two guesses left."

"Hey, not fair," protested Holly.

"You snooze you lose, princess."

"Let's see. Frank is a local college student who is interning for the head honcho, but his secret plan is to take over this holiday empire one day."

"Nope. But you're getting warmer."

"Oh, I've got it! Frank is actually the boss and he's gone

undercover to make sure we're all doing our jobs. Hey, maybe he'll agree to be an investor in my collective art space if I tell him about it at the concert."

"I can assure you, he's not the boss."

"Shoot."

"But he *is* the boss's grandson. And he just may run the family business one day. For now, he's in charge of purchasing. Tomorrow, the moon."

"You're kidding me. Frank is a Neumann?"

"Nope, he's a Walker. His mom was a Neumann before she married Drew Walker."

"The meteorologist?"

"Yup, The Weather with Walker on Channel 5."

Just then Miss Congeniality walked by, spotting Holly.

"We'll have to continue this small town gossip later," said Holly quickly and carefully, trying her lackluster ventriloquist skills again, in case Lena overheard.

"Oh hi, Holly."

"Hi, Lena."

Play it cool. Don't let her know that you know she's dating an ex-felon. But does she know? How could she not?

Holly tried to recover. "Can I help you with something?"

"No, thanks. I have a meeting upstairs in a few minutes, but was just looking around since I'm early."

Holly didn't have the courage to press about the meeting.

Lena continued. "Hey, since karaoke didn't pan out, we'll have to try a night out again sometime. It'd be good for Nik to get his mind off his previous residence. He relocated recently from out of state." Lena looked around before quietly adding, "Let's just say it wasn't an ideal situation."

You can say that again. Being locked up for a crime is not at all ideal.

"Yeah, well, keep me posted on your plans," managed Holly, trying to keep things as normal as possible.

"Our plans?" Lena's brow furrowed.

"About a night out?"

"Oh yes, that," chirped Lena nervously. "I'm a little busy lately…."

Holly glanced down at the order sheet on her clipboard as if it were a script that would cue her next line.

Then Lena added, "Oh! I know, there is something you could help me with. Maybe you could volunteer with this new program we're doing at work. I think you'll like it. It'd be easier to show you than tell you about it. Why don't you stop by sometime this week after work around 6, and you can see it in action?"

"Yeah, maybe."

"Great! Hey before I go, would you mind wrapping this for me?"

Lena laid a singing angel ornament on the counter. "It's for Chase. You'll get to meet him when you stop by Music Keys. And can you put one of those curly bows on top?"

Reason 123.

CHAPTER 6

Code Rudolph

"I THINK IT'D BE FUN," ELAINE SAID TO HOLLY REGARDing Frank's concert invitation.

"You sure?"

"Oh, come on, Frank's quirky cool. His three-point shot isn't too shabby, either. And we'd be crazy to pass up front row seats."

"You're right. And it's not like I'm agreeing to a lifelong commitment to a hometown boy who'd keep me stuck here. It's just a date. And you'll be there, too. What else would I do anyway, stare at my bedroom ceiling and listen to depressing songs while feeling sorry for myself?"

"You know I'm in your corner, girl, but you seriously need to snap out of this. You're not a failure. Repeat after me: A failed project does not make me a failure."

"Why is that so hard to believe?"

"Listen, I know it stinks that the creative space thing in Chicago didn't work out. But you can't let one dead end hold you back. Let's call it a detour instead. One that led you back here, where you get to hang with fun people like me *and* Frank, sing your heart out at weekend karaoke, and custom paint ornaments for purebred pets."

Holly laughed out loud, then imitated Hildebrandt's cocky pose in the picture that Mrs. R. had shown her. The laughter lowered Holly's guard. "All right, I'll tell Frank that we're in for the concert."

"You don't have to twist my arm. It's a date."

✻ ✻ ✻

"I'm treating you to lunch at Stocking Stuffers'," announced Andy on Wednesday. "Bratwursts are in your near future— unless you're vegetarian?"

"Nope, not anymore. I was for a few years in college, but that had more to do with the questionable meat they served," explained Holly.

"Then brats it is!"

"It's nice of you to offer lunch, but if we take a break at the same time, who's going to keep our station running?" asked Holly.

"Never fear, Holly dear. I worked it out with Betty Jo. She's sending someone over."

A few minutes later, Leslie from Customer Service arrived to take over while Andy and Holly went to lunch.

They walked over to Stocking Stuffers' near Station 11, which was crowded with customers. Holly managed to snag a table while Andy ordered.

He eventually returned, precariously juggling four plates of food.

"That hungry, huh?"

"Well, yes, but I'm trying to slim down a bit. This is actually for the other two who will be joining us. Did I forget to mention that?" Andy asked.

Just then Betty Jo spotted them and jingled her way over to their table.

"Ooh, doesn't that look good?" Betty Jo wiggled into the chair next to Andy, making herself quite comfortable.

Holly tilted her head at Andy as if to ask why he had invited the jovial store manager to join them during their break.

Andy diverted his attention. "I'm so glad you could come."

"It's not often other employees invite me to lunch. You both are so kind," she beamed.

"Sorry I'm late," apologized Frank as he slid into the seat next to Holly, nearly stepping on her foot.

Holly tried to take Frank more seriously now that she knew he was upper management, but his boy-next-store vibe mixed with his inability to gracefully maneuver his lanky frame made it challenging.

As they ate, the coworkers made small talk about the weather and work until Andy interjected.

"So, ladies and gentleman, truth be told, I invited you to lunch to ask for some advice."

"Ooh, I'm all ears," sang Betty Jo.

Frank rubbed his palms together, fidgeting beside her. Holly tuned out the hubbub around her as Andy proceeded with his predicament.

"I'm trying to make a decision, and I think some woman-ly input will help. And Frank, I think your spirit of adventure will come into play."

"Bring on the fun! That's my motto," agreed Frank, putting his arm on the back of Holly's chair. She pretended not to notice, but she was most certainly aware.

"Is this about a certain someone who needs her cold car warmed?" smiled Holly.

"Well…kind of yes and kind of no. I don't know. Maybe this isn't a good idea."

"Oh, do tell," chimed Betty Jo.

Andy stroked his lumberjack beard, as if deep in thought.

"Okay, well…when Tammy and I split, my whole world split in two. It was hard to imagine life beyond what we'd built. Oliver was only four at the time. It was so unfair to him. I even suggested that Tammy and I take turns staying at the house so Oliver didn't have to be the one to shuffle between us. Since we had uprooted his stability, I thought we should be the ones to inconvenience ourselves for him, not the other way around."

"I think that sounds quite sensible," stated Betty Jo.

"Fast forward three years, and here we are. I think Bill is about to propose to Tammy. I've been living in an apartment since the divorce, but Tammy asked me if I wanted to move back into the house or sell it after she moves out."

"What do you think you'll do?" pressed Betty Jo.

"Well, here's where it gets weird. I have this strong sense that I'm…"

Andy looked around to see if anyone was listening in. Betty Jo's eyes were as big as Shopkin dolls. Holly tapped her foot under the table in anticipation. Frank scooted closer to Holly, his extended forearm grazing her back.

"…that I'm supposed to give the house to someone." Andy delivered the outlandish news so quickly that Holly wondered if she heard him correctly.

"Rad, man!" approved Frank. He nearly clocked Holly in the head as he offered Andy a fist bump from across the table.

Holly ducked.

"You okay?" asked Frank, patting her head in a gesture of concern.

"I'm fine." Holly assured him.

"I concur," muttered Frank, with a tilted nod at Holly before turning his attention back to the conversation at hand.

Subtlety is not his strong suit.

"Oh my stars, Andy. This sounds like a scene from *Miracle on 34th Street*. The black and white version, not the latest one. The original is so much better, in my opinion."

Leave it to Betty Jo to add her two cents about a Christmas classic when a whole lot more than pocket change was on the table—that, and the mostly devoured bratwursts.

"Say that again?"

"That black and white version is far superior…."

"Not that, I want to hear what he said again." Holly's eyes were fixed on a nervous Andy.

"I know it sounds crazy, but I feel like I'm supposed to give the house to someone. And I want to know what you all think about that. Not that I need your permission or anything, but I mean, I've, um, never done anything like this before and to be honest, I don't want to come across as a lunatic to the person I think I'm supposed to give the house to."

"Oh my stars *and* bars, you already have someone picked out for the house? Oh, do tell! I won't tell a soul." Betty Jo leaned so far over the table that Holly was afraid her "girls" might land in the ketchup of her half-eaten brat. Three dramatic words followed to solidify the store manager's promise to secrecy: "*To the grave.*"

Holly held in a burst of laughter. Work was never dull, that was for sure.

"Spill it!" egged Holly, a little too loudly, as evidenced by some concerned customers who looked her way. She waved them off and quickly turned her attention back to slightly squirming Andy. He was typically easygoing, but this give-the-house-away epiphany and subsequent confession had him out of sorts.

"Well, let's see…it's someone who could really use the house. But I don't want her to get the wrong idea."

"A her, huh?" Holly's eyes danced. "I knew it!"

"Smooth, man. Totally smooth," approved Frank.

"Ooh la la, what a Romeo! Some guys ask a girl for her digits, but not you, no siree, Bob…*you*, Andy Schroeder, give a girl the farm—I mean, your house. Well, technically the house that you and your ex-wife used to live in. But I digress. Whew! What I'm trying to say is, it's a grand gesture of love that's sure to make the lucky girl swoon."

Good grief.

"Oh no, I was afraid of this. All due respect, Ms. W., but this is not a grand gesture of love. Well, I guess it kind of is, because it was the Big Man's idea for me to help this person out. But I definitely don't want to scare her off or give her the wrong idea. Obedient? Yes. Romantic? No."

"I think it's amazing. Almost tempts me to like Christmas again."

"Oh Holly, this is no time for jokes. This is serious business. Not liking Christmas? That's not funny at all," scolded the store manager.

Andy and Holly exchanged a knowing smile.

Frank leaned closer to Holly, "Not liking Christmas, huh? I'm pretending I didn't pick up on that. Not sure I can take out a girl who has an aversion to Christmas…." He paused before adding, "No matter how fantastic she is."

Holly raised her eyebrows to Frank as if to challenge the validity of his claim.

"Good thing I'm not that shallow. My invite still stands." He patted her back before returning to his plate to reach for the last few fries.

"Does it now?"

"Besides, now my mission is clear…to make you fall in love with the best holiday ever."

"Good luck."

The store clock chimed, signaling 12:30.

"Gotta run, man. But I say go for it! Who wouldn't want a free house? Let me know if you need help pulling off the big surprise," offered Frank.

As he rose to leave, he gave a casual salute, "I've got my eye on you, Holly Noel."

She was pretty sure the color of her face looked more festive than desired as a result of Frank's obvious flirting. Thankfully, he left Stocking Stuffers' before reading her conflicted expression—one part apprehensive, another part amused.

"Oh dear. I'm afraid I have to go soon. A manager can't munch for long. Duty calls! But I'm all ears if you're going to tell us who *she* is."

"Yes, do tell," Holly agreed.

"I will, if you promise to keep it a secret."

"Like I said…*to the grave.*"

"Pinky promise."

"It's—"

Only in "a mile of Christmas joy for every girl and boy" at the pinnacle of a fascinating conversation would a trio of employees be interrupted by the announcement over the loudspeaker: "ATTENTION EMPLOYEES. CODE RUDOLPH. CODE RUDOLPH."

"Promise me we'll finish this later?" asked Holly.

"Deal," said Andy as he sprang into action.

Code Rudolph did not mean there'd been a red-nosed reindeer sighting or a bloody nose incident. It meant that a small army of red-aproned employees were needed to search for a missing child in the store (all five-thousand two-hundred and eighty feet of it).

"I've gotta skedaddle. Can you clean up?" asked Betty Jo.

"Sure thing," Holly assured her.

As a member of the Code Rudolph team, Andy had already pulled up the store app on his phone to gather the details:

- 10-year-old male
- Blond hair
- Hazel eyes
- Down syndrome
- Last spotted near lighted houses display at Station 6
- Part of North Star Elementary School field trip

Wide-eyed, Andy mouthed to Holly, "It's Chase. A boy from Oliver's school." And with that, he darted out of sight.

As Holly cleared the table, she shot up a prayer for lost Chase to be found. On a whim, she decided to take the last few minutes of her lunch break to clear her head with some fresh air before relieving Leslie.

She grabbed her down coat and gloves before heading outside. Warmth and cold collided as she left the store and stepped onto the sidewalk surrounding the Christmas mecca. As she walked past the life-sized Nativity figures, she tried to sort through her swirling thoughts.

Was she still feeling brave enough to say "yes" to Frank's concert invitation? Or should she back out? Did he like her or was he just being friendly?

Who was Andy going to give the house to? She had a hunch but she could be wrong. But was it a good idea?

Who was Chase? Where had he gone? And why did that name sound familiar?

Just then, some movement caught her eye near the Nativity. Kneeling beside a ceramic rendition of baby Jesus, with his head bowed and hands outstretched, was a boy.

Holly drew near.

"Chase? Is your name Chase?"

The blond-haired worshipper looked up but kept his hands straight out. Without coat or hat, he was shivering in his position of adoration. His ungloved, stubby hands held a Charlie Brown tree ornament. An apparent offering to the newborn King.

"Hey, buddy. Wow, that's a really neat thing you're doing. But we need to get you inside. People are worried about you."

Chase looked back at Jesus, then at Holly with his almond-shaped eyes. His lip quivered. She wasn't sure if it was from the cold, because he didn't want to leave his post, or some of both.

"My name is Holly. Let me help you get inside, where it's warm."

A reluctant Chase set the tree ornament on top of Jesus' swaddling clothes and double-tapped it for good measure. Holly offered a gloved hand to steady Chase as he slowly rose from his kneeling position.

"Th-th-th-thank yew."

"My pleasure, young man."

The unlikely pair linked arms and made their way to the west entrance of the store.

Before they reached the double doors, Nik rushed toward them, his blue eyes frantic with concern.

"Oh, thank goodness. There you are, Chase." He let out a sigh of relief into the crisp air.

"Holly?"

"Hi, Nik."

"What are you doing here?" they asked simultaneously. Nik's inquiry sounded more curious, while Holly's was more accusatory. She adjusted her tone slightly in an effort to ward off any suspicion that she knew about his shady past.

"I work here," explained Holly. "I was on a quick break when I found Chase."

"I'm serving as a chaperone for the school field trip," Nik said. "I was supposed to be keeping an extra close eye on this guy, but another student tripped and I got tied up helping them, and then Chase was gone."

An ex-con working with children...surely he had to fill out a background check first?

"S-s-sorry," stammered Chase, looking down at his VELCRO sneakers.

Nik bent down, putting his arm on Chase's shoulder. "Listen, buddy. You're okay. We were worried but you're here now. I'm so glad Miss Holly found you. Just don't go disappearing on me again. All right?"

"J-j-jee. Jesus."

"What's that, Chase?"

"I found him by Baby Jesus. I think he was trying to gift him with a 'borrowed' ornament from the store," Holly explained, gesturing with air quotes.

Nik's concern faded into amusement. "Oh, I see, buddy. That was really special. Next time, just let me know and I'll come with you, okay?"

Chase nodded.

"It's cold out here, let's get you inside."

Nik put his arm on Chase's back as Holly held Chase's other hand, tying to keep him warm. Holly's nurturing instinct kicked in as she gently pulled Chase closer to her than Nik, trying to widen the distance between this precious boy and his chaperone with questionable character. Once inside, they escorted Chase to the information station, where the attendant's tense expression melted into relief at the sight of them.

"Attention neumann's employees, rudolph has landed. I repeat, rudolph has landed."

Chase looked up to the rafters, as if he anticipated a reindeer sighting.

After the red-aproned brigade was called off and Chase had been safely returned to his teacher and classmates, Holly went back to her post.

* * *

After a debriefing with the Code Rudolph team, Andy joined Holly back at their station.

"Well done, Holly girl. Maybe you should join our team."

"I don't know about that. I'm just relieved Chase was found. I have no idea how long he would have stayed out there."

"What made you look near the Nativity?"

"Nothing in particular. I was just getting some fresh air—trying to burn off calories from that delicious lunch—when I spotted him. He was so sincere, kneeling beside baby Jesus."

"Reminds me of one of the songs Oliver's class is practicing for his school Christmas concert."

With a slight country twang, Andy sang the last verse:

> *What can I give Him,*
> *Poor as I am?—*
> *If I were a Shepherd*
> *I would bring a lamb;*
> *If I were a Wise Man*
> *I would do my part,—*
> *Yet what I can I give Him,—*
> *Give my heart.*

"'In the Bleak Midwinter'! Grandma Bea loved that song. Gabe and I sang it each year, while she played the piano."

"Maybe Chase's version went something like this: Yet what I can I give ceramic Jesus, give Him a stolen Charlie Brown tree ornament."

"Way to ruin the moment."

"Consider it my specialty."

"Hey, that reminds me…who's the lucky lady?"

"Whatever do you mean?"

"You're not going to tell me?"

"Tell you what?"

"I think you and Gabe are long lost brothers after all, with graduate degrees in teasing."

"4.0, baby."

Oh brother.

The rest of the work day continued like clockwork. Andy acted like he had never disclosed anything about his grandiose house plans at lunch, so Holly decided to try—or pry—again tomorrow.

She turned her attention to the steady stream of custom orders. After avoiding an important business matter all day, time was running out. If only she could decide what to do: say yes to Frank or no? One minute she felt good about it. What was the big deal? She didn't have to decide if she wanted to spend the rest of her life with him. It was just a date to a local concert. But on the other hand, what were Frank's intentions? Was he just trying to be nice or was there something more there? Was he secretly plotting to gift her a house…or his heart?

Reel it in, girl. One baby step at a time. Stop overanalyzing it.

Holly's feelings ping-ponged inside as she tried to maintain a steady hand while painting ornaments.

✳ ✳ ✳

A few minutes before 5:00, Holly headed upstairs to the Neumann's family offices. Hoping no one would notice her, Holly kept her head down while she located Frank's office. As she lifted her hand to knock, the door opened simultaneously. She nearly fell into Frank's chest.

"Well, well, hello there, Holly Noel. Fancy running into you here."

Oh dear. Her flushed face was its own sort of Code Rudolph.

"I'm sorry. I just was, uh…"

"Oh no, I'm sorry. I should look before I leap."

Holly tried to tidy up her appearance and composure before announcing with auctioneer-like speed, "Hey Frank, you've got two yeses for the concert. Elaine and I will be there. Okay, thanks."

"Why, that's fantastic! You sure know how to make someone's day."

"Gotta go." She turned, trying to collect her pride off the floor.

"Alrighty. I'll see *you* there."

"And Elaine!" she added without turning around.

And with that, Holly hurried down the stairs with a spring in her step—in the opposite direction of Frank.

CHAPTER 7

Music Keys

IN TRUE LENA FORM, THE INTERIOR OF THE MUSIC KEYS building was tastefully decorated in calming hues of cream and tan. Pops of emerald were present in a few statement pieces. The focal point of the Pinterest-perfect reception area was large bronze keys that spelled out "Music Keys" mounted on a background of classical sheet music. Lena never did anything halfway—except when it came to her most recent selection of a boyfriend.

Has she been so consumed by her work at Music Keys that she's gotten sloppy in her choice of companion? That seems unlikely.

Deceptively handsome Nik was plunked down on a stool in the reception area at Music Keys, feigning interest in Lena's passion project. He was probably crafting a master plan to line his pockets with the grant money Lena had been awarded—swindling innocent children like Professor Hill in

The Music Man.

"Earth to Holly. You with me?" Elaine waved her hands a few inches from Holly, trying to get her attention.

"Uh, yeah, sorry."

Elaine followed Holly's gaze to Nik.

"He's taken," she whispered, much to Holly's shock and disgust.

"I *know.* I also think this town's about to be taken—" Holly stopped herself mid-sentence, realizing she had almost broken her promise to Nik's Aunt Claire.

"What are you talking about?"

Busted.

"Never mind, forget what I said," Holly backpedaled.

Regal Lena entered the room. Nik rose to greet her.

Per usual, she looked polished as a porcelain doll…her posture, the glow of her skin. A coordinating pencil skirt and blazer complemented her silky jade blouse. Lena's raven hair was parted down the middle and pulled back in a tidy bun at the nape of her neck. Dainty pearl earrings served as the crowning finish.

Holly usually felt pretty comfortable in her own skin. But in the presence of people like Lena, she reverted back to the thirteen-year-old version of herself, at least on the inside—feeling somewhat frumpy, clothed in an oversized sweater of insecurity. Her signature messy bun didn't feel so fun and attractive at the moment. She—and it—felt a little too messy.

"I'm glad you're here. I can't wait to show you around," announced Lena.

Elaine was 2 and 0 when it came to getting her way. First, she had convinced Holly to branch out and say yes to Frank's concert invitation. And now she had swayed her to stop by Music Keys to hear about Lena's new initiative. Both of these "yeses" went against Holly's better judgment, but the alternative was less than appealing—home alone, minus the threat of burglars and Kevin McCallister's arsenal of booby traps.

Just then a few measures of Puccini's "O Mio Babbino Caro" rang in the air. Lena reached for her phone and answered the call. Suddenly deep in conversation, she exited the entryway.

After a few moments, Nik announced, "Well, ladies. Looks like I'll be your tour guide."

Or prison guard.

Nik led Holly and Elaine past the reception area and down a short hallway. The emerald accent pieces matched Holly's envy as she was confronted by Lena's success on display throughout the tour. She tried to wrangle her wayward thoughts by turning the channel to a lively pep talk.

Don't let Lena intimidate you. Her success doesn't mean you're doomed for failure. Things come more easily for her. Don't let her accomplishments trip you up. Lena isn't flawless. Whether she realizes it or not, she's fallen in love with a convict. Hopefully Nik won't get her locked up, too. Hmm, I wonder if they have female prisoners in Leavenworth? Well, she definitely won't be able to wear her coordinating pantsuit there. Unless it's orange.

"You look a million miles away." Nik's observation halted Holly's internal dialogue.

"More like eight hundred miles away," she muttered under her breath.

Holly had Googled it, discovering that it was exactly seven hundred and ninety-two miles from Bavarian Falls to the

U.S. Penitentiary in Leavenworth, Kansas.

She smirked at her inside joke. Nik looked confused. Elaine wasn't amused.

"What's with you, today?" inquired Elaine.

"Must be the brats talking, or the adrenaline wearing off from the Code Rudolph."

Nik smiled, "You really saved the day, Holly. How can I repay you?"

Oh, now you want to give me money? Are you a bank robber or Robin Hood?

"Code Rudolph, huh? Do tell," pressed an intrigued Elaine.

Holly recounted the story of lost Chase being found kneeling beside baby Jesus.

"Truly, you were an answer to prayer," Nik patted Holly's shoulder in admiration.

She resisted the urge to recoil and brush off the convict's cooties.

"Well done, you," added Elaine.

"I was just trying to clear my head during my break, and there was Chase, shivering in the cold."

"Did you say Chase?" asked Lena, rounding the corner.

"Yeah."

"I'm assuming we're talking about the same one. The ten-year-old with blond hair and the voice of an angel?"

"Well, I can vouch for the first two descriptors, but he didn't break out in song during our interaction," explained Holly.

Lena smiled, linking her arm through Nik's. "Let's show them, shall we?"

"We shall! Right this way."

Nik held open the door to the newly refurbished studio. Lena entered first. She slowly spun around, gesturing gracefully to the various features of the soundproof space. On the wall hung a professional photograph of a motley crew gathered around a microphone, grinning from ear to ear.

"This is where the magic happens," added Nik.

Lena went on to explain that Music Keys had been the recipient of a large grant, enabling them to record a Christmas album with their attendees. The grant covered the cost of the equipment needed for the studio, hiring a sound engineer to produce the album, and the funding for the mastering, distributing, and marketing of the project. The sales from the album would be used to provide scholarships to cover voice and music lessons for participants with special needs throughout the year.

"It's a win-win," beamed Lena, stating the obvious.

"The best part is how stoked the kids are to be a part of a professional recording. They think they're rock stars," added Nik. "The other day, little Julie asked me if I'd be her bodyguard when the paparazzi come to town. I told her that her wheelchair is so fast, she'll probably get away from them pretty easily."

Lena pointed to one of the young people in the portrait, who towered over the rest. "You should hear Tony's rendition of 'What Child is This?' Cue the waterworks."

"He's on the spectrum," she added. "Pretty much nonverbal except when he sings. It's amazing. Music has unlocked so much for him."

"I see what you did there," Elaine piped in. "Music Keys… unlocked his potential."

"Exactly. So here's where you two come in...I hope. One of the grant's requirements is for veterans to benefit from the project in some way. I've been wracking my brain to come up with a creative way to include some of Bavarian Falls' military personnel. I know both of you have family members who served. I could use your help incorporating this important element."

Black and white war-torn scenes projected in Holly's mind. At the mention of military personnel, the flashbacks strobed through conversational fragments from her childhood:

"There's been an accident, Holly." Her mom's voice wavered as she pulled young Holly in close. Her whole frame shook as she continued, "Your dad is alive, thank God, but he's not the same. I'm so sorry, sweet girl." She rocked her daughter back and forth, like a metronome.

Gabe erupted a few weeks later. "I want Dad back! Why can't things be like they used to be?!" Glass exploded as Gabe flung a basketball through the living room window. Holly looked up from her coloring book in stunned silence.

Next, the voice of the counselor assigned to her and Gabe hung in the air. "How do you really feel, right now?" Holly blinked, keeping her guard up. She was afraid she'd break like the living room glass and Daddy's brain, if she answered honestly.

And then, the most painful soundbites of all: "Daddy, are you awake? It's time for Saturday Workshop. Can we listen to our favorite song? Can we...Daddy, why are you still in bed?" Holly had bounded into her parents' bedroom, holding hope that their favorite pastime could continue.

"Hol-Holly, stop it! I-I-I can't. Go play with Gabe. My

ha-ha-head hurts. Be quiet!" Dad yelled in exasperation.

Holly couldn't remember an instance of her daddy losing his temper prior to the aneurysm. But his verbal explosion that morning rattled her, as did his subsequent, sporadic outbursts throughout her childhood.

"But Daddy—"

"Quiet! Can't you s-s-see I'm not the same?!" he moaned.

At that moment she felt as if an arrow had ripped through her chest, exposing her harsh, altered reality. The gaping hole became a dull ache over time, but the conclusion was the same—something was missing that once belonged to her and she didn't know how to get it back, or if it was even possible.

Silence hung thick between father and daughter for a few uncomfortable moments.

Holly wanted to crawl into her own skin, like a cocoon, never becoming a butterfly. Maybe a moth though, so she didn't have to stay in the dark forever. But if she was a moth people might shoo her away or even squash her with a paper towel…or their foot.

Her dad closed his eyes and laboriously rolled away from her. Holly backed out of the room slowly, as to not further disturb her father.

Holly never did play with Gabe that day. Instead she ran to her room, closed the door, and ripped up a damp painting. The one she had made for Dad of a caterpillar on a leaf.

As the replay of heartache crescendoed, the studio walls seemed to be closing in on Holly. Lena's voice became muffled and distant. Holly's ears rang and she felt hot from the inside out as the room started to go dark. Like a tree that had been hit just right by the final blow of a lumberjack's ax, she started to go down.

Timber.

Two strong arms grabbed her as she began to sway. "Holly!" Elaine called out.

Fifteen minutes later, Holly was feeling somewhat better. Chalking it up to low blood sugar, she assured her companions she was fine. Holly didn't tell them that Lena had unintentionally triggered the grief that she'd tried to suppress for decades. Grief is like that—an unwelcome house guest that barges in, knocking you off balance.

It was like Holly's body remembered what her mind was trying to ignore. The holidays were coming, and with them came a wave of grief that hadn't dulled as much as she expected. Her dad wasn't who he used to be, yet even after all these years, she wanted to rewrite the story—to rewind to B.C. Not Bible times, although that might not be half bad, but *Before the Christmas* when Dad left and didn't return the same—*Before the Crisis* that rocked her childhood. Instead, Holly was forced to live in A.D., in the *Aftermath of Dad's aneurysm.*

Holly thought she'd been doing okay, but her near fall seemed to connect the dots between her brain's avoidance techniques and her body's muscle memory of the pain. Fascinating, how the days on a calendar can alert grief in the soul, long past tally marks and vigil keeping.

After catching her fall, Nik had walked her to the pleather couch in the studio so she could regroup from a sitting position.

"Are you sure you're okay?" Lena asked for the third time.

Elaine sat beside Holly, rubbing her back in a gesture of comfort and understanding.

Holly was not a wimp. She hated how her episode might've given her present company a different idea.

"Would you look at the time? I've got to get going. My mom is expecting me to swing by Greta's Grocery before I head home."

"I'm not sure you're in any condition to drive," stated Captain Obvious.

"Oh, I'm fine. Really. I'm feeling much better after sitting here for a while and drinking this carrot juice. Thanks for that, Lena."

"Nik is right. Why doesn't he drive you home? I'll grab the items your mom needs and meet you back at your house."

Holly hoped Elaine would come to the rescue, but she was no help.

"I wish I could take you, but I picked up a shift at the Inn tonight and I'm going to be late if I don't leave now. I'm sorry! I'll text you after work to see how you're doing. Take it easy, okay?" Elaine hugged Holly then reluctantly grabbed her coat, heading for the door.

Unfortunately, Elaine added one more thing before leaving. "Thanks so much for thinking of us. I'm sure once Holly is feeling better, she and I can come up with a plan to help with the grant."

The childhood friends were usually in sync, but Elaine was now 0 and 2. First of all, she was leaving Holly with Miss Congeniality and The Jailbird (although to be fair, Elaine only knew about Lena's claim to fame, not Nik's). And secondly, she had volunteered them to help with the veteran component of the grant. How was Holly's heart supposed to heal when she was thrown headlong into dealing with her source of hurt?

"Wonderful! It's settled then. I knew you two were right for the job." Lena clapped her hands daintily. It was about as uncomposed as she allowed herself.

"Now, where's your mom's list?"

"Hang on, it's on my voicemail," groaned Holly.

"She doesn't text?

"I'm working on it."

Nik and Holly pulled into the driveway of the Brighams' brick home on Kühn's Way.

Great, now the criminal knows exactly where I live. Maybe I should text Lena to see if she'll pick up some glue, feathers, and a blow torch so I'll be prepared for a home invasion.

The ride had been pretty uneventful, much to Holly's relief. The weirdest thing that happened was that a Harry Connick Jr. song came on, and both driver and passenger admitted he was one of their favorites.

Was he a favorite before Nik's incarceration or did Harry come and do a concert in the slammer? The latter seemed less likely.

Holly shifted in her seat, looking in her chauffeur's general direction, but avoiding eye contact.

"It was nice of you to drive me home. And thanks again for catching my fall."

"Any time. Well, I guess I should ask first—does the fainting thing happen often? You know, just so I'm armed and ready with my guns…."

It took Holly a few beats to realize that Nik was referring to his muscles, not actual firearms.

"No, I'm not prone to it. Haven't done that in years. Like I said, I probably just needed a pick-me-up."

"If you say so. Sure there wasn't more to it?"

Holly wasn't ready to admit the other reason to herself, much less to Nik.

"Lena should be here soon. I'll walk you in."

"That's really not necessary."

"Selfish motives. I don't really want to stand out here in the cold or sit creepily in your car until Lena gets here."

"Oh yes, of course. I mean, come on in. I think you met my parents at church? They'll be surprised I brought you home—err, I mean that you came home with me. I mean…."

"You better stop while you're behind," laughed Nik.

Holly's cheeks flushed for the third time that day—first in front of Frank, then when she fainted at Music Keys, now standing in her driveway with a guy whom she knew very little about yet enough to not let her guard down. It didn't help that he was handsome.

Where did that come from? Lasso that stray thought to the ground, girl. Stay focused…just not on his eyes, guns, or charming nature.

"Think fast," announced Nik, right before throwing Holly's car keys in her direction.

Plunk.

Apparently Holly didn't think fast enough. And Lena

wasn't returning fast enough.

Holly picked up her keys and bolted toward the front door. Feeling a little childish and unsteady, she was determined not to let it show.

"I'm home!" she called out a little too cheerily as she entered her childhood home and current residence.

"Oh hi, honey. How was the tour? Thanks again for grabbing the groceries. I really—"

Spotting Nik, Anna Brigham stopped talking.

"Hi, there Mrs. Brig—I mean, Anna. Lovely to see you again."

They're on a first name basis? Oy vey, thought Holly. *This is the weirdest—and longest—day ever.*

"Welcome to our home. What brings you here?" Anna kept her voice light, but her eyes searched Holly's for answers as she rose from the table and moved to the sink.

"Well, ma'am, Elaine and Holly were at Music Keys and Lena was recruiting them to help, when…"

Holly could see where this was going, and she definitely didn't want her mom to know about her incident.

"Nik rode with me because I wasn't feeling well and Lena should be here any minute with your groceries. I wonder what in the world is taking her so long."

"Well, technically I drove, but…."

"I didn't realize you were allowed to do that yet," began Anna, much to Holly's horror. Holly's piercing eyes and pursed lips alerted her mom of her near blunder.

Mrs. Brigham seemed to realize she had nearly blown it by admitting her awareness of Nik's incarceration. Thankfully, she dodged a bullet by doing what moms do best.

"Snacks, anyone? I just made some chocolate chip cookies, and if Carl didn't get into it yet, there should be some vanilla bean ice cream to serve with them."

"Sounds great, thanks!" Nik agreed a little too enthusiastically, while Holly resisted the urge to make a swift exit. Nik didn't seem to pick up on her mom's slip-up. That, or he was just as thankful for the culinary diversion as the Brigham women were.

After the cookies, bowls, spoons, and mostly-full ice cream container were retrieved, Anna left Nik and Holly sitting around the Amish-built kitchen table while she checked on her husband in the den.

"We're livin' the dream," Nik said mid-bite.

"I don't know about that."

"Seriously, we're living in such a welcoming community. I tried finding this kind of camaraderie in Leavenworth, but unfortunately my time there was cut short."

Holly almost choked on her mom's famously soft chocolate chip cookies, dumbfounded that Nik would freely admit to being locked in the slammer. And why did it sound like he regretted his early release? Wasn't it a good thing to not have more time there? It wasn't exactly the place you'd go to look for a new bestie.

Ding dong.

Glenda—er, Lena—finally arrived in all her goodness with the bag of groceries from Greta's. The only thing missing was her wand and bubble encasement as she floated in from Oz.

"Let me help you," Nik offered, rising from his seat.

"Thanks. But I'm more than capable of carrying it," Lena scolded as sweetly as honey. She carefully set the bag on the counter.

"Sorry it took me so long. No less than three people stopped me to talk about all that's happening with Music Keys."

"That's my girl. The hometown hero, unlocking kids' potential, one music note at a time."

"You sound like an infomercial."

"Hey, that's a good idea."

"It's already on my to-do list."

"The one with 101 items on it?" teased Nik.

Lena's serious expression melted into her awarded-winning smile—the one that had, along with her nightingale voice, won her several beauty pageants.

Anna returned to the kitchen with Holly's precious dad in tow. His anger had mostly subsided over the years as his brain made healing strides, but the gaping hole between "what was" and "what is" still ached.

"Lena, thanks so much for doing the grocery run. Is there *anything* you can't do?"

Holly willed her eyes to not roll back in her head as her mother gushed praise. Holly's annoyance and insecurities were magnified under the lens of the two high-achieving women, cut from similar, color-coordinating cloth. She brushed stray cookie crumbs off her sweater.

"Actually, she's lousy at bowling," offered Nik. Lackluster bowling skills were hardly kryptonite, but they were a start.

"Hey now," protested Lena.

"I, on the other hand, am basically a pro. I took a bowling class in college for one of my electives," boasted her boyfriend.

"Impressive," responded Holly's dad.

"Mr. Brigham, we meet again." Nik rose to extend his

hand to Holly's flannel-pajamaed father. "I don't know how you keep your figure with your wife's famous cookies around the house. They're delicious."

Carl patted his wife's arm.

"Can I help you put away the groceries?" cooed the nightingale.

"I'm feeling better now. I got it," intercepted Holly, not letting on that her head still throbbed a little.

"Glad to hear it. We need to get going, but let's touch base soon about your creative ideas for the grant requirement."

"Ooh, do tell."

"Later Mom, okay?"

"Oh, all right. Please, take a few cookies for the road."

Nik obliged; Lena politely declined. Within minutes the unlikely couple had left the house.

"Well, that was delightful," commented Holly's mom as the door closed.

"Mom! Have you forgotten Nik's history? Don't let him fool you! Aren't you concerned that he knows where we—and your famous dessert—live? He's bound to come back, either to steal Dad's flat screen or a dozen cookies."

"Now, now, ladies. Nik seems ha-harmless."

"And not too hard on the eyes, either."

"Mom!"

"Oh dear, did I say that out loud?"

"Now Anna, I think…you and I need to find some…pr-pre-season mistletoe," coaxed Carl.

"Don't worry, dear…he doesn't hold a candle to you."

With that, Holly's parents retired for the evening.

Holly grabbed her AirPods and listened to some Harry

Connick Jr. while she put the groceries away. She wasn't sure how to process the strange evening. But she was sure of one thing: she was determined to say no to Lena's invitation. She didn't want to risk another painful walk down memory lane—or fainting spell around Nik—again.

CHAPTER 8

Inside and Outside Work

THURSDAY FLEW BY, AND NOW IT WAS FRIDAY THE 13TH.

"Ready for your hot date?" prodded Andy.

"I don't know if I'd call it a date, exactly. Just some friends and I are going to a concert, that's all. Besides it's cold outside, not hot—thank you very much. Don't you have a deer to hunt or something?"

"Soon…very soon. I'll be back on Tuesday with a photo of a trophy buck to prove it. Never fear, they'll send someone over to fill my place while I'm gone."

When Holly lived in Chicago, November 15th was an ordinary sort of day. But in Bavarian Falls, opening day of rifle season was pretty much an official holiday.

Holly was relieved she wouldn't be winging it on her own while Andy was occupying his hunting blind. With Thanksgiving approaching, the die-hards were already

Christmas shopping. Ornament customization orders were stacking up faster than you can say "Christmas ornaments" in German—although that wasn't saying much, since "Weihnachtsschmuck" doesn't exactly roll off the tongue.

As an artist, Holly had adopted her high school art teacher's philosophy that "art takes time." But the in-store "Countdown to Christmas" clock wouldn't allow for that. There was no time for art to take time in this case, as impatient shoppers flocked to Station 8.

There were the typical requests that came in:

- *Personalize a child's name on the Baby's First Christmas ornament.*

- *Paint the wedding date on the Mr. and Mrs. wedding bell ornament.*

- *Write a teacher's name in calligraphy on the chalkboard ornament.*

- *Add grandchildren's names to the back of snowman collectables.*

Just yesterday Andy had received an order to add a couple's first names to the "We Still Do" ornament for their tenth anniversary. Picking up on Andy's subtle sadness, Holly offered to take that one for him. Andy and Tammy hadn't made it to their tenth, and the customization request seemed to prick her co-worker—even though he tried to appear nonchalant about it.

As Friday the 13th continued to unfold, the custom ornament requests went from slightly weird to full-blown mind-boggling:

There were the more unusual requests, like:

- *The non-traditionally spelled names: Jennyffer, Justeen, Caspurr, and Tommee, to name a few (all humans, not pets).*

- *The Senator's wife who wanted to add her kids' names to a donkey ornament: Kennedy, Carter, Wilson, and Rosie (she explained that their daughter was named after Roosevelt).*

Holly wondered if Clinton or Obama were next.

And then there were the ones you really didn't want to ask about, like:

- *The request to add "Will you pluck my chicken?" on the farmer ornament.*

While the demands on her time were a bit stressful, Holly was fascinated to learn a little about the customers through her interactions with them and their requests for customization (except that last one).

There were many requests to add Mrs. Jackson to teacher ornaments. Holly safely concluded she was a favorite among the local students. One customer came in and bought fourteen figurines, for her daughter and son-in-law's slew of children. Holly marveled at how each of the children came to the family: a blend of international adoptions, biological children, and several sibling sets adopted through the foster care system.

All the talk of children reminded Holly that she wasn't exactly a spring chicken anymore. She tried to mute her biological clock that tick-tocked louder than her singleness could shush.

It helped that she had a date tonight. Frank struck her as the kind of guy who would want a baker's dozen when it came to offspring. Not that she was imaging their future or anything. Besides, she couldn't picture herself driving around a 15-passenger-van, although she did love children.

As her shift neared its end, an attractive middle-aged couple approached the counter. They held up a glass ornament—a stocking with gifts pouring out the top. There were ten spaces on the stocking, ready to be customized with tiny letters by an artist's steady hand. The couple was visiting from Tennessee, and within a few minutes they hit it off with Holly.

They confided in her, recounting their newlywed life as Broadway stars and their transformation from fame to faith. They had left their success in New York to lead a quieter life and start a family. In the wake of heartache and health issues, they were unable to fill their home with the children they longed for. Miraculously, they conceived one child. A daughter. They raised her to develop her innate talents and work hard, without compromising her integrity. Now she was a successful musical artist, with her name in lights at concert venues all over the country. But more importantly, she and her husband had been blessed with five children of their own.

The couple beamed with pride as they pulled up a picture of their adorable grandkids.

"We once thought our names would be on marquees and that we'd have a minivan full of our own children. But we have no greater joy than to see our only child shining brightly in a dark world, filling the world with wholesome music and filling our hearts—and vehicle—with grandchildren. It wasn't the story we would have written, but in many ways, it's better."

Holly was stirred by the sincerity and transparency of this couple. It was clear they had faced disappointments, yet it was evident how grateful they were to be a part of a bigger and grander plan.

"When we saw this ornament, we knew it was the one. Look! It has exactly ten slots to be filled with names—for my daughter, her husband and their houseful of kids, and for us, too."

"And what would you like on the last line?"

The husband chimed in, "That one's for Rocky. Our dog."

Holly laughed easily, "No problem. Dogs are my specialty."

"Do you know how long it'll take? I know this probably isn't typical, but we really need it before the weekend is over. We're only in town through late tomorrow."

Holly glanced at her ever-growing stack of orders. The current wait time was two weeks out.

"For you guys? It'll be ready tomorrow morning by 9. I'll leave it up at the Customer Service desk with Leslie. Just don't let on that you ordered it today, or my manager will give me the naughty elf slip," Holly joked.

"Thank you so much. We really appreciate it. I know it might seem silly, but it's pretty special to have an ornament like this, serving as a tangible reminder of God's faithfulness and how He brings good out of difficulties."

"It's my pleasure, truly. Thanks for coming in today."

And with that, Holly's mind was changed. Maybe she could make something helpful and useful out of her dad's difficulties. Maybe she would look beyond her past and herself, and invest her time in others, for the greater good.

She'd call Lena tomorrow.

✳ ✳ ✳

Holly had convinced Frank to meet her *and Elaine* downtown, near the life-sized Glockenspiel clock, instead of picking her up at home. It was bad enough that Nik knew where she lived. She didn't want to add to the list of ineligible suitors showing up unannounced at her front door or inviting themselves in for dessert. Well, at least, she was trying to convince herself that Frank was an ineligible suitor. She rehearsed her list again: He's younger, he's committed to Bavarian Falls long-term because of his job *and family*, he's funny, he's amusing, he's…

Wait—this is supposed to be a list about the reasons why this shouldn't go anywhere. Oh dear, I need to get out more.

Bavarian Falls felt like Christmas all year long—even in mid-July, minus the snow. However, as the end-of-the-year holidays drew near, an electrical current radiated from the Christmas enthusiasts who crowded the streets and filled local businesses. The intensity permeated the air. There was no avoiding what was coming.

Holly didn't even attempt to park at Edelweiss Inn because it was the night of the big concert. Instead she opted for public parking near the visitor's center, then walked the few blocks to the Inn to meet up with Elaine.

"Sorry, I know I'm cuttin' it close," Holly apologized.

"Almost thought you backed out."

"Nope—had a rush order I needed to finish before my shift was over."

"Well you're here now and this is going to be fun," Elaine reassured her.

"I think you're right. Thanks for giving up karaoke for this."

"Don't get used it," joked Elaine. "I doubt Klingemann's will be hopping tonight, anyway. It's not every day that an artist of this caliber comes to town."

A rush of people swept past the friends.

"Let's hurry, it's almost 6!"

Elaine and Holly crossed Main Street to the iconic landmark, the Glockenspiel Clock, located near the Engel Haus Restaurant. The monumental clock was housed in a bell tower. Several times a day, wooden figurines emerged on a moving stage, portraying the story of the Pied Piper of Hameln. Gabe used to make fun of his younger sister for being afraid of the trail of ceramic rats that were a part of the Pied Piper depiction. Holly still wasn't a fan of the life-size rodents, but thankfully they no longer haunted her dreams.

Rats aside, the wonder of the clock delivered joy to the year-round crowds, young and old alike. The illuminated clock face brought locals and tourists together in close proximity, as they indulged in a Bavarian-style slice of history. Even Christmas-averse-Holly appreciated the Glockenspiel's cheerful carillon bells and Westminster chimes that echoed throughout town. The German and American hymns it played were part of the soundtrack of her childhood.

The intricate time-keeping hands clicked into place on top of the gold-covered numerals of six and twelve. This shift in time initiated the music, proceeded by the presentation of the tragic tale.

Frank snuck up on Holly and Elaine while their attention was fixed upward.

"Never gets old, does it?"

"Ahh!" erupted a startled Holly.

"What, the rats or my sneak attack?" grinned Frank.

His timing was the worst—or impeccable, depending how you looked at it.

"Both?" shrugged Holly.

"We've got about an hour until we need to be at the concert. VIP tickets have their advantages…we can bypass the line. So, my question is: carriage ride or dessert?"

"Dessert," both Holly and Elaine blurted out.

"Jinx!" yelled Frank, rather amused with himself.

It wasn't that Holly was opposed to the carriage ride itself. But it sounded romantic, like something you'd do with a boyfriend, not the boy-next-door—or in this case, the boss's grandson.

"It's really nice of you to treat us to a night on the town," offered Holly.

"My pleasure."

What was this? Chick-fil-A? Or just a fun-loving guy trying to improve his social life?

"You sure, no carriage ride?"

Apparently Frank had booked both a carriage ride and a table at the Engel Haus restaurant ahead of time so they'd have no waiting with whatever option they selected. He was either overeager or thoughtful. Over Black Forest torte, he admitted he clocked about sixty hours a week during the holiday season, so perhaps it was a good excuse for him to take a break.

"Doesn't the store only close four days a year?" inquired Elaine. "When do you get a break?"

"When Great Grandpa was alive, he instituted a mandatory family break so we could all have time off together. He trained other staff to fill in during that two-week period. After his business took off, he acquired some land. He eventually built a place big enough to house all of us."

"Please tell me it's in Florida, where you can thaw out and chill at the beach," insisted Elaine.

"Do you know my family? We're basically the official Christmas ambassadors."

"So not a beach house?" deduced Holly.

"No, a chalet in—wait for it…North Pole, Alaska."

"Stop it!" reacted Elaine.

"Not joking. Population 2113…or 2147-ish, when the Neumann entourage arrives every June."

Wow, vacationing with extended family every year at the same place? Sounds equal parts sentimentally sweet and slightly suffocating. And definitely far removed from my vacation experiences.

Besides the Mackinac Island trip and a few other day trips to nearby cities, Holly's family had stayed close to home because of her dad's health complications. One time, Grandpa Dale and Grandma Bea surprised Holly with a thirteen-year-old adventure trip to Chicago, where she experienced a new art museum each day. Holly felt like she had been transported to another country. Her senses were wide awake, painting with a broad stroke of diverse colors, while a cacophony of different languages swirled overhead and the "L" rattled as it approached its next stop. Holly's soul was stirred as she took in the varying styles, textures, and feelings of each museum exhibit. Pursuing art as a career went to the forefront of Holly's mind, as did a resolution to not stay in Bavarian Falls after high school. She had seen a glimpse of what was out there, beyond the borders of her hometown, and she couldn't wait to leave her mark—preferably on the bottom right corner of a canvas hung in The Art Institute of Chicago.

After more small talk and the last bites of Black Forest torte, the trio exited the restaurant and drove to the packed concert venue. Frank pulled up to the entrance and instructed Holly and Elaine to give their names at the window to pick up their tickets. He'd meet up with them at their seats after he found a parking space.

"I'm surprised he doesn't have VIP parking with his family connections," Holly commented.

"Looks like he's a VIP in your book," teased Elaine.

"Can't a guy and girl be friends without everyone assuming there's more?"

Elaine raised her hands in surrender.

"Can you imagine vacationing with your immediate and extended family for two weeks straight in Bavarian Falls' sister city?"

"Is that true?"

"The sister city thing? I don't think so. But it might as well be. On the drive over, I did a little investigating of North Pole, Alaska. You should see the Santa house there."

"Sorry about teasing you. I think Frank's just a nice guy looking for some friends outside of work."

"Well, technically, I'm from inside his workplace."

"That's true, but—"

"Hey there, ladies. We meet again."

Holly pulled her prickly shell up like a turtle neck in the presence of the guy who had once been guarded himself—literally.

"Oh hi, Nik."

Everywhere I go, he shows up. Is he following me? Maybe I'm just being paranoid. It is a small town, after all—must be a coincidence that we keep running into each other.

"Lena's meeting me here after her video call with a non-profit out of Atlanta."

Of course. He's here for Lena. Get out of your head, girl.

"She's definitely committed," offered Elaine.

Nik crossed his arms and rocked back on his heels, and then forward again. It looked like he was tired of waiting.

After a few uncomfortable moments, Holly offered, "Well, hope you enjoy the show."

She led Elaine over to the ticket window. An elderly man with an official-looking name badge that read Barry handed them their tickets along with swag bags filled with merchandise from the headliner and her opening act.

Once they were settled in their front row seats, Elaine started cracking up.

"What's so funny?"

"It's really too bad that Barry was too old for you."

"The ticket guy? I think he was in his seventies. What are you talking about?"

"Holly and Barry sound like a match made in heaven. Get it? A holly berry?"

"Oh boy."

Speaking of "oh boy," a few minutes later Frank and his lanky legs arrived and sat next to Holly.

He leaned over the arm rest and asked, "Ready for this?"

His pepperminty breath lingered and Holly fought the

urge to back away. He wouldn't try to kiss her here, would he?

Think fast, Holly! "Um…for the concert?" Holly blurted. "Yeah, it's a good change of scenery. Thanks for inviting me."

"No problem-o. I'm glad you said yes, by the way. You kept me guessing." He sat back in his seat.

"I like to keep things a bit mysterious."

"Well, it's no mystery that you're beautiful. You know that, right?"

"Thanks, Frank." She patted his arm, acknowledging his compliment yet trying to put the brakes on the freight train of thought barreling down on her.

She turned her attention to the stage, taking in the elegant beauty of the set design. Her appreciation for the various stage elements was interrupted by what was becoming a familiar voice.

"You sure it's okay, man?" Nik directed his question toward Frank.

"Totally. I'm just sorry that your girlfriend had to bail." Frank stood up to give Nik his seat while he moved to the empty seat on the other side of Holly.

Mayday, mayday! What's happening?

Frank quietly explained to Holly, "Nik and I ran into each other in the lobby. Lena canceled on him so he was going to leave, but I insisted he come sit with us and not miss out."

Holly kept her voice low, "Where did you get the extra front row ticket?"

"I've got connections." Frank tilted his head slightly, pointing at Holly while clicking his tongue on the side of his cheek and adding a wink for emphasis.

Elaine initiated some small talk with Nik, probably to

distract him from Lena not showing.

Thankfully the show was about to start. Holly wondered if Frank would try to hold her hand in the dimmed venue. Her hands beaded with sweat at the thought of it.

Sandwiched between a boisterous Frank and a stood-up Nik wasn't ideal, but in actuality, Elaine had it worse—although she didn't know it. At least Holly was also sitting next to someone who hadn't broken the law…well, not that she knew of, anyway.

Soon after the concert began, the less than ideal seating arrangement was forgotten.

The five-piece band started playing, unleashing joy into the atmosphere—it reverberated off the walls and bounced back to the crowd. Holly realized that since returning home, she had allowed a gray cloud to loom overhead, tempering lightheartedness. It was like she was stuck on the side of a back road and needed a push out of the ditch. The wailing trumpet served as that shove, as Holly willingly let her guard down, drinking in the wonder of the concert. She laughed freely as the crowd rose to their feet. She clapped to the beat and danced as if no one was watching.

A few times during the show, Holly looked over at Elaine, who was having a grand time. She couldn't help but notice that Nik seemed to be enjoying the experience too, as evidenced by his bright eyes and steady smile. She couldn't imagine what he might have done to land in jail, but she could definitely see why Lena was attracted to him. And there was no doubt Frank was having the time of his life with his flailing dance moves and loud, slightly off-key singing. He nearly gave Holly a black eye during one zealous spin. He profusely apologized with a quick peck on her temple that left her paralyzed.

He'd basically claimed her as his without asking how she felt about it.

Holly glanced to see if Elaine had witnessed Frank's unusual concoction of clumsy mixed with spontaneous affection. Elaine's attention was elsewhere, but Nik raised an eyebrow at her and shook his head a bit. Holly flushed and shrugged, turning her attention back to the stage.

If the lead singer, Jana Bonparente, hadn't been so talented or authentic, Holly might have mulled the moment for the rest of the night. Instead Holly was mesmerized by Jana. In a culture of celebrities compromising their morals and toppling under the weight of fame, there was something different about Jana. It radiated from within.

As the concert neared its conclusion, the band members faded into the background, except for the musician at the grand piano. Jana's heels clicked on the stage as she walked over to a stool positioned under a flood of sapphire lights. The audience seemed captivated by Jana's crystal voice as she performed a ballad that built and swelled as it unfolded:

The key to peace is turning to face that which holds you down.
The way to freedom is not out of reach.
Turn the knob, let yourself be found.

There's an echo of hope that you've all but forgotten
As you've lost your way in the crowd.
But don't give up, I've come for you.
I'm your Everything…even in this.

I never leave. I never change.
I see you.
Even when life causes you pain.
I'll be with you.

The key to peace is turning to face the One who loves you best.
The way to freedom is not out of reach.
Take a seat, let your soul find rest.

There's a pattern of purpose that you've overlooked
As you've made your way back home.
But don't miss out on what's to come.
I'm your Everything…even in this.

I never leave. I never change.
I see you.
Even when life is not like you planned
I'm here with you.
I'm your everything.
And that's everything.
Ooo…everything.

The hush of the crowd replaced applause. Sacred silence was their amen. Nik on her left, Frank on her right, and thousands at her back, but Holly felt like the only one in the room. It was as if the song had been written for her, for this moment. A gift from above, carried on sound waves and tucked inside her heart for safe keeping.

The way to freedom is not out of reach. Turn the knob, let yourself be found.

CHAPTER 9

Let Me Be, Frank

As Holly set up her station Monday morning, she wondered who had been assigned to fill in for Andy. Whoever it was, she hoped they'd be able to keep up.

Was it Teresa? No.

Was it Leslie? No.

Was it Betty Jo, accompanied by her jingling feet and bubbling enthusiasm? No!

It was…*Frank?!* He who had sent one hundred texts in three hours after the concert Frank.

"I'm all yours," he announced as he approached Holly's work station. He had exchanged his crimson vest for an apron that matched hers, minus the "Holly Noel" name tag.

Holly spent forty minutes trying to teach Frank how to paint customized ornaments, but there are some things you can't teach; they're innate. It wasn't that Frank wasn't trying hard enough; he was trying too hard. The apprentice stopped his sensei frequently, making sure his brushstrokes were up to standard.

"Thanks again for the concert. Jana was amazing."

"You're welcome. I liked the first band better 'cuz I could jump around like a fool to their sick beats."

Touché.

"So, how about that carriage ride sometime?" asked Frank.

Gulp.

She willed Andy to fill his hunting tags early, come show off his prize deer, and relieve Frank of his duties.

"Uh…well, I'd need to check with Elaine first. Her work schedule's pretty crazy at the Inn right now."

"Elaine is nice and all, but I was meaning you and me. Like a date."

Double gulp.

"Oh no! I just remembered I have to check with Leslie about something. You're doing great on that order, by the way. Keep it up. Be right back."

Holly tried to keep her stride to a swift walk instead of a full-on sprint, as she bolted over to Customer Service. She needed to buy some time to process what had just happened and to figure out what to do next.

"Hi, Les. I wonder if you can help me with something?"

"Sure can."

"Did a middle-aged couple stop in on Saturday morning?"

"Let's see, there were about two hundred and some middle-aged couples here from all over the country, and the world. So you're going to have to specify."

"They were picking up a custom ornament. The stocking

one, with presents in it. They were from Nashville and just as kind as they could be."

"Yes! They were here! Why didn't you just ask if Jana Bonparente's parents stopped by instead of being so elusive?"

"Are you kidding me?"

"Come on, surely you knew who they were?"

"No way! I had no idea."

"Look them up, you'll see. There's a great photo that pops up online of them with their grandkids. Looks like the sweetest bunch."

Holly replayed her conversation with Jana's parents, making sure she hadn't said anything stupid.

"By the way, your secret is safe with me."

"What do you mean?"

"You obviously rushed their order, and gave it priority over others to get it done."

"Guilty as charged."

"My lips are sealed."

"I owe you!"

"Oh, don't worry about that. The shock on your face was worth the price of admission."

Holly walked *slowly* back to her station, shaking her head along the way. Who knew? Apparently everyone in the store but her.

She'd left Frank hanging long enough. It was time to respond to his direct request for a solo carriage ride.

"What was that all about?" asked Frank, playing it cool.

"Looks like you're really getting into your work," Holly diverted, pointing to the stray paint mark that had wound up on his temple.

She grabbed a cloth from the drawer and offered it to him, trying to avoid his probable request that she wipe it off for him…or return a temple kiss of her own.

"Did I get it all?"

"Almost. One more spot, right there," directed Holly.

"So, back to my question. How about you, me, and a horse and carriage?"

So much for Elaine's idea that Frank was just looking for friends to hang with outside of work. He was trying to work it, in his own sort of way. Holly didn't want to be mean, but she also wanted to be clear. She decided to rely on a bit of humor to lighten the blow.

"Let me be frank…"

"Wait a minute. I'm not sure I like the sound of that. In my estimation, it could mean one of three things:

"1. Let me be frank: Meaning you're going to shoot straight and give me your answer, either declaring your affection or aversion to me, or telling me you can't go because of a horse allergy or something.

"2. Let me be Frank: Meaning you think I'm so dope you actually want to be me.

"3. Let me be, Frank: Meaning you want me to leave you alone, forever. Auf Wiedersehen."

Holly laughed. "I see what you mean. So many options. Let's see…I'll take what's behind Door #1. I'm going to be frank…"

Frank gave a quizzical expression.

"Whoops…I see how that's still confusing. What I mean is, let me be direct. There, is that a better word choice?"

He nodded.

"Thanks for asking, but I'm not interested."

"Not interested in the carriage ride, or me?"

"That sounds a little harsh when you put it that way. It's just that I'd like us to be friends, Frank."

"Famous last words."

"I'm sorry…it's just that—"

Frank held up his hand like a patrol guard stopping traffic for young children to pass. "You don't owe me an explanation. I'll just speculate the reason:

"1. I'm too young for you.

"2. It's a conflict of interest to date the boss's grandson.

"3. I'm out of your league and you'd feel insecure around me.

"4. The thought of a honeymoon in the North Pole is not your cup of tea—I mean cocoa."

"Uh, whiplash! We went from 0 to 60 there. First a carriage ride, now we're getting married?"

Holly's timing was impeccable—or the worst, depending on how you look at it.

Ingrid Meyer, the pastor's wife, was shopping within earshot when Holly delivered her last line.

"Holly? And Frank! How are you, darling? I still can't get over how tall you are. It seems like yesterday when you were in Sunday School, keeping things lively and terrorizing poor Mrs. Schulz."

"My claim to fame!" boasted Frank.

"I didn't know you two were an item?! I can't believe your mom didn't tell me."

"Nope, we're just partners today," Holly assured her.

"Oh dear, young people are so progressive these days…."

Holly, horrified by her own word choice, added an important clarifier. "We're *work* partners today—not an item, just checking off line items for these one-of-a-kind ornaments. That's all."

A nervous, chatty Holly tried to undo what had been overheard by the well-meaning but slightly meddling pastor's wife.

"Is that a fact?" she looked for confirmation from Frank.

He decided to keep things interesting with his own brand of illusion.

"It's a fact that Betty Jo is, as we speak, adding the newest additions to the clergy ornaments at Station 10. You won't want to miss snagging up the latest and greatest for Pastor M."

"Thank you! I'll head over there right now. And don't worry, you two...mum's the word," she glinted.

Holly's stomach felt like a string of tangled Christmas lights. It wouldn't be long before Ingrid told Holly's mom what she'd overheard—and had clearly misunderstood.

"We're working side by side, but Mrs. Meyer acted like we were hand in hand."

"You think?" Holly said a little more sarcastically than intended.

"Come on, it was sort of funny, right? Who else could we convince that we're an item?"

Oh dear. Here goes Round 2.

"Let me be, Frank...."

"I hear ya loud and clear. Friends, it is. I hope?"

"Sure thing. But can you lay off the antics a bit?"

"Your wish is my command. Wait...let me try again. How about, 'As you wish'? Nope—romantic movie line, too much. How about this—final answer—'You've got a friend in me.'"

The eye roll, coupled with a smile, communicated Holly's feelings precisely. Frank was both annoying and slightly amusing.

The rest of the morning went off without a hitch, and without any more talk of them getting hitched. On her lunch break Holly decided it was time to act on the important decision she had made after her encounter with Jana Bonparente's parents.

I'll bet they were at the concert! It would have been fun to see them there. Heck, they were probably in the front row, too.

Holly pulled out the Music Keys business card that Nik had given her on the tour last week. Like Lena herself, the business card exuded professionalism and poise. It was baffling how Lena could walk hand in hand with the likes of Nik. Although, had Holly not known about Nik's dark side, she would've been easily won over herself.

Holly decided to be a big girl and call instead of text, after she asked herself, *What would Lena do?*

After several rings it went to voicemail. "You're reached Music Keys, a 501c3 committed to unlocking children's potential through the universal language of music. Please leave a message and we'll get back to you as soon as we're able…*Beep.*"

At the sound of the tone, Holly told Lena that she could count on her to come up with a creative solution for including veterans in the grant-funded project.

She sighed as she hung up. It wouldn't be easy to face what had held her back—and had literally knocked her down—the last time she was at Music Keys. But she was committed.

✳ ✳ ✳

Andy arrived back to work on Tuesday without bragging rights of a trophy buck, but satisfied with a good-sized doe, which meant meat in the freezer. He relayed to Holly how Oliver had helped him process the deer in their garage.

"You're a straight up pioneer."

"You know it. Hey, how'd it go when I was gone?"

"It was entertaining, all right." Holly shared the bullet points, including the inordinate number of texts she'd received from Frank. How anyone could type that fast on a phone was beyond her. and more than a little suffocating.

Andy's raspy laugh swelled when Holly got to the part about the pastor's wife misinterpreting her and Frank's relationship status.

"You're going to start a town scandal, Holly-girl."

"That's the last thing I need!"

"Frank's a great guy, though. I hope you let him down easy."

"I tried, truly. He seemed like a pretty good sport about it. I might have considered another date with him after our concert experience, but it's all a little—or a lot—too much. Besides, Frank belongs in Bavarian Falls, and well…I'm just passing through, ya know?"

"That's what you keep saying. We'll see."

"Not you, too!"

"Just kidding, Holly. We'll be lining up to pay admission to view your art exhibit one day."

"Well at this rate, my art might only make it onto local

Christmas trees."

"Speaking of, let's tackle these orders so we don't get backed up."

After they worked in silence for a while, Holly broached the subject of Andy's house. "So, since I shared with you... Are you finally going to let me know more about the mystery woman?"

Andy explained how he did some of his best thinking in the woods. With looming oaks and squirrels as witnesses, he was able to slow down long enough to gain perspective and clarity.

"It's Teresa," he blurted out.

"I knew it!"

"But please don't say anything to anyone about it."

"Do you like her? Is that what this is about?"

"See, that's what I'm afraid of."

"Liking her?"

"No...that she'll *think* I do if I offer her the house. This is more about being true to the prompting I had. I know this house would be an answer to her prayers. She has confided in me about her difficult financial situation—mainly due to all her unexpected medical bills because of her arthritis."

"Oh, Andy—this is big. So how are you going to present it? With a mile of ribbon wrapped around the house?"

"I'm not sure. I'm still thinking that through. Any suggestions?"

"Maybe dinner at Edelweiss Inn and a letter from Santa that lays out the details? That way you'd just be the messenger."

"I think you've been getting ideas from Betty Jo and that movie she likes. Hopefully Teresa won't shoot the messenger!"

Andy chuckled.

"Obviously you've still got hunting on the brain."

"Always."

"When do you think you'll ask her?"

"Before the end of the month. Oh, did I tell you that Bill proposed to Tammy this weekend?"

"You thought that was coming, right? How are you feeling about it?" asked Holly carefully.

"I can't change the past. But this arrangement has been our reality for a while now, so I'm making the most of it. Trying not to live with regret."

"How's Oliver doing?"

"Ebbs and flows. Bill bought a new puppy, so he enjoys chasing the dog around. He'll be with me for Turkey Day and we're going to go hunting, just us. That'll be fun."

"Gabe, his wife, and my niece will be home for Thanksgiving. It'll be nice to be together again under one roof." As soon as the words were out of Holly's mouth, she regretted what she said. Andy would give anything to have his family under one roof. She put her head down and tried to erase the unintentional hurt she might have caused.

"I think that's great, really. When you don't have something you once did, you appreciate the small things even more."

"How profound, Mr. Pioneer. Or should I call you Mr. Frost?"

"Why, because I'm ice cold?"

"No, because you're a poet and you don't even know it!"

"Far from it."

The next few weeks were packed with thousands of customers and what felt like thousands of ornament projects. There was little room for friendly banter between Holly and Andy as their attention was needed elsewhere.

Andy mentioned that he was formulating a plan for telling Teresa about the house, based on Holly's suggestions. He'd let her know if he needed further assistance.

Holly was counting down the days until November 26th, a much-anticipated day off for all Neumann's employees. She was also looking forward to her brother's arrival, and more than ready to let him gobble up Mom's attention for a while.

CHAPTER EIGHT

CHAPTER 10

Gobbling the Attention

ON HER DAY OFF, HOLLY PLANNED ON SLEEPING IN—but her mom had other plans, starting with an early intrusion into her adult daughter's bedroom. Her conspicuous objective? To locate the fancy Thanksgiving placemats, housed in a plastic storage container under Holly's bed. The retrieval process was more like a search and rescue mission than a covert operation.

"Mommm, seriously. It feels like I'm on a waterbed."

"Oh, don't mind me. Just sneaking in to grab some decorations."

There was a lot of tugging and pulling, and not much sneaking. With one last tidal wave of exertion, the stowed container was finally freed.

"You'll be up soon, right? So much to do, so little time!"

"Twenty more minutes. Is that too much to ask? And could you please knock next time?"

The door closed, leaving a wide-awake Holly in its wake.

✳ ✳ ✳

"Auntie Holly! Are you up?" the exuberant voice of her six-year-old niece, Claudia, called out not more than five minutes later.

"Just a minute, sweetie."

"Nana told me to come wake you up."

Happy thoughts. Think happy thoughts. You can do it. You can make it through today without a meltdown. You're a grown woman. You can cooperate without being controlled. Deep breaths.

"It's gobbly bird pick-up time!" Claudia added.

Holly's mom, in her high-achieving, gold-hearted fashion, coordinated a collection of thirty cooked turkeys for the local shelter on Thanksgiving Day. Her friends and neighbors dropped off the "big birds" (as Claudia called them) that they'd cooked the day before. It was a sight to see, as giant coolers lined the front yard, proof of the early morning turkey drop-off. A truck from the shelter was due to pick them up mid-morning, which was what Claudia was anticipating and urging her auntie to get up for.

Holly finally rose to the occasion. Her hair nest and dragon breath were proof of her disgruntled awakening. She left the nest but opted to brush her teeth in hopes it would freshen her mood.

She emerged in tapered gray sweats and a monochromatic orange crewneck, ready for comfort food and a day at home. The televised parade was going strong in the Brighams' household, as was the savory aroma of turkey and stuffing.

"Hey, little sis. About time you joined us," Gabe bear-hugged her and added a few noogies for good measure.

His wife of eight years, Monica, greeted Holly with a normal hug void of noogies, thankfully. Her ginger beach waves reached her mid-back and had long been a source of covetousness for her sister-in-law.

"Auntie!" was the only warning Holly received from her freckle-faced, pigtailed niece who snuck up from behind, squeezing her around the waist.

"Claudi-boo. It's so good to see you!"

"Not Claudi-boo. Just Claudia. Or Claudia Ann."

"Hey now, don't be rude to your auntie," Monica instructed her daughter.

"Claudia or Claudia Ann, *please.*" And with that she curtsied and ran to the bay window to look for the truck.

"Kids these days," added Gabe. "Speaking of, when are you springin' this place and moving out of your old room?"

Monica elbowed him.

"Nice, Gabe. Way to make me feel awesome within the first few minutes of our reunion. That hurt."

"So did my wife's side jab."

Holly's pursed lips and flared nostrils communicated precisely what she was feeling…fuming anger.

How dare he waltz in here with his precious family and rub it in my face that I'm such a loser because I moved back home for a hot minute? Never mind the fact that I tried my best to avoid a scenario like this.

Holly's stare down and her concerted effort to bite her tongue instead of lash out like usual seemed to help Gabe realize his teasing had crossed a line.

"Look, Sis. I'm sorry. I'm sure this isn't your end goal."

"You think?"

Old habits die hard.

"You were just so insistent that you'd never live here again, and now..."

Holly stood, armed crossed, trying to hold her ground. But she couldn't hold the tears back anymore. They fell freely, locked up for too long.

"Hey, Hol—look, I'm sorry, truly. Can we have a redo?"

Silence.

The altercation between the Brigham siblings was Monica's cue to attend to her daughter. She shot Gabe a look as she left.

"I know it's like our 756th redo, but what do ya say?"

Holly swiped at her tears, trying to brush away the vulnerability.

"It's me. Your big bro who acts like a jerk every now and then but cares about you, more than you know."

"That was really low."

"Hey, maybe Dad still has that triple XL shirt they used to make us wear when we fought."

"Oh man, that was the worst!"

"Right? What was it called again?"

"The Get Along Shirt—oh, the memories."

"For sure. We have a long history, you and me. Let's not give up now."

"No more snide remarks about my living arrangements?"

"Deal." His hand shot out to take Holly's and she couldn't help smiling when he nearly shook her arm out of the socket.

"I've been looking forward to you being here so Mom can micromanage somebody else for a change."

"She means well, Sis."

"I know, but my tolerance has gone down with age. I'm a grown woman now…even though my current circumstances don't exactly scream "adult." But I'm saving up and trying to make the most of my short stint here."

"Does that mean you're dating again?"

"GABE!"

Her brother held his hands up in surrender as Holly reached for the decorative "Give thanks" pillow from the couch. Gabe, anticipating her next move, counter-attacked with the "Count your blessings" pillow from the recliner.

"Kids! Knock it off. Come on, the truck is due any minute. I need help loading the birds," hollered their mom from the kitchen, with a mix of amusement and irritation.

Anna Brigham's partially empty nest was now full again—*temporarily*—and both her smile and instinctual bossiness signaled that she felt quite at home with the arrangement.

Dad wasn't saying much, per usual, but his pleasant expression indicated that he was enjoying the holiday hubbub.

✳ ✳ ✳

Claudia's round face was pressed up to the cold glass of the bay window as she tried to get as close as she could to the outdoors without actually being there. Her mom had vetoed her plea to wait in the yard for the shelter's truck. She was surprisingly more dedicated to the truck's arrival in the driveway than she was to witnessing a life-size dog balloon float down Fifth Avenue in the televised Thanksgiving Day Parade.

Finally the big moment arrived, and Claudia squealed with delight, "It's Turkey Time, everybody!"

In a scurry and flurry, Anna, Holly, and Gabe and his family threw on their coats, mittens, hats, and boots, and tumbled out the front door to greet the truck's driver, Stan.

Gabe was the first to reach him. "Stan the Man, good to see you again."

The passenger door opened as Stan's helper got out.

"My sidekick is going to help us load up. Everyone, this is Nik Beckenbauer."

And here he is again. Does he help everyone in this town? First his aunt, then Chase, then Lena at Music Keys, then he drove me home, and now he's volunteering at the shelter? Are you casing this town, Nik, or have you turned over a new leaf and now you're trying to make up for lost time?

"Oh, we know, Nik," cooed Anna.

"Sure do. Already been a recipient of the Brighams' wonderful hospitality and Anna's famous chocolate chip cookies," affirmed Nik.

"Great to meet you," Gabe said as he shook Nik's hand. "A friend of mom's cookies is a friend of mine. This is my wife, Monica, and my sweet and spicy daughter, Claudia."

"Claudia Ann…please."

Nik bent down to her level. "It's certainly nice to meet you, Miss Claudia Ann."

She giggled before running over to grab her auntie's hand.

"When I insisted Stan let me tag along, I had no idea where we were headed. But when we turned on Kühn's Way, I should have known this is the street where you live." Nik spoke directly to Holly.

Monica's turn of the head and raised eyebrow were not subtle.

Holly couldn't help but notice Nik's nod to the Harry Connick Jr. song, "On the Street Where You Live"—or was it just a coincidence?

"I assume you're also a friend of my single sister?"

And there it was: Gabe's knack for throwing her under the bus…or in this case, the shelter's truck.

"Yes, you could say that. We're getting to know each other through my girlfriend's nonprofit."

Nik seemed to emphasize "girlfriend" a little more than necessary, probably trying to set the record straight that he and Holly were just friends.

Famous last words.

Where did that come from? Probably just a little word association from my interaction with Frank. Nik has a GIRLFRIEND. And even if he didn't, I am not interested in dating an ex-con. Get it together, Holly. Sheesh!

Holly's face felt as crimson as the pick-up truck in her driveway. She tried to act unfazed by her brother's teasing and her own stream of consciousness.

"Hey folks, it's cold out here. Let's get these birds en route."

Stan to the rescue.

The crew set their mittened hands to the good work so the needy in Bavarian Falls would not go without for Thanksgiving.

Halfway through the loading process, Nik almost dropped one of the turkeys that Claudia insisted on handing to him. Holly rushed in to intercept the near spill at the same time that Nik was adjusting his grip. Their hands collided, Nik's insulated gloves covering Holly's as they both held on to the foiled pan. Time seemed to stand still for a moment.

Pull away! Resist his captivating eyes. Back away from the turkey pan.

"Why are you staring at each other?" Claudia asked, cocking her head to the side.

Holly and Nik shifted their eyes.

"I've got it," Nik assured Holly as he repositioned his hands.

Holly nodded and turned back toward the waiting turkeys.

$$* * *$$

After Stan and Nik drove away, the Brigham women gathered in the kitchen to finish their own Thanksgiving meal prep.

Holly had long been annoyed that the men got to sprawl out on the couch, half-watching the dog show, while the women cooked. She knew it wasn't like this in every household. Remembering her resolution to not revert back to a tween or toddler, she bit her tongue for the second time and chose to look at the bright side, like the protagonist from the movie, *Pollyanna.*

In Holly's childhood, applying Pollyanna's "Glad Game" used to include things like:

- I'm glad we went out for ice cream today.
- I'm glad that Mom let me stop taking clarinet lessons.
- I'm glad that Gabe stood up to Penelope Jorgerson for me on the playground.
- I'm glad Daddy didn't die from his aneurysm.

Today, it included things like:

- I'm glad my brother married someone so nice.
- I'm glad my parents have stuck it out for all these years.
- I'm glad I have a sibling, even when he drives me crazy.
- I'm glad Dad didn't die from his aneurysm, even though things aren't the same.

"Do you think you guys will ever move back to the area? Bavarian Falls is such a wonderful town to grow up in. Claudia would fit in well at the elementary school," Anna primed her daughter-in-law.

"Mom, can't we just enjoy the time we have right now?" intercepted Holly.

Monica mouthed a quick and silent, "Thank you."

"Oh, I am! Isn't it wonderful to be together? Sure wish Dad and Mom were still here."

"Me too. But aren't we glad that Grandma Bea's corn casserole recipe lives on?"

"Yes and amen," added Monica.

"It makes me miss her, but it also feels like—in some small way—she's still with us," sniffed Anna.

"Remember when I turned ten and she decided I was old enough to learn the secret recipe? It was a rite of passage of sorts."

"A very messy one, I might add," laughed Mom.

Holly retrieved Grandma Bea's handwritten corn casserole recipe from her mom's recipe box. Her flawless cursive and the buttery-smudged fingerprints comforted Holly as she gathered the necessary ingredients.

Not long after the casserole was in the oven, Mom assigned the women other tasks—Monica peeling potatoes, Holly the apple pie. As Holly cut butter into the flour for the pie crust and rolled it out, her mom recounted the success Gabe had achieved in basketball, baseball, and as a leader on the award-winning debate team. She mentioned that Holly had been selected as a 7th grader along with a few upperclassmen to design and paint a mural of Bavarian Falls for the Bavarian Festival. She reminisced about holiday traditions, like visiting Santa at Neumann's and getting their annual family picture taken by the covered bridge. The long monologue was most likely to fill Monica in on stories she hadn't heard yet.

But what her mom didn't include was how long it took Dad to get into position for the family picture, or Gabe's near expulsion after Dad's incident, or how much pressure her mom had put on Holly about her contribution to the mural. Holly remembered many sleepless nights due to her mom's insistence to always put her best foot forward. The pressure had nearly imploded Holly on more than one occasion. Now, her mother's sidelong glances at her "back at home" daughter and "helpful" hints on slicing the apples thinner didn't help matters.

"Well, I'm glad all your memories are rosy—or that you've somehow managed to view them through rose-colored glasses. But mine aren't like that. Some of them still sting," Holly admitted, slamming the cupboard door for emphasis.

Her mom's slanted recollection had pricked holes into Holly's outer shell. It was inevitable that the steam was about to escape as the conversation heated up.

"What do you mean?"

"I know you were doing your best, Mom. But I didn't feel like I could compete with Dad's disability. It felt like it was all about him. And no matter what I did or didn't do, it didn't hold up when compared to this big thing that none of us asked for or expected, but we all had to deal with. I know no one asked for this and we were all just trying to find our way through. But it hurt. And I feel guilty for even saying any of this. But I can't keep it in anymore."

Holly sat down at the table, crumpling up a tea towel she had been using to clean up her mess.

"Oh, honey."

"And while I'm laying it all on the table, I might as well say that I felt like you were too busy for me. But I don't want to say that because it will make you feel bad. But if I don't admit it, I'll just grow more resentful."

Holly gripped the towel as if trying to draw strength from it.

"Can't you put yourself in my shoes just for a moment?" her mom responded.

"My feet are two sizes bigger than yours!" countered Holly.

"Dad needed me, you and Gabe needed me, and our dwindling bank account needed me to work, once we had some respite care for Dad. I never wanted either of you to feel like you were on the back burner. It was just so…" She gasped trying to hold back the floodgates of tears. "…So hard. I was trying to be enough for everyone, but there wasn't enough of me to go around."

"I feel like a jerk."

"You're not, Hol. It was hard on everyone. And as much

as it hurts to hear, I'm glad you're letting it out. I mean, I think we've all tried to hold it together but eventually, the hurt has to escape our hearts so it doesn't break us in half."

"Did you hear that in counseling or something?"

"That obvious, huh?"

They both smiled, breaking the thick-as-flannel tension in the room.

"Honey, I love you so much. I'm so proud of you. And I am truly sorry for the hurt."

"I guess I never really thought about it from your perspective. I was young and it's like I got stuck there. Cycling 'round and 'round, rehearsing the pain, then feeling bad about how I felt. I just wanted Dad back...and you back. And our life back before all of this."

"I know. My coping mechanism was to muscle forward, to do the next thing so I wouldn't have to face the pain. Because if I did—like, *really* did—I was afraid it would overtake me and paralyze me."

"I was oblivious to all that, Mom. How lonely that must have been for you."

Tears fell in place of words. Strong and put-together Anna Brigham let her guard down. The crack in her armor was showing, and it wasn't a flaw. It was light.

Holly had put her mom on a pedestal, even when she was annoyed with her. The pedestal had a light shining up on it, like an art piece in a museum display. But until now, Holly couldn't recall ever noticing light radiating from it.

There in the weakness, in the humanness, in the break, a ray shone through. The drone of the dog show could be heard from the den. In the kitchen, a few wall-demolishing swings at the past liberated the women gathered over corn casserole batter.

It wouldn't fix everything, but it was a start. A pivot away from resentment and a lunge toward honesty and health.

Monica cleared her throat, gently reminding the mother and daughter that she had served as witness to the emotionally-charged exchange. Though usually soft spoken, she sounded like she was gearing up to speak.

"I wanted to let you both know something. Please hear me out. This isn't easy, but I think it's important to consider how all this has affected Gabe. He was ten when it happened, and all of a sudden he had to grow up overnight. He said Grandpa Dale and Grandma Bea helped a lot. But at the end of the day, he strapped on a layer of responsibility that he tried to mask with his jokes and charisma. But in the quiet moments—before bed, on a walk, on long car rides—it's there. The face like flint. The tense jaw bone. The distant eyes. The 'am I doing this right?' The 'do I have what it takes?' The second guessing."

Monica's blotchy face and shaking voice indicated that this admission was uncomfortable. But it was necessary.

In part, Gabe had fooled them. There was more to the story than his apparent steadiness and frequent punchlines. He was hurting in his own way. Of course he was.

How have I been so blind and oblivious to the pain of my family members?

"It's been a long time since it happened, yet it's fresh in many ways." Monica paused, as if calculating her words. "But this is good, to get some of it out in the open so we can get stronger and softer, too. Gosh, this is hard for me."

"For all of us," added Anna.

"Mom, you always seem to have it together," interjected Holly.

"Ha! If only you knew the persistent, inner critic that reports its exhaustive commentary about my missteps."

"I don't get it," Monica added, peering into the den where the other half of the family watched TV.

"What's that, dear? Haven't you read about the Enneagram? Type 1's have a strong inner critic and try to improve everyone and everything—mostly themselves."

"Oh, I'm well-versed in all that. I was talking about the dog show. I just don't get all the hype."

Holly blinked a moment, processing what her sister-in-law had said, then a giggle escaped. Leave it to Monica to break the ice and melt the room with her warmth and a well-placed conversational reset. It wasn't that she was trying to avoid the tough stuff altogether, but headway had been made. The rest of their time together didn't need to be dominated by discord.

"I'm grateful for you girls. I know this lot isn't easy, but it's ours, and God will help us at every turn. Now, I think this calls for some hot cider and a slice of butter almond stollen."

"Let's not let the couch potatoes know we're slicing into dessert," schemed Holly.

Over their indulgence, Mom stirred the pot. "It's really too bad about Nik. He seems like a great guy."

"You mean, too bad he has a girlfriend, right?" clarified Monica, cupping her steaming mug of cider while once again assessing her sister-in-law's expression.

Holly made eye contact with her mom, as if telepathically trying to decide whether they should share the inside scoop.

"It's a little more than that," started Anna.

"Mommy! Mommy! Look!" Claudia rushed in the kitchen, tugging on her mom to come see. "The golden doodle is going to win! That's the one I picked!"

"Just a minute, sweetie."

"Please, Mommy. Come on, you're going to miss it!"

Holly had expected Gabe to be the center of attention, but it was his daughter who gobbled it up—and that was just fine with her.

CHAPTER 11

Shop 'Til You Drop

THE WEEKEND AFTER THANKSGIVING WAS THE BUSIEST of the year for the mile-long Christmas store. Thousands of customers descended upon Neumann's to tackle their holiday shopping lists.

Hundreds of employees were aproned and ready to make spirits bright and exude the love of Christmas, melting grinchy hearts with hospitable smiles and helping hands.

"Oliver is coming to the store to see Santa," announced Andy.

"Today?" asked Holly.

"Yup. Tammy insisted, even after I told her the line for Santa will feel like it's a mile long today."

"No FOMO for him."

"Or her. Listen, I'm all for Claus spreading holiday cheer and my son getting a keepsake photo with him, but of all days,

Black Friday is not the day I would choose for him to do so."

"Agreed."

Andy manned the counter, taking orders and answering questions so Holly was free to execute the custom orders. Holly tucked a stray hair behind her ears as she leaned over an ornament shaped like a fir tree and plotted how to fit Merry Christmas in German—"Frohe Weihnachten!"—on a Tannenbaum ornament.

Holly wished she could put in earbuds to tune out the peppy sleigh ride music and the peppering of questions Andy received while she tried to work:

"Can you change the date on my ornament from last year to this year, so I can re-gift it?"

"Can you personalize this ornament with 'Baby Girl VanHusen' for a gender reveal party? They're going to pull this out of a stocking and be tickled pink. Her family has all boys in it. Bring on the tutus and crowns, right? And the Legos and trucks for good measure, of course. We have to prepare her to be an engineer, not just a ballerina."

"S'il vous plaît ajouter Voulez-vous m'épouser? À cet ornement?" A phone translator helped Andy understand that this request was to add "Will you marry me?" in French to the customer's ornament of choice.

The questions got weirder as the day went on.

"How long will it take to personalize twenty black ornaments with 'Doug Doug the Tattoo Thug' for my work party?"

"Sir, can you fit her full name on the ornament? It's a bit above the letter count, but my goddaughter doesn't have anything with the whole thing on it, so it'd be really special. It's Matilda Janae Gertrude Perry-Harrison."

For once, Holly was thankful for the larger-than-life showroom. Its high ceilings helped curb claustrophobia as the waves of shoppers kept surging.

During one such tidal wave, Andy's ex-wife, Tammy, fought her way through the crowd with Oliver hanging onto her faux leather purse. Bill stood a few yards away, unusually preoccupied with the stocking display.

"Psst. *Psst.*"

Andy tried to politely excuse himself for just a moment from the godmother of Matilda Jane Gertrude Perry-Harrison.

"What is it, Tam? I've gotta get back to work."

"I know you're maxed out right now, but you'll never believe what your son asked Santa for."

"A Red Ryder carbine-action 200-shot range model BB rifle with a compass in the stock?"

"Come on, I'm serious."

"So am I."

"Your son asked St. Nick for a six-pack."

Oliver shook his head in disagreement. "No, I didn't ask Nik the Elf, I asked Santa Claus."

"Nik the Elf?!" gasped Holly, interrupting the conversation between Andy and his ex-wife.

Nik is in the store interacting with all those kids?!

"St. Nick and Santa Claus are basically the same thing, buddy," Andy calmly explained. *But definitely different from Nik the felon.*

"Andy! Back to the six-pack."

"What?"

"I was mortified by his request. We were standing there in line by Pastor Meyer, his wife, and their grandkids."

A sheepish Oliver peered out from behind his mom.

"And get this," Tammy continued, "when Santa asked him to explain further, Ollie said, 'My dad has some of those, so I want 'em, too.'" Her voice was escalating with each syllable.

Holly set down her brush and squared her shoulders, preparing to step in to defend her friend from the woman who had broken his heart.

"Listen, Tammy. I told you before, I sometimes have a few cold ones on the weekends. That's it. Maybe he saw them in the garage fridge."

"It was humiliating."

Oliver tugged on his mom's arm. "Mom...*Mom!*"

"Just a minute, Bud."

"I've gotta go Tam, can we talk about this later?"

"Mom!"

"What, son?" Tammy snapped.

"Why am I in trouble? I just wanted some of these, like Bill. And I think Nik the Elf has some, too." Oliver lifted up his shirt and pointed to his abs. "A six-pack of abs. I've been trying to do sit-ups but they aren't doing much. I thought Santa could help."

Tammy's cheeks pinked. But Andy, who had every right to be angry at his ex-wife's accusations, burst into a merry laugh that could've rivaled the big sleigh driver himself. Tammy tittered and glanced at Bill, who joined in. Holly released a snort and bent over her work.

Oliver looked confused.

Andy assured his son, "Oh Buddy, you'll get there. But maybe not this year."

Slightly embarrassed but more relieved than anything,

Tammy collected Oliver. "I'm sorry I jumped to conclusions."

"It's okay. I'm used to it."

"Andy, don't start."

"Gotta get back. Come here, little man." Oliver ran over to do his part in their father-son secret handshake.

"I love you just the way you are…two-pack and all."

"Thanks, Daddy. Love you."

And with that, Oliver left with his mom and his soon-to-be-stepdad, Bill with the six-pack abs.

"You okay?" asked a flustered Holly as she tried to juggle her projects and the line of people who were growing more impatient by the minute.

"Later," Andy replied, turning his attention to the god-mother whose stern expression resembled Marlon Brando in *The Godfather*.

Station 8 was so riddled with traffic, "later" ended up being a few hours later. When Andy and Holly finally had a chance to recount the six-pack mix-up, they had another good laugh. Then Andy suddenly got quiet.

"What's wrong?" Holly asked with concern.

Andy muttered, "Oliver called him Dad."

"Who, Santa?"

"No, Bill. Oliver said he wanted a six-pack like his dad. Tammy thought that meant me. But Oliver meant Bill."

Words escaped Holly at her co-worker's realization. She offered a comforting hand on his shoulder. He briefly acknowledged her sisterly gesture with a double-pat on her hand.

"Excuse me, sir." The female Brando lookalike was back.

Holly hadn't forgotten how Andy had saved her hide when Mrs. Rasmussen needed help, so she stepped up and took one for the team. "I'd be happy to help you, ma'am."

"We're getting ready to load the tour bus, but I came back to make sure he spelled Matilda's first middle name right. It's J-A-N-A-*E*, not J-A-N-A-*Y*. People mess it up often. But she was named after my second cousin once removed and it's important to me that it's spelled correctly."

Attention shoppers. Last call for all riders on Bus #1228 headed to Oak Haven for the North Pole Express tour. Doors will be closing soon. Please finalize your purchases at checkout #4.

"Oh Mylanta, that's me."

"Andy is one of the best there is, ma'am. I'm sure he wrote it down just as you spelled it out."

"If you're sure…"

"I'll double check myself if that will make you feel better," added Holly definitively.

"Oh, it would. Thank you."

And with that, the godmother left the station.

During a brief parting of the seas, Mrs. Rasmussen sauntered up to the counter decked out in a red and green business suit, a Christmas hat, and elfin heels. She'd make Betty Jo herself look like she didn't have enough holiday spirit.

"I'm back!"

"Yes, you are," replied Andy. "Anything I can help you with?"

"Honestly, I'm just taking a stroll around the store to give Doc some breathing room. He said I was driving him crazy. And he wasn't meaning it in the usual way. He shooed me away from Santa's line. Apparently, I was trying to 'squash the vision of sugar plums dancing in little heads' with my timer and whistle."

"A timer and whistle?" asked Holly.

"I thought these tools from my former profession would help keep things running smoothly so the little darlings wouldn't dillydally in line, but I guess not."

"Your dogs are here?"

"No, of course not—they'd destroy the place! I was referring to all the kids in line waiting for Santa."

"Mrs. R. used to be a gym teacher at North Star Elementary," clarified Andy.

"Wow! I never would have guessed that," said a thoroughly amused Holly.

"I know. It feels like another life. I'm glad to have exchanged my windbreaker getup for fancy clothes, but I do miss wearing tennies on my dogs—my feet, not my pets," she clarified. "Heels have taken their toll on these Cinderellas." She lifted her feet, twisting her four-inch heels back and forth as proof.

Holly was trying hard to keep her face neutral, but Mrs. Rasmussen's vernacular wasn't making it easy.

"But I wouldn't trade this life for anything, even when Henry drives me nuts. He's good to me. I just wish he would've let me go to that special school so I'd be more prepared for my role today."

"I guess I'm a little lost. What is it that Dr. R. is doing at the store?"

"You don't know? I guess you're a little old for it, but I thought everyone knew. He's on his fifth year, after all."

"He's wearing the beard and velvety suit," explained Andy to his confused sidekick.

"That's right, Santa Claus has the best-looking teeth in the store. Gosh, he looks good in red," sighed Mrs. R.

"Well, he's a patient man, that's for sure," observed Andy. Realizing how his admission could have been misinterpreted, he added, "I mean, because he's coming in contact with so many kids and all."

"Yes, he is. I practically forced him to take his Vitamin C, D, garlic capsules, and kale smoothie this morning, to ward off any potential germs from snotty hands and close talkers."

"He's definitely a trooper."

"By the way, did you hear what Oliver asked for?"

Andy's jaw clenched. "About that, I'm really sorry...."

"Sorry for what? I didn't catch the second thing he said, which seemed to cause quite a stir with Tammy. But the first thing he asked for was a BB gun. I was a little shocked myself, but when Santa asked him why, he explained how he loved spending time in the woods with his dad looking for deer. You should have seen the adoration on his face. He sure loves you."

Andy, visibly moved yet trying to appear macho, quietly thanked Mrs. Rasmussen. "That means a lot. Thanks for telling me."

"Of course. Now, I think I've stayed away long enough. It's time for the chief elf to take her place back at Santa's side—minus the timer and whistle," she added sheepishly. "Nice talking to you two. Just let me know if you want to pop a few Vitamin C tablets for good measure—let's just say I'm amply supplied."

"Thanks, but we're good," Andy assured her.

"Well, I'm off. Ta-ta!"

Mrs. R. returned to her post next to Santa, Andy's burden was eased, and Holly had some quirky material for a Bavarian

Falls tell-all book one day—that is, if she decided to give up art and take up her other childhood dream of writing a novel like Jo March and Anne Shirley did in two of her favorite books. Grandma Bea used to read them aloud to her. It was the books' covers that ultimately drew Holly to pursue art. She was awed by the way they encapsulated a slice of the story, serving as gatekeeper between imagination and reality.

Not long after Mrs. Rasmussen left, a masculine elf ran up to Station 8.

It was Nik the Elf, decked out in a red belted top with striped sleeves and evergreen shorts, complete with candy cane leggings and belled felt shoes.

Sheesh! He even looks good in that ridiculous outfit!

"Hey guys! Santa got called in for emergency dental surgery and Mrs. R. sent me to find a fill-in for a few hours until Doc can get back," Nik explained. Turning to Andy he asked, "Can you do it?"

"Well, I've never suited up at work…."

"Listen, you'll do great. I offered to fill in myself, but Mrs. R. insisted my lack of beard and the fact that the kids will recognize that the elf is now Santa could cause some issues. So she sent me to retrieve you."

"I could do it, but I don't want to leave Holly hanging here."

"I can step in for you; Holly can show me the ropes. There's another elf named Teresa over there who can hold down the fort while I stay and fill in for you. Can you let her know I've been detained?"

Andy's conflicted expression morphed into confident determination. "Absolutely. I'll go get changed!"

"Thanks, man. There's about to be a mutiny over there."

Here they were again. Holly going about her business, then *bam!* Nik appeared out of thin air, now in a different role, yet once again offering his time to help others.

This small town keeps getting smaller.

"Sorry you lost your partner in crime," joked Nik.

"How many hours do you volunteer a week?" drilled Holly, suddenly realizing that his helpful spirit might cloak the fact that he was actually fulfilling required community service hours. She discreetly tried to spot a tether hidden near his ankles, where his elf leggings met his felt boots. Nothing appeared out of the ordinary—except that she was working side by side with Lena's elf boyfriend.

"Honestly, I've lost count. I don't mean that in a prideful way. It's just that with this relocation, I'm committed to figuring out what went wrong in Leavenworth."

"By volunteering at as many places as possible?"

"Well, when you put it that way, I now realize that I've filled my schedule with so much volunteering and a few side jobs too—like this gig," Nik gestured to his elf getup, "that I haven't had much time to sit and figure out what I really want."

"Speaking of not having time to figure things out, I don't suppose you're a student of Bob Ross?" asked Holly, picking up her paintbrush.

"The happy little tree painter? Um, nope. Is there another way I can help?"

"Sure. You take down orders, and I'll paint happy little names and phrases on these ornaments. Just ask the questions on this form, then record the customers' answers on this spreadsheet. Make sense?"

"You got it, boss. I'll do my very best."

After a few more instructions, Nik quickly caught on. Holly attended to her pile of mounting orders. They managed some sporadic conversation as they worked. Nik proved more than competent as he systematically took orders and engaged in kindhearted small talk with customers. Holly noticed he was very good at the job.

"What's Lena up to today?" Holly forced herself to think about her friend—his girlfriend.

Nik smiled. "Oh, you know…changing the world one song at a time. I'm headed over to Music Keys after this, but Lena had meetings scheduled all morning, so I told Frank I could help out here today. You and Frank are a thing, right?"

She remembered that Nik had most likely observed Frank's kiss on her temple at the Jana Bonparente concert and made the probable conclusion that they were an item.

Holly heard herself reply, "Stranger things have happened."

Why did I say that? Maybe it's just a protective response from years of being single? But why would I say that to Nik? It's not like he's someone I need to impress or a well-meaning yet meddling friend of my mom.

Thankfully, no more strange encounters happened. In some ways the rest of the day flew by; in other ways it dragged on, as customer after customer oohed and awed and hemmed and hawed. Andy returned shortly after lunch to swap places with Nik, and reported that no punches had been thrown or hair pulled, even in the endless line of antsy kids waiting for Santa. But maybe that was because Mrs. R.'s whistle was still around her neck, ready to intercept shenanigans with a shrill warning.

Mid-afternoon, the familiar face of Ms. Claire Weber surfaced from amid the flurry of shoppers.

"Holly! I'm glad you're here. I have a special order and it needs a real artist's touch. No offense, Andy."

"None taken, ma'am. We all know that Holly's skills are authenticated, with an art degree and all."

"It appears that my nephew is in it for keeps with Miss Lena Albrecht, so I wanted to do something special for them."

From behind her back, Ms. Claire produced a circular emerald ornament and a bronze key charm.

"I'd like you to affix this key with a ribbon to the top of the ornament and also hand letter 'Nik & Lena' on the front in gold foil."

"That'll be beautiful," Holly admired. She wasn't sure if she should stop there or continue verbalizing her thoughts. She realized she cared too much about Claire and tolerated Lena enough to not speak up.

"Pardon me, Ms. Claire. But aren't you a little concerned about this?"

"Don't worry about a thing. I've been saving up for this. I know it's a bit extravagant, but I think it will mean a lot to them."

"I wasn't talking about the price." Out of the corner of her eye, Holly made sure Andy was still occupied with other customers before she continued, "I meant Nik's history…with Leavenworth."

"Ah yes, I see what you mean. It definitely was upsetting, but I think he's recovered from that quite nicely, don't you?"

"Well, I don't know all the details of his release, nor is it my business really, but Lena is okay with it?"

"I'm sure they've talked about it and worked through it. Even though Lena is successful now, she started Music Keys from the ground up. She had to move out of the nonprofit's original building before moving into its current location. It was a huge setback. So I think she, like you, knows what it's like to be forced to relocate and start over when things falls apart."

Holly couldn't believe a smart woman like Ms. Claire would minimize time behind bars as a relocation and a crime as things falling apart. Wait a minute—maybe Nik had been accused of something he didn't do? Based on her interactions with him, he was either a professional deceiver or he was actually the considerate and kindhearted guy he appeared to be.

This new possibility gave Holly courage to ask, "Was it his fault?"

"It's hard to tell. Maybe partially, maybe not. These sorts of things can be unclear."

Again, Holly was taken aback by the nonchalant way Ms. Claire conversed about this serious matter.

"So you don't think he'll return?"

"I don't think so, dear. At least not now. I think it would take a lot for him to go back. It's hard to face that which has hurt you most, isn't it?" Ms. Claire's compassionate inflection signaled that she knew her last sentence hit close to home.

Holly was temporarily distracted by the lump in her throat. The lyrics to Jana's song, "Everything," swirled in her mind from memory:

> *The key to peace is turning to face that which*
> *holds you down.*

"That's it. That's the key I've been missing."

"What, this one?" replied Ms. Claire, still clutching the bronze key.

"Not exactly." A rebel tear escaped down Holly's cheek.

"Are you okay?"

"Yes, ma'am." Holly collected herself as best she could, before adding, "This is going to be the loveliest ornament."

Upon Ms. Claire's exit, and with throes of Black Friday shoppers as oblivious witnesses, Holly decided that she was going to face what had been holding her back. Come Monday, she was going to schedule a counseling appointment, after a dozen-year hiatus.

CHAPTER 12

Heart-Breakery

Holly, Andy, the other Neumann's employees, Elf Nik, and even Doc and Mrs. Rasmussen were still standing after the shop 'til you drop weekend.

Before the store doors opened to customers on Monday, Holly and Andy were already counting down the days until the coming weekend.

"My friends Elaine and Shayla have convinced me to join them for a Christmas movie marathon on Saturday. I tried to tell them my eyes are already strained from painting a gazillion ornaments, but they insisted."

"Don't shoot your eye out!" warned Andy.

"Huh?"

"Probably the best line from *The Christmas Story*. Please tell me you're going to watch that one."

"It's a rom com marathon, so I doubt it will make the cut."

"What did you say?"

"Rom com—you know, romantic comedies?" clarified Holly.

"Like Christmas chick flicks? Why didn't you just say so? Yeah, I don't care for those. It never turns out like that in real life."

"I couldn't agree more."

"Want to know my weekend plans?" asked Andy.

"Of course! Gotta be better than mine."

"I'm going to offer the house to Teresa. Just like you said…dinner at Edelweiss Inn, note from Santa—the whole nine yards."

Holly punched Andy's arm playfully. "This is huge! Wow, let me know how it goes. You could even dress up like Santa again."

"I think my Santa days are over. That was intense! You can pray I don't need to overdose on antacid to get through it."

"You'll do fine. But maybe avoid the grilled onions on your bratwurst this week…for more than one reason."

"Duly noted."

"Are you going to the work party tomorrow night?" asked Holly.

"Absolutely I am. Mr. Neumann does it up right. I won't give anything away, but let's just say you don't want to miss it."

"I don't mean to sound ungrateful, but I was kind of surprised to hear that the party is going to be here. I mean, it's already decorated, so that makes sense. But we spend a lot of time in this place, especially this month."

"I hear ya. But where else can you house five hundred employees at this time of year?"

"Good point."

"It's lot of fun, you'll see."

During her morning break, Holly made good on her promise to herself and scheduled an appointment with a counselor. She'd chosen one that she'd seen advertised on the church bulletin board. Thankfully the counseling office was about forty minutes away. The miles were a welcome buffer between that which she was trying to distance herself from and that which she was attempting to face.

Holly had been to counseling briefly as a child and then again after she graduated from high school, but now she was more determined to face the fog.

The counseling office was especially busy during the holidays, but miraculously they had a cancelation and Holly was scheduled for later that week.

Relief and anxiety duked it out as she typed the appointment into her calendar app. Before she closed down her phone, she spotted an invite reminder for the work Christmas party. She moved her response from "Interested" to "Going."

✳ ✳ ✳

Droves of employees arrived for the big event. The arena-like showroom felt even more festive than usual. Through the sound system, a synthesized orchestra amplified songs from *The Nutcracker*. Servers in tuxedos walked around with silver trays filled with mouth-watering appetizers. Bacon-wrapped water chestnuts, figs stuffed with goat cheese, and crispy flat-bread crackers laden with pesto were headliners in the aromatic food prelude. A bird's eye view would've captured a real-life

Whoville minus the sky-high hairdos of the Whos—unless of course you took Betty Jo's bouffant into consideration.

Holly entered the party with the ambition to blend in. She was thankful that the absence of a guy on her arm would not be noticed in a crowd this size. After hors d'oeuvres, plated with a side of mingling, Frank's grandfather—the son of Neumann Sr., the store's founder and North Pole vacation acquirer—stepped up to the mic.

"Good evening, everyone. What a great turnout. We know this is a busy time of the year, especially as a Neumann's employee. We host this annual party to express our deepest appreciation for each of you. We wouldn't be successful as a company without your commitment to making spirits bright for all those who visit our store.

"Folks, you're in for a real treat this evening. Over the years, I've rubbed shoulders with many well-known people all over the globe, from actors to business owners, from political figures to musical artists. But it especially blesses my heart to discover talent right here in the Falls. I've invited a special guest to grace us with some holiday music. Ladies and gentleman, our local angel, Miss Lena Albrecht."

In walked Lena, with the posture of a ballerina. Apparently she had listened to her mother's advice about standing up straight as a child. That, or she took a lot of dance classes growing up. Probably both. Her sleek French twist, white cashmere sweater, black leggings, and high boots exuded elegance.

The room erupted with applause.

"Thank you for that warm Neumann's welcome. What an honor to sing for you this evening. Shayla Johnson is going to accompany me on the piano."

Shayla, Lena's karaoke comrade and pianist at Music Keys, gave a full-faced smile to the crowd as she took her place at the grand piano bench.

"The first song I'm going to sing is a familiar one to many, but you may not know the history behind it. 'I'll Be Home for Christmas' was recorded in 1943 by Bing Crosby. It was written from the point of view of a World War II soldier who wouldn't be able to celebrate Christmas with his family because he was serving overseas. The holidays looked different than he would have liked. His heart was home, but his feet were a world away from those he loved.

"Millions of people visit Bavarian Falls every year, and as you know, most of them come to Neumann's. You play an important role in helping them get a taste—or rather, a feast—of Christmas. In some ways, the tourists are like that soldier, wanting to remember the childlike wonder of the season, even if they are far from home. Even when life hasn't turned out as they planned, it's here that they can reconnect with that which grounds us all, the love of God and the hospitable hearts of people. Thank you, Mr. Neumann, for overseeing a place that welcomes the world and offers them the uncomplicated message of the true meaning of Christmas: good news of great joy, for all people."

The audience erupted into cheers and applause.

It was evident that Lena had participated in many beauty pageants. Her wording, inflection, and gestures worked in unison. It was also clear this wasn't an act; Lena's sincerity and admiration for Bavarian Falls was genuine.

"For this first song, one of my friends at Music Keys is going to accompany me on the cello. Come on up, George."

George, head down, arms at his sides, marched to the front and took a seat near Lena. A man, most likely his dad, carried his cello and bow and placed them in front of him. Once he was situated, George placed his left hand on the neck of the cello and lifted the bow with his right. He waited for his instructor's cue.

With an assuring nod from Lena, George began the first few measures of "I'll Be Home for Christmas." The rich tones of the cello served as a current of lament, paired with Shayla's floating arpeggios and Lena's lilting soprano voice. Holly broke her gaze from the stage to glance at the audience and noticed that the rest of the party attendees seemed entranced. She spotted Andy across the room and waved to him, but he appeared to be deep in thought.

Holly looked around for another familiar face. Leslie was by the punch bowl, laughing about something with another employee. Teresa was nowhere to be found. And she wasn't sure she wanted to hang out with Frank all night. Although he had honored her "just friends" request, she couldn't be 100% sure that he wouldn't try to lead her over to the mistletoe, which she had spotted hanging from the rafters, a little too close to the food table.

Continuing to survey the showroom, Holly spotted Ms. Jingle Jangle herself, sniffling over her eggnog.

"Everything all right?" asked Holly as she approached.

"I'm sorry for this less-than-cheery display," replied Betty Jo, "but that song gets me every time."

"It was lovely, wasn't it?"

"Yes, it was. Lena's voice is a gift straight from heaven. But it also made me sad, reminding me of a dream that never came to fruition."

You and me both, Betty Jo.

At Betty Jo's admission, Holly felt the familiar longing of unfulfilled ambitions surface. She kept the attention on her boss, intentionally avoiding the spotlight that could expose her own disappointments.

"Did you want to be a singer?" deflected Holly.

"Not really, but my choir teacher did say I could break glass with my overactive vibrato."

"Did you want to start a nonprofit, like Lena has?"

Like I wanted to.

"That's a nice idea, but no, not that either."

"So what made you sad?" asked Holly. Her voice cracked as she willed her vulnerability to behave.

"Well, dear. I'm just going to blurt it out. I was almost engaged once. But it didn't end well."

"I'm so sorry. What happened?"

"Oh, you don't want to hear about it. You should go be with your friends, not stuck here listening to the store manager's sob story."

"I'm not going anywhere. And besides, this sounds a lot like one of the storylines from *Anne of Green Gables*, so I'm here for it."

The truth was, not only was Holly interested in hearing what Betty Jo was about to reveal, she couldn't shake the feeling that there might be a key dangling in this conversation that she was meant to find.

"If you're referring to Marilla and Mr. Blythe's courtship not working out, then you have an inkling of what happened."

"Oh, no."

"I met Clark Köhler when we were both working at Rudolph's Reindeer Farm. I was in charge of the holiday tours and he was training to be a large animal veterinarian—like that charming Dutch doc on TV.

"We hit it off and started dating in the off-season. A family emergency called him back to Milwaukee. Once things settled down, he invited me to come visit him in Wisconsin. It sounds silly now, but the city intimidated me. I'm just a simple lady who is comfortable in the country. Navigating that way of life was easy for him, but it was out of my comfort zone. I was scared to commit, not knowing if we had enough in common for the long haul. I waffled. I was preoccupied with losing what I had always known, not willing to leave the safety of home to make a new one. He ended up not finishing vet school and our phone calls became fewer and farther between. And with no way forward, because neither of us would budge, the relationship disintegrated."

Betty Jo's distraught expression was enough to make Holly sob herself. Her heartbreaking story of missed love, all because she couldn't picture herself flourishing elsewhere, was a tragedy.

Holly wrapped an arm around Betty Jo. "I'm so sorry."

They stood there side by side for a few moments before Betty Jo added, "I can't change what happened, and I try not to let it get the better of me. But when I hear that song, it reminds me that my home could have been somewhere else. Yes, it would have been different, but it might have been even better. Love takes guts, doesn't it?"

"You've got that right, especially when there's no guarantee it will end up like you envision," admitted Holly.

Holly felt compassion toward her manager, as well as a newly discovered kinship.

Passion for art and a hunger for adventure had driven Holly to put herself out there and relocate to Chicago, even though there were enormous obstacles in the way. Securing competitive grants, navigating the bustle of city life, and cutting through the red tape of bureaucracy was no picnic. Month after month, Holly persevered, determined to find a way to make her dream a reality. But eventually the little grant money she was able to secure ran out, the doors closed shortly after they opened, and her vibrant imagination had to face reality. Reflecting on the unsuccessful launch of her community art space in Chicago was a prime example of things not ending up the way she'd envisioned.

Betty Jo turned to face Holly. "Over time, I was able to take the love I had for Clark and use it to help others. It brings me such joy to see each face, young, old, and in between, different nationalities and languages all coming together here, under the banner of Christmas and what it means."

"You know what I just realized?"

"What's that, dear?"

"Even though you were afraid to go out into the world for love, you have been strategically entrusted with a position where the world comes to you! You impact people from all over with your kindness and care. The circumstances are not like you thought they'd be, but the impact reaches far beyond these walls."

Betty Jo's jovial demeanor returned to its rightful place as she processed Holly's profound conclusion. Holly longed for that same kind of impact...one that reached beyond herself and the walls she felt barred behind.

"I think you're right. All this time I felt like I missed the boat, but actually, trains, cars, planes, chartered buses, minivans, and maybe somehow, a few boats have made their way here. The void caused by my parting from Clark hasn't necessarily gone away altogether, but all is not lost. Repurposed, not wasted. Maybe I haven't missed my one chance, but have been given thousands of opportunities to love."

"That's the most beautiful thing I've heard in a long time," sighed Holly.

"Well, now—Lena's voice, *that* was something," reiterated Betty Jo.

"I prefer your epiphany."

"Thanks, dear. Now, you better run along. Go hang out with some people your age. Frank and Nik spent quite a bit of time hanging that mistletoe over there."

Oh boy.

Holly avoided any mistletoe mishaps by heading over to the Christmas tree display during Lena's next two songs. Never had she imagined she'd have a heart-to-heart with her manager during the party, and that their conversation would teach her so much—not just about Betty Jo, but about herself.

Holly couldn't help but notice the contrasts between her history and Betty Jo's. While her manager had never wanted to leave Bavarian Falls, Holly had never wanted to stay. But here she was, in the place from which she had tried to distance herself.

Lena's rendition of "I'll Be Home for Christmas" had touched something deep in Holly's heart, too. No longer hearing the song as a verdict on her detour back home, she heard an invitation to come home to who she once was—not an exact replica, but one that was repurposed, as Betty Jo had said. She wondered what it would be like to allow herself to uncover joy in her present circumstances, even when the circumstances felt lopsided and unfinished. Even when they weren't wrapped up with three pieces of tape and a symmetrical bow.

"Deep in thought?"

"Andy, you scared me!"

One look at her coworker and she knew something was wrong.

"You okay? Did Lena's song do a number on you, too?"

"Kind of. But probably not in the way you're thinking. While she was singing about not being home for Christmas, I got the impulsive idea to speed up my weekend plans. I didn't want Teresa to have to wait any longer, wondering how she was going to make it. And I didn't want to delay the inevitable. So I found her across the crowded room—"

"*South Pacific*?"

"Huh?"

"Never mind...keep going."

"I was already feeling nervous and the change of plans made it more so, but I didn't want the moment to pass. It felt right, ya know?"

"So what'd she say?"

"Well, I tried some small talk, but it fell flat. And since Teresa's pretty shy she wasn't providing much feedback. So I just kind of went for it. I said, 'Look, I know this sounds weird, but I feel like I'm supposed to offer you my house to live in.'"

"And what did she say? You're killin' me, Smalls!"

"*Sandlot?*"

"Ding ding."

"She didn't punch me, but what she said next pretty much did."

"Oh no, why?!"

"Well, at first she thought I was asking her to move in with me. But once I assured her I wasn't, she thought my offer was too much, assuming—as I feared—that I was declaring my affection. Then because I was flustered, I started mumbling stuff about the Inn and dinner and a note from Santa. And I think I lost her."

His jaw clenched as he paused, obviously affected by Teresa's negative reaction. "It was awful. Reminded me of when Tammy and I were trying to work through things but it was like we were speaking different languages. I was just trying to follow this crazy prompting and help a friend out, but it backfired."

Holly couldn't help but notice the juxtaposition between the celebratory work party in the background and the gravity of the current conversation.

"I don't know what to say. I mean, I'm just so sorry about the misunderstanding. Do you think she'll come around?'

"Doubt it. She seemed pretty overwhelmed. And that's what broke my heart. I was trying to ease her mind and her load, but I guess I messed it all up and made things worse."

It pained Holly to see her friend this way.

"So, you want a house?" said Andy, half-joking, half-serious, obviously still hurt.

"What?"

"Just thought I'd see if I had better luck with someone

else. But I know deep down it's for Teresa. I can't force her to receive the gift, though. That's up to her."

"I hope she comes around. But maybe just give her some time?"

"Well, I'm certainly not planning on putting myself out there any time soon."

"This work party is breaking my heart," admitted Holly.

"Don't say that, it's one of the highlights of the year. Just wait. I'll be fine, promise. And if Teresa doesn't change her mind, well, I'll put the house on the market and see what happens. I just don't like playing the fool, especially when I had noble intentions."

"You're a good guy, my friend."

"I don't know about that, but I try. Hey, since I won't be using the Edelweiss Inn dinner reservation this weekend, why don't you and your gal pals take a break from the movie marathon and eat up. My treat."

"See what I mean? That's so nice. Here's the thing, though—and I don't mean to sound ungrateful…but I think we're going to pass. Elaine works at the Inn and I'm pretty sure it's the last place she'll want to hang out on her day off, especially since it's December."

"Makes sense. Don't blame her."

"Thank you, though. That was really thoughtful."

"Maybe I'll see if Nik wants to use it for a date with Lena. I hear she's been putting in a lot of time after hours, with the album coming up. They could probably use a night out together."

"Probably."

"Hey, this is your first work party. You should go have fun

and not worry about me. I'm fine, really. Pride's just hurt. I'll bounce back."

"You sure?"

"Positive. You won't want to miss out on the Bavarian feast and the after-dinner entertainment."

"You're not sticking around?"

"I think I'm going to call it a night."

As Andy turned to leave, Holly stood in place, contemplating how the night had unfolded. Bittersweet conversations had induced so many feelings—she felt inside out.

Just then the new guy in town, who had exchanged his elfin garb for handsome party digs, caught her off guard.

"Hey, Holly. Have you seen Frank? We've got some drooping mistletoe and I'm looking for the ladder before it drowns in the punchbowl."

"Nik to the rescue again, eh?"

Nik rubbed the back of his neck as if trying to divert Holly's observation.

"I actually haven't seen him—which may be hard to believe, but I've been detained with…" her voice trailed off with a sniff as she processed the weight of Betty Jo's and Andy's disappointments that mirrored her own.

"You okay?"

"You must think I'm a piece of work, huh? First nearly fainting, now a mess of emotions at the Christmas party. I'm usually a lot more fun than this, but coming home has magnified what's missing and it aches, ya know?"

Why am I telling him this? He is the last person I should feel safe to talk to—he's dangerous, right? Or was? Maybe all that's behind him now?

"I do."

"You do?"

"Yeah, I get what you're saying. Of course I don't know exactly what you're feeling, but I've been through some hard stuff, too."

Don't let on that you know what that hard stuff might be.

"You have?"

"Let's just say my old job nearly killed me. I put it all on the line, but it wasn't enough. I tried doing the right thing but it all went south. Nothing like I pictured, you know?" Nik rubbed his neck again and looked back toward the party, clearly conflicted.

"I do."

"You do?"

"This is definitely *not* how I pictured my life turning out. Since I was thirteen, I dreamed of my big move from small town to big city. I wanted to use my art skills for the greater good and inspire others to exercise their creativity, too. But when my execution of a collective art space in Chicago fell through and the money ran out, I was forced to come back home to regroup. Let's just say this was not part of the plan," Holly confessed, crossing her arms and pulling them in close as if to hold in further vulnerability.

"I think it takes courage to regroup. And hey, you're still using your talents for the good of others. I heard that you're the best custom painter on staff. And just think of how many homes your ornament art will be displayed in this season."

"Huh, I guess I've never thought of it that way."

"You're spreading a whole lot of joy in spite of your disappointment. And if you ask me, that's pretty cool."

"Thanks," replied Holly, amazed that Nik was able to pivot her perspective with a simple observation.

"Now, I've really gotta run and find Frank. The mistletoe mission awaits!"

"Go get 'em. Save the party from the droopy—or already drenched—mistletoe."

With a determined nod, Nik headed toward the heart of the showroom. But after a few steps he turned back, adding one more piece of encouragement: "Whether in Bavarian Falls, Chicago, or somewhere else, you're an artist, Holly. That's all there is to it."

As Nik walked away, Holly uncrossed her arms and straightened her shoulders. Never would she have imagined that an ex-con's compliment would make her feel like a real artist.

CHAPTER 13

Chasing the Blues Away

WITH HER COUNSELING APPOINTMENT SCHEDULED FOR the next day, Holly knew she had to expedite her plan to help Lena before it was too late. Questioning her sanity for adding more to her already full plate with work, Christmas approaching, and trying to enjoy a smidgen of a social life, Holly resolved to do the hard thing of helping Miss Perfect in her time of need. Besides, Holly found satisfaction in spotting an inch of Wonder Woman's humanity showing.

After work, Holly pulled up to Music Keys. As she approached the steps, she noticed that the window boxes housed pine boughs, white-capped pinecones, and realistic-looking holly berries. Leave it Lena to make time for intentional decorating in the midst of a demanding season.

Holly knocked before opening the Bavarian-styled door that led to the reception area.

"Come on in," said Nik, approaching the ornate door.

"Elaine here yet? I came over as soon as I got out of work."

"She texted Lena and said she was running a few minutes late. Coffee?"

"Tea for me, thanks."

"Let me guess, chai?"

"How'd you know? Am I that predictable?"

"Truth? I noticed it on the counter at your house when the groceries were unpacked."

"You're quite the spy," replied Holly.

That or you're casing the joint. If the chai goes missing with the TV, you're sunk, Nik.

"Oh good, you're here," announced Lena as she rounded the corner.

"Elaine's not far behind," added Nik, noticing his girlfriend's scan of the room.

"Come on back, Holly. I've got a spot set up for us to meet."

"I'll bring your tea back when it's ready. Just call me Barista Beckenbauer."

Lena offered what looked like a rehearsed smile and gestured for Holly to follow her.

Once settled, the meeting began.

"Thanks again for offering to help. Late starts are not usually my style, but with the grant coming through at the last minute and our recording window being limited, it couldn't be avoided. So, what are your thoughts?"

"Well, I contacted the local VFW to see if they'd like to participate. They loved the idea, but couldn't commit because most of their volunteers are being utilized to set up for the annual craft show."

"This is what I was worried about—everyone's already at capacity. Please tell me you have some more ideas. We can't stop now. The kids have been looking forward to recording for weeks." Lena tapped her fingers on the desk, letting out nervous energy.

Knock knock.

"A chai for you," Nik said as he set the steaming mug next to Holly. "And an almond soy milk steamer for you." Nik kissed Lena on the temple as he handed her the beverage. Holly couldn't help but notice that Nik's kissing ability appeared more tender and refined than Frank's had been.

"That was sweet, thank you," noted Lena, this time with a genuine smile.

"I just saw Elaine pull up. I'll let her in, then I'm headed to shoot some hoops with Frank and some of his buddies."

"Okay, have fun. We'll be solving the world's problems while you sweat."

Nik paused in the doorway, obviously trying to decipher whether Lena's statement was passive aggressive or playful. Holly almost felt bad for him.

A knock on the door sped up his departure as Lena's finger tapping got louder.

"So, any more creative solutions for this complex problem?" she asked.

"I think Elaine has been working on a few angles but I did have one more. What if we partnered with—"

"Sorry I'm late." Elaine barged in with a bottled water that displayed the Music Keys logo. Apparently Barista Beckenbauer had fulfilled her order as well.

"It's understandable. This town is on overdrive this time of year."

"Nik asked me to give you this." Elaine handed Lena a While You Were Out slip. "He said it was from Chase's mom?"

Lena read the message audibly: "Chase has horse therapy today and will be twenty minutes late to rehearsal. So sorry! See you then."

"Horse therapy?" asked Elaine.

"It's wonderful—except when it conflicts with rehearsal. Sorry, I shouldn't have said that out loud. It's truly amazing. Adoptive children, individuals with disabilities, and veterans have all benefited from it. The horses and instructors help them process trauma through intentional exercises that develop trust and confidence. The Ranch is a big supporter of what we're doing, too. Horse therapy and music therapy are similar in some ways. They both aid clients in getting unstuck and rising to their potential. The horses seem to understand what's going on, even when the clients can't articulate it with words."

Holly wondered if she could switch her counseling appointment to The Ranch instead. Horse therapy sounded much more appealing.

"So, ladies, any other ideas to move the needle forward?"

Elaine added her findings to the think tank, but after some deliberation none of them were quite the right fit, either.

"I hate to cut this short," said Lena, looking at her smartwatch, "but the clients will be arriving shortly for rehearsal. I need to step out, but if you're able to strategize a bit more, I'd really appreciate it."

"We can. Don't worry, we'll figure this out...somehow," insisted Elaine.

Holly knew Lena was busy, but she couldn't help feeling like they'd been brushed off.

"Great! I knew I could count on you two. As you can see, most of my time is accounted for, and then some."

"I don't know how you do it all," Elaine said, shaking her head.

"When you really believe in something, you'll put in whatever time is needed to see it through," Lena stated matter-of-factly.

Back to the drawing board, Holly and Elaine put their heads together to come up with a creative idea to include military personnel in the grant project. It hadn't seemed like a difficult task at first, but they were coming up short and time was running out.

In their focused brainstorming session, they nearly missed the soft knock on the door of the office.

"Excuse me. Hi, I'm Chase's mom, Rosalee, and I'm wondering if you could help me with something? Lena's tied up with rehearsal so I don't want to interrupt her. They should be taking a break pretty soon so Chase can join them then, but he's having a hard time and I'm wondering if one of you might sit with him? I hate to leave him like this, but my husband needs our spare set of keys, and Chase doesn't want to miss any more rehearsal."

"No problem at all, I can do that," volunteered Holly.

"Oh, thank you. I don't usually leave Chase with strangers, I promise, but I just don't know what else to do."

Extending her hand, Holly introduced herself to Rosalee so they weren't strangers anymore.

"Besides, Chase and I bonded at Neumann's during a little

field trip excitement there."

"Are you Chase's angel? The school filled me in on my escape artist's daring act of worship. They didn't know the name of the woman who found him. But it sounds like it was you?"

"In the flesh," confirmed Elaine, pointing at Holly.

An unexpected shyness came over Holly in the presence of Rosalee's shower of gratitude.

"As you can imagine," Rosalee continued, "it's hard to send Chase off to school and to things like field trips and extracurricular activities. He's usually fine, but it's a leap of faith to trust that others are going to care for him like we do. We want him to be as independent as possible, but learning when to let go and when to hold on sometimes feels like a physics equation—and math was never my strong suit."

"We'll definitely keep a close eye on him," Holly assured her.

"Does he like hot cocoa?" asked Elaine. "I saw some out front. My mom used to add as many marshmallows as my age until a few years ago because it was getting a little out of hand."

"He's a cocoa fan for sure. Thank you. I'll be back as soon as I can."

Rosalee explained to Chase what was going on. He smiled when he heard about the cocoa, which Elaine was busily getting ready.

When he saw Holly, he said, "Ba-ba-baby Jee-jee-susss."

"I've never been called that before. But yes, that's where we met each other. You have a good memory. I'm Holly, remember? It's good to see you again."

Rosalee tiptoed out the front door with a small wave.

"So, I hear you were at horse lessons."

Chase's downtrodden gaze seemed to perk ever so slightly.

"I'm not much of a rider, but they are beautiful, aren't they?"

Holly noticed something in Chase's hand. It was a photograph of a reddish-brown horse.

"Who's that?"

Chase rubbed the photo like he was petting the animal. He slowly turned it over, revealing the name: Solomon.

"Is Solomon the horse's name?"

Chase nodded.

"Is he your favorite?"

"Yup-uh."

"Well, he's very handsome."

"Sss-sick," added Chase, his lower lip turned downward as he searched Holly's face for comfort.

"Solomon is sick?"

Another nod.

"I sure hope he gets better."

"Is that why you're feeling sad?"

"Yup-uh."

"It's hard when those we love are sick, isn't it?" The irony was not lost on Holly. "You know what helps me when I'm feeling sad?"

Chase waited.

"I like to listen to jazz music. Not the sad and slow kind, but the upbeat, dance party kind. You like music, right?"

More nodding.

"Well, what do you say we chase our blues away with some big band tunes?"

Holly pulled out her phone and looked up one of the

happiest songs she knew. She stood and danced to the music, complete with shoulder sways and snaps on the off-beat. Chase soon joined her, tapping his head and feet, still holding his beloved photo, as Sinatra flew them to the moon.

The front door jingled while the dancing duo was in full swing.

"Hey, you two…nice moves." Nik shut the door and stomped off his snow-tipped boots, a few packages in one arm.

"F-f-for me?" asked Chase, eyeing the supposed gifts.

"Sorry, this is for my special lady."

He thrust his tongue on the "L" as he answered with, "Ma-ma-miss Lena?"

"That's right, my man."

"Lena still in rehearsal?" Nik asked Holly, hanging up his coat.

"Yes, we're just waiting until their break so Chase can join them."

"Good to see you again, Bud." Nik extended a high five to Chase with his free hand before heading to the back office.

Holly admired Nik's knack for connecting with Chase. If she didn't know he was an ex-con and if he wasn't attached to Lena, he'd be exactly the kind of guy Holly was looking for.

The last chords of the song rang out, cueing Holly to bow to Chase. He mimicked her final movement.

They took a seat, satisfied by their spontaneous dance party.

Elaine appeared with a large mug of cocoa—not too hot—and a candy dish full of marshmallows.

"How old are you, Chase?" she asked.

He handed the horse photograph to Holly, then held up

both hands.

"Ten marshmallows coming right up."

Chase rubbed his hands together in anticipation, rocking back and forth in his chair. His grin communicated Christmas-morning delight as he watched Elaine *plop, plop, plop* ten marshmallows into the festive mug.

Holly held onto Solomon as Chase enjoyed his drink, right down to the last drop. Soon the other clients took their break, and Chase joined them for rehearsal—cocoa mustache and all.

* * *

It was time to face the past. Not that Holly hadn't tried before, but if she was going to get unstuck she needed to stop spinning her wheels, rehearsing the same hurt over and over.

Holly had gotten out of work early on Thursday to make it to her counseling appointment. She was thankful there wasn't such a stigma about seeing a therapist these days, but she also didn't feel like plastering it on a billboard, splattering it on social media, or telling her parents or coworkers.

Finding someone to fill in at work hadn't been easy. Thankfully, Betty Jo ended up helping out. Andy would probably need an ear detox afterwards from all her chatter, but at least he and Holly would have some good material to laugh about together the next day.

An unassuming woman with salt-and-pepper hair and kind eyes greeted Holly as she entered her office.

"I'm Nina. It's nice to meet you. Feel free to have a seat."

Holly and Nina gelled quickly, which was good because

Holly was ready for a deep dive. Well, she thought she was, until the ugly cry burst out and the snot started pouring, but by that point it was too late to turn back.

Holly started by sharing what life was like before Dad's incident, and how much had changed since he returned from his deployment. She talked about how Christmas triggered her grief. She mentioned her confession at Thanksgiving with her mom and how she had felt pushed aside as a kid because of her Dad's issues, yet felt guilty for feeling that way. And how even though she knew it hurt her mom to admit that, it felt freeing to no longer avoid the elephant in the room. The egg shells. The tip-toeing around landmines, which her family had become so proficient at. Holly brought up the failed start-up in the city, which led to her addressing her singleness and how she hoped it wasn't a permanent fixture. She admitted that it was hard to keep her hopes up, not just in the guy department, but in general. A lot had gone wrong. She had spent so much time and energy wishing things were different. Her soul felt fatigued.

Nina listened intently, nodding, taking notes, and pausing to ask a few clarifying questions.

Holly had assured her that she was ready to deal with things.

"I don't usually recommend something like this in the first session, but I can tell you're determined. And Holly, you're strong." She paused for emphasis. "What you've faced is not easy, but it's evident that you're resilient."

Determined. Strong. Resilient. These were not words that Holly would have used to describe herself, but hearing them from the counselor caused her to stand up on the inside.

"This might sound strange at first, but I want you to bury your dad."

Holly just about came out of her chair, thoroughly shocked.

"I don't think I heard you right, say that again?"

"I want you to bury the version of your dad that no longer exists. Picture yourself at his coffin. Remember the good memories before the crisis. Let yourself grieve what has been lost. Let yourself feel the letting go of that which you can't bring back."

"Woah, this sounds really sad. I'm not sure I can do that."

"Your dad's aneurysm was really sad. Have you given yourself permission to feel the weight of that sadness?"

"What if I get stuck there, in that layer of grief?"

"Well, there's another piece to this exercise. But its effectiveness is contingent on you seeing the first part through."

"Okay. What is it?"

"After you bury what will never be, you accept what is. You let your dad off the hook by burying your expectation and longing for him to return to who he was. And then you celebrate who he actually is, post-aneurysm. You find the good in his limitations and become acquainted with him in the here and now."

"Kind of like the Glad Game?" asked Holly.

"I'm not sure I follow."

"Actually, I think you might be on to something. Not gonna lie, the burial thing sounds a little hokey—no offense. But I think what's tripped me up and held me back for so long is the underlying frustration that things are not as they should be. And no matter how much I wish or plead, or even try to distance myself from it all, I can't change what happened."

"And how does that make you really feel?" Nina waited for her to continue.

"You know what—it makes me so mad! Why can't I have my Dad back?!" Holly yelled, taken back by the force with which she shot out the words.

"Holly."

"Why do I have to say goodbye? I'm just a little girl inside who wants her daddy to be the strong one for her again. I'm tired of being brave! I need him to help me believe that being back home after my failure to launch is not the final say on my worth."

Holly felt as if she'd been lugging around a gallon of paint for years, and her outburst had hurled it all into the air. They sat in silence as Holly's gut-wrenching honesty covered the office walls, dripping down slowly until it pooled on the floor at her feet.

Her heart pounded from the surge of adrenaline. She took in some stabilizing breaths and let them out slowly.

She had finally turned the knob and let herself be found in the place where she was stuck. Everything wasn't fixed, but in the aftermath of Holly's unedited confession, the pent-up pain finally released from its sealed container, and an instantaneous peace filled the void.

CHAPTER 14

Kris Kringle Academy

THE DAY AFTER HER COUNSELING APPOINTMENT, HOLLY was tempted to take a mental health day instead of returning to work. She felt a strange blend of contentment and emotional depletion after her intense session. Relieved to have started the counseling process, she knew she had more work ahead of her—and not the ornament personalization kind, but allowing a fresh perspective to be written on her heart and mind.

While Holly tried to resist the nap that was calling her name, she caught a glimpse of a very realistic-looking Santa wearing a t-shirt. Upon closer examination it read, "If you want to sit in the chair, you've gotta grow the hair." Apparently this Santa lookalike took the slogan literally. He sported the prettiest head of long, white hair Holly had ever seen. She thought she spotted a bicep tattoo that read, "Mrs. C.," but he wasn't close enough for her to confirm or deny.

Just as Holly returned to the ornament in front of her, another Santa lookalike walked in front of the counter. This Santa wore a Hawaiian shirt and shorts—in December. He looked like he ate more salads than cookies, and his hair was shorter. Maybe he didn't take his chair time quite as seriously as Santa #1? But the "Ho ho ho!" that he voluntarily offered on his way past Holly was the most authentic-sounding Santa voice she'd ever heard.

Soon after the trim, healthy Santa walked by, a third Santa-type moseyed her way, decked out in sweatpants and an oversized red hoody with a larger than life button that read, "Mo cookies, mo presents. No cookies, no presents."

Good grief, Charlie Brown. Is this for real?

Holly rubbed her temple and wondered if her time in Christmas Wonderland had finally gotten to her. Or was her decision to face old wounds having residual effects? Were the Santas part of a hallucination?

To be fair, all three Santas had two things in common: white hair (whether real or wigged) and a jolly countenance about them. They seemed to be on some sort of field trip. Maybe they were Frank's distant relatives, or his neighbors from North Pole, Alaska?

Andy had been out running an errand for Leslie. When he returned, Frank was with him.

"Just wanted to check on our supply of Christmas holly ornaments," winked Frank, as forthright as ever, even after their "frank" talk.

Contrived pick-up line or legitimate errand?

Frank's lingering at Station 8 confirmed the former. Holly decided to risk sounding like an idiot to get to the bottom of the chimney—er, mystery.

"Either I've been putting too much time in, or I've lost it."

"Do tell," encouraged Frank as he leaned on the counter.

"I think I'm starting to see things that aren't there. No less than three Santas have crossed my path today. Doesn't Neumann's use one at a time?"

"I haven't seen more than one here today," Andy insisted with a mischievous grin.

"Spill it. What's going on?"

"It's the annual Kris Kringle Academy field trip," Frank explained.

"That sounds made up."

"I swear upon my hunting blind, it's the truth. The Kris Kringle Academy is only about an hour from here, as the crow flies," insisted Andy.

"How did I miss that? I grew up near a training center for Santas and didn't even know it?"

"It's too late for enrollment for this year. And I hear there's usually a waiting list." Frank waggled his eyebrows, thoroughly enjoying himself and his present company.

"Very funny."

Andy added, "This is Betty Jo's favorite day of work. She highly anticipates the arrival of the Kris Kringle Academy students. She told me so yesterday. I have a hunch she wishes she were Mrs. Claus, in another life."

"She'd be perfect for that," Holly concurred. "She could jingle the whole year through."

Just then Frank's walkie talkie went off and he was summoned to the warehouse to address a pressing issue.

"Duty calls! See you kids around!" Frank power-posed

with one fist on his hip and the other extended into space, making a dramatic exit.

Holly shook her head at his over-the-top—mostly annoying, yet slightly amusing—departure.

"So where were you yesterday, anyway?" Andy asked. "It was a bit dicey here with your temporary replacement."

"I'll bet. Anything to report?"

"Are you avoiding the question?"

"That obvious?" smiled Holly.

"You tell me, I'll tell you," Andy reasoned.

"Are you bargaining with me?"

"I'd say it's an even trade."

"That depends on what you have."

"Ladies first. I insist."

"I'm going to counseling to face some things I've been trying to run from."

"Cool. Me too. Several years in. Not fun, but necessary."

"We agree again. Now tell me something good," urged Holly.

"Well, if you promise to keep it between us. Our store manager may have wanted to attend the same school as Mrs. Rasmussen."

"To be a gym teacher?"

"Not that. Kris Kringle Academy."

"They both wanted to be Santa? They'd have to stop waxing and plucking, then."

"Funny, but no. I did a little fact checking on the school's website and discovered that you can enroll as a couple to get trained as Santa and Mrs. Claus."

"That makes more sense."

"Yes to waxing and plucking continuing, please and thank you," added Andy.

"I'm not so sure about Mrs. R. in that role, but I can totally picture Betty Jo as the quintessential Mrs. Claus."

"That's what I thought. It doesn't sound like the dream has died, either…I think it's alive and well."

"So why hasn't she pursued it?" posed Holly.

"Not sure. Timing, maybe? No Mr. Claus? And can you imagine this place without her?"

"No way. She's part of the total package."

Andy added, "No one sings the theme song with as much gusto as she does."

"And no one jingles quite like she does, either."

"But on the other hand, everyone deserves a shot at their dreams."

"Yeah, and she's missed out on some already."

"What do you mean?"

"Just a hunch."

The conversation halted as Santa #4, clothed in a three-piece reindeer-print suit topped with a fedora, asked for directions to the restroom.

"A little too much eggnog on the bus ride," he chuckled.

Andy pointed the way toward relief.

"So how many Santas are here?" asked Holly, after suited Santa was out of earshot.

"Hard to tell. Let's look it up."

Andy pulled out his phone and searched for the website as Holly looked on.

"Hey guys, have you seen Frank? He's not answering my texts and I need to finalize something with him for Lena."

Nik is so supportive of Lena. I'm not sure she knows how lucky she is. He sure bends over backwards for her, but without cramping her style. Either that or he's buttering her up in an effort to scam her somehow. But that's hard to picture, now that I've gotten to know him better. Or has he tricked me, too? Oh Nik, you're still a mystery in so many ways.

"He's over in the warehouse, but I imagine he'll be back soon. He's taken a special interest in the store's Christmas Holly," snickered Andy.

Holly rolled her eyes.

"If you're sticking around to wait, you want to do a little investigating with us?"

"Sure, why not?" conceded Nik.

With a few clicks while bringing Nik up to speed, the coworkers found their answer on the Kris Kringle Academy's website.

"100 Santas?! I've only spotted four so far. People who aren't from around here would never believe this is our real life. It's like we're living in a holiday cartoon special."

"Or a Christmas novel turned movie," responded Andy.

"That too. Although I hear they usually film those in Vancouver in the summer."

They returned to the website to mine for more material.

"One of the classes they offer is Santa sign language. I wonder what that entails?" asked Holly.

"It probably includes laying one finger aside of the nose, with the pointer finger of the other hand beckoning children to come sit," demonstrated Nik.

Three-piece suit Santa returned. "Couldn't help but catch that last part. You're right on the money," he confirmed, laying a finger above his right nostril for emphasis.

"So, Santa. Let me ask you this. What's the weirdest request you've gotten for a present?" Andy asked, as he and Holly exchanged knowing looks, thinking about Oliver's six-pack wish.

"Well, there's the usual weird requests, like one little girl from North Carolina who asked for a dolphin and a rainbow. The rainbow was above my pay grade—and well, the dolphin was too, for that matter. But as I recall, a dolphin poster and necklace may have found their way under her tree. Her brother asked for a golf cart. I'm not sure how much weight he thought the sleigh could take. Pretty sure the little tikes don't factor in the total poundage of everyone's gifts when they make their requests.

"One boy, although his hands were fully functioning, asked for a fake hand and some dirt from Wyoming.

"And then there's the one I'll never forget. A sweetie from Fort Hood climbed up on my lap. Her dad was deployed somewhere overseas. I prepared myself for her request, wondering if it'd be a letter from her daddy or to bring her daddy back home. But instead, she looked up at me with the sincerest expression and said, 'Santa, I'm just asking for one thing, so it shouldn't be hard to remember. World peace, please.' It seemed out of reach, but definitely worth asking for. And I've never forgotten it. It should be on the top of all of our Christmas lists, don't you think?"

"A grown-up Christmas list of sorts," Andy said.

"Not that song again! And don't get me started on 'Last Christmas' or 'All I Want for Christmas is You.' *Gag.*"

"Where's your sense of romance, Holly girl?" teased Andy

as he started humming the first few lines of the last song mentioned.

"Romance to me is more like steadiness and tenderness, versus hype and lavish displays of affection."

"Oh come on, you mean to tell me you wouldn't get weak in the knees if a guy made a fool of himself for you?" ribbed Andy.

Santa inched closer to hear her response, a twinkle in his eye.

"Well, I suppose an over-the-top moment or two would be okay, but I want a guy who gets me and who will get along with my family—or at least tolerate them—so holidays won't be tense. I also hope he's good-looking and a hard worker with a sense of humor. And, this is very important—is at least three inches taller than me."

"Sounds like an online dating service profile," Andy commented.

"Don't act like you don't have one, too," Holly warned.

"Guilty as charged," admitted Andy.

"I used to, but no need for it anymore," smiled Nik.

No way! Did Lena and Nik meet on a dating site? I can't imagine Lena doing that. But then again, she's always so busy. How else would she meet someone from across the country? Mental note: Investigate this theory with Elaine.

Santa leaned toward the single employees and cupped his mouth with his right hand. "If you can keep a secret, you're not the only ones," he winked.

"You have a dating profile?" asked a surprised Holly.

"Been looking for a new Mrs. Claus for a while now. The original took her last sleigh ride in the sky about a decade ago.

But 2.0 has to be special—strong enough to keep up with the rigors of the season and tender enough to connect with all our children."

"You want children?" Holly reacted.

"At my age? Oh, no. Already have a handful back home and mini-grands running around, too. I was meaning all the children at the shopping mall who come for a visit and a picture with us. She needs to be welcoming but not a pushover, since the line needs to keep moving so everyone has a turn. Takes a special lady to become Mrs. Claus. A real blend of grit and grace, laced with gentleness and blessed with wit. I'll know her when I see her."

"I bet you will," said Nik.

"And natural white hair is a plus. Although we learned in the Mrs. Claus breakout session that the right combination of at-home hair color can fix that. Oh, and there's one more piece of criteria that is of utmost importance," added Santa, adjusting his fedora. "It might seem nitpicky but it's actually a big deal."

"What's that?" egged Andy.

"She has to look good in red."

"Of course she does! Comes with the territory." Andy held an even tone, but Holly knew him well enough by now to recognize he was teasing.

"Well, Santa, thanks for telling us what's on your grown-up Christmas list," continued Andy.

"Your secret is safe with us. In fact, I'm kind of a professional secret keeper," Holly assured him, avoiding a sideways glance at Nik.

"If I can offer one piece of unsolicited advice, it's this:

don't despise grand displays of love. Yet hold on to the everyday kind of love, too. His hand in yours, a listening ear when you're stressed, a shoulder to cry on when you're sad, and a smile that makes you feel like you're home, even when you're miles from it. Stick with someone who gets you and loves you as you are, and with whom you can laugh and dream."

"Did you rehearse that?" asked Andy, interrupting the sage wisdom of Santa #4.

"Thank you," responded Holly. "I'll definitely keep that in mind."

"Me too," added Nik. His voice was thoughtful enough that Holly glanced up to see his serious face. *What was he thinking?*

With a nod, wink, and a bit more sign language, Santa #4 left to meet up with ninety-six of his bearded brothers who were gathering outside for their annual Kris Kringle Academy group photo.

"A Mrs. Claus breakout session? Sure he didn't mean a Mrs. Claus make-out session?" joked Andy.

"You're terrible!"

"But that was fantastic. Wait until Ollie hears that I got some face time with the big guy."

"You should've asked him for your own BB gun," teased Holly.

"Now you can see why I keep working here. It's never boring."

"That's for sure."

"I think we should recruit that Santa to fill in for Doc next year. That way there's no chance of emergency dental procedures," suggested Nik.

"Right on. My brief stint filling in for Doc was no picnic. I'm telling you, that red velvet suit does not breathe!"

"I'll bet! My elf leggings weren't the most comfortable, either."

"So, Holly-girl, you think you'll be back here next season? Just think, you'll have more quality time with the likes of me and this cast of quirky characters."

"It's been real. Well actually, more like make-believe, but you know what I mean. Here's the thing, though…I'm working through some stuff, and I'm determined to see it through. And I'm saving up some more. As soon as I can, after those things are taken care of, I'm planning on starting up again elsewhere, further from Bavarian Falls."

"Say it ain't so. You're sure gonna be missed 'round these parts, little lady," twanged Andy.

Nik pulled his phone out of his back pocket and read an incoming text.

"If you promise not to tell—about Santa's online dating profile, or about what I'm about to say…" Holly began.

"Scout's honor," Andy saluted.

"Then, I'll admit—only to you—that this place has grown on me."

"Ha! Knew it."

"Even Betty Jo's holiday radiance will be missed."

"And Frank's showmanship?" pushed Andy. "Talk about lavish displays of affection…that kid would be one to propose on a hot air balloon ride during the summer festival."

"You're on thin ice, Bucko."

"Couldn't resist."

"Hey guys, this has been fun. But that was Frank. I'm

going to meet him now and I'll be sure to fill him in on Santa's relationship advice." He smiled in Holly's direction.

Nik still thinks Frank and I are a thing. Please don't encourage him with relationship advice regarding me. He doesn't need any motivation to flirt more.

Once Nik was out of earshot, Holly turned on Andy. "Frank and I are just friends. Seriously, stop encouraging him. Besides, I'm kind of rooting for him and Elaine—that is, if he can get it through his head that I view him more as the younger brother I never had instead of a love interest."

"Like Star Wars?"

"Eww, don't get me started on Luke and Leia."

Betty Jo waved as she walked by, more chipper than ever.

At that, Holly and Andy turned to each other and exclaimed in unison, "Mrs. Claus!"

CHAPTER 15

The Scavenger Hunt

IT WAS ONLY THREE DAYS UNTIL CHRISTMAS. HOLLY WAS doing some very last-minute shopping downtown after work, trying to find the perfect gift for her mom who never seemed to need anything, except for her daughter to meet her expectations. No pressure.

Bzzzt. Bzzzt.

Dare I hope that Mom has started texting? Probably needs something from the store.

Bzzzt. Bzzzt.

Holly set down a pine-scented candle at the gift shop on Main to read the message. She was surprised to see the sender was Frank.

Can u do me a favor?

What's up?

I'm supposed to unlock the showroom for a
friend at 10.

After hours? Sounds mysterious.

Yes. I'm tied up.

Literally?

No. ;-) Tied up w/ big shipping ordeal in warehouse. Can u?

Unlock showroom? Sure.

U da best.

Where do I get the key?

Promise u won't tell?

To. the. grave.

What?

Nvm. Yes, I promise. Where is it?

In a secret compartment under Baby Jesus #1.

Dude, there's a lot of Jesus on the
property. Which one?

The one out front, under the store name and motto.

Chase's Jesus?

That's the one.

U owe me.

A carriage ride? ;-)

> Ha! How about a hot cocoa
> voucher for Stocking Stuffers'?

Done.

Holly concluded the conversation with a thumbs up emoji and pocketed her phone. Her mom had introduced her to the Nancy Drew books as a child, and now it seemed Holly had been invited to play a supporting role in *The Case of the Christmas Store Caper*—except the boss's grandson knew about the break-in. And it wasn't really a break-in, since Holly had been asked to unlock the door. But a girl can still pretend.

After stowing away her last-minute gifts, heating up leftover pot roast from their Sunday lunch, working on a painting for Claudia, freshening up, and tossing her pepper spray into her purse for good measure, Holly headed back to work. Cocoa instead of cash would be her prize, and maybe a glimpse of the mystery that was unfolding after hours at Neumann's.

Holly parked her Prius around the corner. If there was anything weird going on, she didn't want to get mixed up in it. Although, Frank was a friend and she was sure he wouldn't put her in danger.

Calm down. This isn't Chicago. It's the capital city of

Christmas, remember?

Holly realized she'd been cooped up a little too long in this Norman Rockwell scene. She made a mental note to schedule time in the city with Elaine as soon as Christmas was over.

Avoiding the temptation to treat this favor as a spy mission and sneak through the shadows, Holly opted for the run-as-fast-as-you-can approach, as she sprinted over to Baby Jesus #1.

Sure enough, there was a doorbell-type contraption under the statue that released when pressed. Out dropped a key.

Holly's pulse quickened as she grabbed it and replaced the secret compartment. The nativity scene was lit up like a Christmas tree even when the store was closed, and she didn't want to be caught red-handed and confused as the Christmas Store caper herself. It was almost 10, so she sprinted again to the west entrance as Frank had instructed her.

The wintry evening air in her nostrils and her shaking hands added to the drama as she fumbled to unlock the show-room door. Thankfully the timed exterior and interior lights allowed her to make contact between key and keyhole, and she pushed open the door.

Inside, Holly was determined to warm up. As she did, she peered into the empty parking lot, anticipating the arrival of the mysterious guest.

She realized that Frank had failed to give further instructions past the request to unlock the door. Was she supposed to wait for someone to show up? Was she supposed to lock up afterwards?

That's when she noticed the music. She had grown accustomed to tuning it out during work hours, but she suddenly realized the cheery holiday tunes had been replaced by Vivaldi's

"Winter" violin concertos. Had someone forgotten to turn off the sound system? Maybe the cleaning crew had changed it and forgotten to shut it down? That seemed unlikely, and negligent.

Tap into your sleuthing skills, Nancy.

Walking further into the store, Holly spun slowly, looking up to where the music cascaded from. In slow motion she started to notice what she had missed upon entering. Thousands of dainty white lights had been added above her, winding around the dimly light store.

She tentatively started following the strings of lights. As she passed through Station 10 she smiled, remembering Frank's clumsy encounter with the display there.

A spotlight from the rafters projected a ray of light onto a white envelope lying on the carpet. Holly stepped toward the envelope and saw that it read, "Open me first."

Holly glanced behind her. No movement. She inched closer. *Is this for me?*

Her hands warmed but now shaking in anticipation and healthy fear, she picked up the envelope. The lettering was more welcoming than menacing; more like an invitation than a ransom note. She opened it.

> I realize this may be unexpected. You've been putting in a lot of hours, so I thought a scavenger hunt of sorts would be fun. Keep following the clues and see where it goes.
>
> Love, Me.
>
> P.S. Clue #2 is hanging with care, with holly on it. It's green like a pear.

Love? Oh dear. It couldn't be for her. Could it?

Was Frank trying to win her over even though she had been careful not to lead him on?

The music continued to play and Holly's heart continued to race, but her steps quieted to a tiptoe. The life-size nutcrackers seemed to stand at attention. The ornaments served as secret keepers, as Holly meandered through the vast showroom.

The next envelope was located just past the customization station. It was clearly positioned in a lime green stocking, with a hand-stitched holly on the front of it. Its contents read:

> I know we haven't known each other for very long, but it feels like forever. You bring light and beauty to those around you and to those who care about you. I think you have more than a clue that I deeply care for you.

Gulp.

Holly steadied herself, one hand on the wall, before continuing.

> If I haven't scared you off yet, keep going. Clue #3 is all about dates. Go find the ones that open and close. And specifically look for Rudolph's nose. P.S. I hope to go on many more dates with you.

Holly had been so caught up in the magical and mysterious experience that her brain and heart hadn't synced until now.

Had Frank set her up—pretending that he was tied up in the warehouse? Hadn't she made it clear there were only friends, with no promise of more?

Her stomach flip-flopped, yet she was determined to see the scavenger hunt through. She would face what was to come when she arrived at the final clue.

Envelope #3 was located at Station 5, near the Advent calendars. The huge Santa and his reindeer calendar stood out above the rest, with an envelope taped to the back.

> We're a few days away from something special on the calendar. It seemed fitting to surprise you with this before you were expecting a gift. This whole evening is to solidify that you are of utmost importance to me. And I hope you feel the same way, too.
>
> Do you have time for a show? If so, enter the theatre and sit at the seat with the bow.

Good King Wenceslas. What is going on?

Holly was tempted to text Elaine, but she just couldn't do it. There was something about the intentionality and the drama of the whole thing that couldn't be interrupted—even by an SOS text. Holly didn't feel like she was in danger—at least not yet. But she paused before proceeding, long enough to wonder if the mastermind behind all this was in danger of heartbreak.

"Let's find out what's behind door number four," Holly whispered.

A string of white icicle lights were dropped in front of a seat in the back row of the dark theatre. A glittery, velvet bow signaled this was her assigned seat.

Holly tentatively sat down. She was the sole audience member from what she could tell. Vivaldi stopped. The string of lights dimmed. Now things were getting a little eerie. She slowly reached inside her purse to locate both her phone and pepper spray, if need be.

The screen in front of her came to life. During store hours, three different movies were shown here on rotation throughout the day: the history of the store, the life story of its founder (Frank's great-grandpa), and the making of the Stille Nacht Sanctuary. During her training, Holly had seen them all. She wondered which one would play now.

It wasn't any of them.

There on the ginormous screen was the man who was off limits to Holly for many reasons. His gorgeous eyes were seemingly fixed on hers as he spoke from his heart:

> "I realize this might be a bit of a shock to you—but don't worry, I didn't break in here. It was basically an inside job. As you can probably tell, this took some work. But you're worth it. And I hope you think I am, too. This might seem like a grandiose way to tell you so, but I think—and hope—that this is what you want, too.
>
> It's a fresh start. A new definition to our relationship, if you're on board. And I hope you are. Because you're amazing. Sometimes I don't think you realize it. I wish you could see yourself like everyone else does. You don't have to have it all figured out. And I don't have it all figured out, but...I guess what I'm saying is, will you take this next step with me?"

Holly wasn't sure she had breathed at all during the movie. She definitely had not moved a muscle, except her mind was racing faster than a horse favored to win the Triple Crown.

She had half-expected to find Frank in the theatre, trying to seal the deal on the carriage ride. Never in a million years did she expect to see Nik projected in megapixels, professing his love for her.

Had he and Lena broken up? He sure didn't waste any time.

While she was trying to make sense of what had just happened, the screen rose and Nik's silhouette appeared behind it.

He dropped to his knee, and shouted to the lone audience member in the dark theatre, "Will you marry me?"

Holly gasped.

From his chivalrous posture, Nik's eyes adjusted to the light change, and all of the sudden he looked like a deer in the headlights.

"Holly? What are you doing here?!"

"What am *I* doing here? I should ask you the same thing!"

"I guess you have a point there...you're usually here, and I'm hardly ever here. But Frank helped me put this plan together to propose."

"Frank was in on this?"

"Are you surprised?"

"Surprised that Frank was an accomplice or surprised by the proposal?"

"Oh! Oh, gosh! This wasn't for you. It was for Lena. What kind of guy do you think I am?"

His words broke the dam on the secret Holly had been keeping. "You're a criminal!" she blurted out.

"Since when has trying to love someone been a crime?"

Nik shouted back.

"Your aunt told me you were released from Leavenworth. I've kept it to myself until now. But you already know anyway, so I guess it's still a secret, kind of. What do you have to say about that?" she challenged.

"About her confiding in you?"

"No, about Leavenworth," clarified Holly.

"What does that have to do with this?" Nik responded, apparently confused.

"Don't you think that affects a relationship with someone trying to run a nonprofit for kids?"

"I hoped it wouldn't." Nik's clear eyes avoided eye contact for the first time that evening.

"Well, it's a big deal in my book."

"I'm sorry you feel that way, Holly."

"What did you do, anyway? I guess it's not my business, but now that you've proposed, I guess it's more my business now that it's ever been."

"I was proposing to Lena, but you showed up in her place."

The two of them locked gazes, trying to read the moment through the lens of their charged emotions.

"You really want to know, huh?"

"Yes."

"Well, everything I worked for was taken from me after a confrontation went south. I didn't know what hit me. I guess I should have read the writing on the wall, but I didn't see it coming until it was too late."

"What…a stray bullet? A drug bust gone bad? A heist?"

"What are you talking about? None of the above. I was

working my way up in a major tourist corporation out west, when…"

"I'm not sure I'd call Kansas 'out west,' exactly."

"Kansas? No. I was working in Leavenworth, Washington, when one of the higher ups at the company called me into a meeting. Apparently I hadn't been filling out part of our contracts correctly, and the company lost money because of it. But the guy who trained me never taught me how. Turns out he didn't have much integrity, but it was too late—the damage was done. They let me go. Released me from my job."

"Washington?"

"Yes, that's what I said. Leavenworth, Washington. The town that looks a lot like Bavarian Falls, in all her themed glory."

Holly's jaw was on the floor, her eyes as wide as her mother's fine china platter reserved for the main holiday dish. And she was beginning to feel like the Thanksgiving turkey.

"What did you *think* happened?"

Dumbfounded that she had been wrong about Nik the whole time, Holly managed to fumble over a few words. "I…I…gosh, this is going to sound awful. See, based on what your aunt said—about you being released from Leavenworth and it being difficult—I thought you had been a military criminal at Leavenworth, the U.S. Penitentiary in Kansas."

"What?" Nik sounded flabbergasted by Holly's admission. "Why on earth would you think that?"

Holly busily replayed the last six weeks in her mind—their interactions at church, Music Keys, the ride to her house, sitting around her kitchen table eating dessert, the concert, Thanksgiving Day in her driveway, working side by side on

Black Friday, their conversation at the Christmas party, and now, this moment when he had proposed—accidentally—to her.

She rolled up the guarded armor around her exposed heart, trying to assemble any ounce of dignity she could muster after her outburst.

This straight-out-of-a-Christmas-rom-com proposal hadn't been for her. It was intended for Lena: his successful, beautiful girlfriend. The one who was not standing under a thousand sparkly lights, with her favorite classical music sweeping overhead while her really good-looking, non-criminal boyfriend asked her to be his wife. Of course it hadn't been for her—the stuck-in-her-childhood-bedroom, working-at-a-temp-job-in-her-30's, plain old Holly.

The rest of the evening happened in fast forward. The ring was returned to Nik's pocket. The key was returned to Baby Jesus #1. The oversized emotions were packed away in a suitcase that wouldn't close entirely.

It was all a big misunderstanding—Holly's wrong assumption about Nik's past, and his accidental proposal to her. In hindsight, she should have just unlocked the door and left. Curiosity has been known to kill the cat, but in this case, it led to an endearing proposal—meant for someone else.

After a few frantic texts with Frank, Holly uncovered more evidence for the truth. She was supposed to unlock the door for Lena, who was coming to meet Nik at Neumann's. Nik's "story" to Lena was that he was having car trouble and needed her to come rescue him. The idea was that Lena would enter the store, complete the Scavenger Hunt, and become a fiancée by the end of the evening.

Apparently, Lena, like Frank, had gotten held up at work with a pressing issue of her own and couldn't get away to meet Nik. She had tried to text, but his phone was on airplane mode so it wouldn't make any noise while he hid behind the movie screen, waiting for her. The last he knew, Lena was on her way. He had no idea Holly would be the one sitting in the back of the theatre—the unexpected recipient of his lavish display of affection.

Holly hurried to her concealed vehicle, trying to put emotional and physical distance between herself and Nik after the major mix-up. She kept replaying the strange turn of events in her mind. She tried to think of anything else, but was drawn back like a magnet to a fridge. There was something in her that wished someone like Nik would care enough about her to actually propose in such a thoughtful way. But the only guy she seemed to be able to attract was quirky and entirely devoted to staying put. Not that he was a bad guy, but Frank was not a solution to Holly's bigger life problem. She had reverted back to her twenties in nearly every way. She wanted a guy who would take her seriously; one whom she could dream with and confide in. She wanted someone who would help her move forward and who she could love with her whole heart.

Holly wondered how she was supposed to act normally around her parents after this debacle, and where in the world was she going to start the narrative with Elaine.

In her not-yet-warmed-up car, she chose to laugh instead of cry.

What a ride.

* ✳ *

When Holly arrived at work the next day, she felt as if she was being watched—not from the security cameras, but from the thousands of white lights that served as witness to the previous night's bizarre experience. She felt like everyone knew...but how could they? She had only told Elaine, and she was pretty sure Nik wasn't going to leak it to the local newspaper.

If he did, she could picture the headlines:

> *The Case of the Christmas Store Caper Solved by Local Sleuth*
>
> *Hometown Holly Accidentally Proposed to Days Before Her 33rd Birthday*
>
> *She Thought He was an Ex-con, He Thought She was His Girlfriend*

With only a few days until Christmas, the procrastinators were on the prowl for the perfect gift—or any gift, really—for their loved ones. The customer flow had slowed down at Station 8, as people realized they'd probably missed their window to get their personalized orders back on time.

"You look different," observed Andy. "Did you get your hair cut or something?"

"Nope," responded Holly, wondering how he could tell something was up.

"Different makeup?"

"Same old, same old." Holly's blush deepened as she tried harder to convince Andy nothing had changed.

"So what's up with all the lights? You think an elf made a late night visit?

Warmer.

This was going to be a long morning. Holly decided she'd better change the subject before Andy discovered she almost became a bride-to-be after hours at Neumann's.

"Do you have Oliver for Christmas?" She prayed he did, otherwise she'd feel like a jerk for bringing up a sore subject. She was desperate to divert the curious sleuth.

"Actually, I do. Bill is taking Tammy to meet his extended family down in Kentucky. They thought it'd be better if Oliver had a more low-key Christmas, and I agreed."

"I'm glad to hear that. About you and Oliver."

"Did you color your hair?" asked Andy, insistent on figuring out what had shifted.

"I'm pretty sure that's not a question you should ask a woman."

The guy who had poor timing the night before had comedic timing today. Nik approached the counter.

"Hi," he offered.

"Hey," Holly replied.

Andy tried to jump in but soon realized he was a third wheel of sorts, so he busied himself by announcing an impromptu errand near Teresa's station.

Alone momentarily, Nik started in. "So look, last night was really weird. I'm sorry you got brought into it. That had to be quite the shock."

"You proposing to me, or me finding out you're not really the criminal I had you pegged for?"

Nik scratched his head. "Just to make sure we're clear, I

wasn't proposing to you, but to Lena…well, imaginary Lena, who was supposed to be there."

"Oh yeah, that's what I meant. And yup, loud and clear…I'm very aware that you were not proposing to me."

Holly couldn't help but feel a slight sting of rejection. It was as close as she had come to being the recipient of a marriage proposal, even though it hadn't been intended for her. She understood Nik wanting to clear the air, but the way that he was overemphasizing that she was *not* the object of his affection felt like being picked last in gym class.

He was watching her, and just to be sure he couldn't read her thoughts, she turned things on him.

"About the criminal thing…I'm truly sorry. It's just that the way your aunt said you were released from Leavenworth only meant one thing in my mind."

"You didn't automatically think of the charming village in the Pacific Northwest? My family vacationed there a lot when I was growing up. We moved around quite a bit when I was a kid, but Leavenworth was a constant. I guess that's what drew me to find a permanent job there—well, it was supposed to be permanent."

"The only association my family has with Leavenworth is my dad's experience transporting military prisoners in Kansas."

Just then Frank walked up. "What did I miss, an inside joke?"

"More like an inside job!" laughed Nik.

Holly joined him. It was a relief to know Nik wasn't living a double life.

They brought Frank up to speed on what went down when he sent Holly in his place to unlock the showroom.

As Nik recounted what happened, Holly couldn't help but analyze Frank's nonverbal reaction. Was that jealousy she saw flash across his face, or just a general disbelief in what transpired?

"That's wild, man! Sorry I wasn't able to do my part like we talked about."

"No worries," he assured Frank. "We sorted it out, didn't we Holly?"

"We did," agreed Holly, wondering why she felt that sting again.

"Thanks again for letting me use the store, even though it turned out differently than we dreamed up."

"We?" asked Holly.

"Oh yeah," answered Nik. "Frank and I plotted out the whole thing over chips and queso at the pub."

"I swung by here to finish plotting my course with Frank, when you, Andy, and I had our encounter with wise old Santa."

"About last night…I've been thinking. Why didn't you just leave the door unlocked, since you were already inside?" asked Holly.

"To avoid something like what happened," interrupted Frank. "Nik didn't want to accidentally propose to Betty Jo or anyone else, so I locked him in when I left work. That gave him time to set up the Scavenger Hunt without any accidental visitors. I was supposed to come back to unlock the west entrance so Lena would enter there and see the first clue. I was scheduled to arrive ten minutes before she did so I could get out of there before she suspected anything."

"But you sent me," stated Holly.

"That I did."

"Hey, it's been real guys, but I've gotta get over to the Eatery. Lena's meeting me there. She insists they have the best chili in town. Time to fess up to the proposal fiasco before she reads about it in the paper." He winked at Holly.

Maybe the newspaper headline would read: *Holly Brigham Unlocks Love Only to Find Out It Wasn't Meant for Her.*

"So now that I have you all to myself," teased Frank, "you still going to be around at the end of January?"

"No offense, but I hope not."

"Well, just in case you are, what do ya say to joining me as a judge for the ice-sculpting contest?"

"That'd be fun, but like I said, I'll probably be gone by then."

"Well, Bavarian Falls won't be the same without you. And Neumann's definitely won't look as spectacular in your absence."

"Aw, shucks. How will I go on without these 'frank' conversations?" laughed Holly.

"I have no idea." With a wink and a surprisingly coordinated pivot, Frank headed toward his office.

CHAPTER 16

Papa's Got a Brand New Band

HOLLY DECIDED AGAINST KARAOKE AT KLINGEMANN'S on Friday. She wasn't physically sick, which was the only thing that typically kept her away, but she was tired from the long days at work and the focus required to keep her brushstrokes steady and names spelled correctly. Who knew there were so many ways to spell names like Hailey, Haley, Hayley, Haleigh, Haylee, Hallie, or Alicia, Alecia, Alesia, Aleesha, Alisha, Alicea. Holly had seen them all.

But even more than that, she didn't want to risk seeing Nik again after the mix-up. Or see him and Lena singing a power ballad love song while she ate humble pie. Although she couldn't quite imagine Nik and Lena gazing in each other's eyes and singing a power ballad together...that was more Frank's style.

Holly had filled Elaine in on everything that happened

the night of the accidental engagement, so Elaine was understanding when Holly opted out of karaoke.

Holly slept in on Saturday, waking up from the weirdest dream about a bachelorette-style show where Betty Jo was trying to find a date for the work Christmas party. She had to choose from a room full of graduates from the Kris Kringle Academy. They tried to impress her with their belly laughs and reindeer handling skills, and they took turns performing a sign language piece set to their favorite Christmas song—kind of like the Happy Hands' Club, from *Napoleon Dynamite*.

I need to lay off the late night cookies and milk routine before bed. It's causing me to identify too closely with Santa. Mental note: I should probably join the gym again in the New Year. My metabolism is bound to slow down the closer I get to 40.

Holly climbed out of bed and stretched. She noticed her binder from counseling on her nightstand and slid it into the drawer. The last thing she wanted was her mom seeing it, then having to talk to her about it.

Holly had an early afternoon meeting at Music Keys, then she'd promised her mom she'd go with her to purchase the paint for the Fellowship Hall painting project at church. Anna wanted her artistic daughter handy to confirm she'd made the right selection.

It would've been more appealing to fill the time with mindless scrolling on her phone or to paint along with Bob Ross as she watched his old videos, like she used to do at Grandma Bea's. But as her birthday drew near, Holly felt an urgency to deal with her stuff. At the first counseling appointment, they'd surveyed a chunk of the iceberg, but there was more to address below the surface. So she pulled out the exercise that her counselor had suggested, about burying what was and accepting what is when it came to her dad.

Here goes nothing.

Holly's counselor had encouraged her to make the assignment her own and do what felt meaningful to her. So Holly reached for her charcoal pencils and started sketching. Three separate images came to mind as she thought about the things she missed most about her dad.

The first was of her dancing with him before everything changed. Memories of attending a Daddy-Daughter dance together when she was Claudia's age filled her mind and poured onto the page. Her head was tilted back, and she was giggling. He looked down at her with a smile. Her feet were on his as they swayed to the music.

I miss this, Dad.

It wasn't just the dancing; it was more than that. The sketch represented a carefree moment before the heaviness fell.

The next sketch was of her mom playing the piano while her dad stood next to her, his trumpet to his lips. They were rehearsing for the Christmas cantata at church. Next to them Holly was painting at a plastic easel. Gabe lay on the floor playing with his action figures and a wooden Nativity set, having an epic battle of some kind. This sketch was a snapshot of tradition and togetherness, of warmth and simplicity.

I'm saying goodbye to this, too. Not forgetting it, but realizing this storybook image is not a part of our present reality. You're different, Dad. It's not your fault. And it's not ours, either. Something awful happened, and in many ways we're still removing the shrapnel. I'll constantly be frustrated and distant if I keep willing you to return to the way you were before. I want to accept you as you are now, instead of resenting what I no longer have.

The last sketch was of a young bride, with a not-quite-as-messy-as-usual bun piled on top of her head. She was standing at the back of the sanctuary at St. Schäfer's, a simple veil cascading down over her elegant, non-fussy wedding gown. Her strong dad stood with his hand on her back, whispering his best advice for the moment she had been dreaming about since she was a little girl.

I'm saying goodbye to what I planned on. Being married before I was thirty and you returning to your pre-aneurysm mind and body. Maybe I'll get married someday and you'll be there to give me away. But it won't look like this. I want to have the courage to sketch a new image instead of fixating on the one I thought was guaranteed. I need to let us both off the hook. Sometimes we can't make things happen, no matter how much we wish, hope, and pray for them.

After the last bit of shading was complete, Holly lined up the sketches on her windowsill. She pretended she was at the Chicago Art Institute, standing before a complex piece, evaluating each element and allowing herself to feel the artist's intention. Each stroke, each detail, each emotion. She let herself feel it all.

And when she couldn't take it in anymore, she knew it was time to do the next step.

With trembling hands, she ripped each sketch, straight down the middle, signifying the breaking of her heart, as she acknowledged what needed to be buried. It wasn't hope she was splitting; it was her bitterness, her expectations, and her presumed right to normalcy. As she tore the strips of paper, she could feel the tug and release on her heart.

She placed the papers in a shoebox and taped down the lid. There was too much snow on the ground to bury it now, so she put it away. The act of closing the top of the box ushered in sharp tears—but they were cleansing tears. She had finally faced that which held her down—not partially, but fully. Sure, there might be times where she had to address more. But for now, she knew she had done the hard work she'd been avoiding for years. And she felt more settled than she had in a long time.

After showering and throwing on her comfy gray sweater and stretchy black jeans, Holly headed to the kitchen. Mom had left a note on the fridge in her near-perfect cursive:

Holly:

At the North Star Elementary Craft Show. See you at 2 at the paint store. Walt is coming to pick up Dad for the day around 12:30. Can you make sure he's ready? Thanks!

Love you always, Mom

Holly had to smile. Leave it to her mom to write handwritten notes instead of texting on her phone. She groaned outwardly but secretly thought it was endearing. When she was in elementary school, her mom snuck notes into her lunchbox. She ended them with her signature "I love you to pieces," but in place of the word "pieces," she drew puzzle pieces. Over the years her mom had changed it to, "Love you always."

Holly devoured some hummus, pita crackers, and carrots, trying to counter her bad habit of late night sugary snacking. Afterwards she checked to see if her dad was ready to leave.

"Hey, Dad." She walked into the den as he was struggling to get his shoe on. "Need some help?"

It was the first time seeing her dad post-counseling-exercise, and while the familiar heaviness threatened to resurface, she took a deep breath and reminded herself of what was true. Her dad had a brain injury. He had limitations, but he was alive and was doing the best he could, given the circumstances.

She focused on helping him then went and grabbed his cane. He despised having to depend on it, but it helped steady him and prevent falls.

"Thank you for the help with the sha-shoes, not cane," he smiled.

That's where Gabe gets it from.

"Walt should be here soon," Holly said. "But I wanted to say something."

Her dad waited.

"I'm sorry." She tried to think of a way to explain more, but she didn't know how to say it without hurting him or it sounding weird.

Her dad seemed to understand all she was saying with her "I'm sorry."

"Me too, Hol-ly."

And that was enough. A line in the sand between her past expectations and her new acceptance.

A loud *honk, honk* came from the driveway. Walt had arrived.

After her dad was on his way, she ran back into the house to get her notebook and purse for her meeting at Music Keys. As she passed the den on her way out the door, something caught her attention. She usually didn't pay much attention to it, but in that moment, her dad's trumpet, displayed on top of the built-in bookshelf, gleamed a little brighter.

She thought back to the sketch of her family around the piano and Dad's confident stance as he let the notes soar to the festive tune.

That's it! That's the missing piece! Hallelujah, a divine download in the nick of time!

Holly carefully grabbed the trumpet and dashed out the door.

What should have been a fifteen-minute drive took only ten. An out-of-breath Holly proudly set her dad's prized trumpet on the table at the meeting with Lena and Elaine.

"What's that?" asked Elaine.

"A trumpet, obviously…and a lovely one at that," answered Lena before adding, "No offense, Holly, but what does that have to do with the issue at hand?"

"Everything," beamed Holly.

The memory of her dad practicing the trumpet had reminded her that her dad used to play in a small band with Walt, the mayor, and Pastor Meyer. They had each served in the military in some capacity and used to play at churches, nursing homes, and local parades. After Dad's incident, the band disassembled and hadn't played together since.

"I haven't heard my dad play in years…but what if we could get the band back together and have them accompany the clients on one of the carols on the album, like, 'Hark! The Herald Angels Sing?'"

"Hmmm. It's an interesting idea for sure. Do you think they'd do it? And pardon me for asking, but do they still have what it takes?" queried Lena.

"I'm counting on it," stated Holly, trying to silence any doubts.

Elaine backed up her friend. "I think it's genius!"

"It's definitely intriguing. We don't have much time, though. Can you jumpstart this and report back?" asked Lena.

"You got it. In fact, my dad and Walt are together right now, so I'll go ask them. Elaine, can you ask the mayor? My mom and I are going to drop paint off at St. Schäfer's later today, so I'll talk to Pastor Meyer then."

"Great, text me to let me know what you find out. Rehearsals will need to be scheduled for early next week. The singers' recording time is scheduled for next Saturday, so we need to record with the band by Friday. Time is of the essence!"

"You got it, boss!" Elaine replied.

"I hope this works out. Not only will it meet the grant requirement, but it'll be really special, too." Lena looked at Holly with empathy.

"Yes, it will."

After all the emotional energy Holly had spent already, she hoped that this idea was not one of wishful thinking. She prayed it was a part of new memories with her dad.

A half-hour later, Holly received a text from Elaine:

The mayor is in! What'd u find out?

> Shopping for paint w/ Mom. I'll let you know as soon as I know.

Sounds good.

Another text came through from Elaine:

BTW, guess who came to the Inn last night?

> Our favorite celebrity?

Nope. The power couple of Bavarian Falls.

> Betty Jo and Santa Claus #4?

Nope. Guess again.

> Nik and Lena?

Winner, winner, chicken dinner.

> Andy gave them his reservation.

Things didn't go well.

> ?

Couldn't help but overhear their argument. Sounds like he's tried to be patient with Music Keys but feels pushed to the side.

> Wow.

Didn't sound like it was the first time they'd had this fight. Looked like Lena got a work-related call during dinner. She walked out to talk and didn't come back for a long time.

> Whoa.

Yeah, poor Nik just sat there with his half-eaten meal.

> For how long?

I tried not to spy on him, but being their server, it came with the territory. He was there for a while before she came back. It looked like he was asking her to stay but she shook her head and left.

That's too bad.

Yeah, trouble in paradise. It's great what Lena's doing with Music Keys, but it might come with a bigger cost than expected.

Think they'll work it out?

Time will tell. Gotta get back to work. Talk later.

K, bye.

Holly slid her phone into her pocket. She wrangled her thoughts away from the overanalyzing zone with regard to her text exchange with Elaine. But she couldn't deny how her heart had leapt at the thought that Nik and Lena might not be a permanent fixture.

Holly and her mom had finally checked out at the paint store after *much* deliberation about which base paint brand was best. She'd not-so-patiently held off on sharing her idea until she had her mom's full attention. As they drove over to St. Schäfer's to give the paint to the pastor's wife, Holly took the plunge. She shared a condensed version of her sketch experience that had been encouraged by her counselor, omitting the first and last sketch and only telling her mom about the trumpet one. Holly went on to describe her idea about the military band reunion.

"So you're in counseling, huh? How long?"

"Mom, I wasn't going to tell you…not yet. I've only had one appointment. Although it feels like five because it was so helpful." Holly anticipated a lecture or a series of pressing questions next, but her mom surprised her.

"I'm glad. That couldn't have been easy…the decision to go or the sketch exercise. I'm proud of you. Always." Anna made eye contact with her grown daughter, as if willing her words to express the full weight of her adoration.

Holly tried to let her protective wall down and receive her mom's words at a deeper level.

"Now about that band idea…"

Here we go, thought Holly. *The caveat.*

"Go ahead, tell me what's wrong with it," muttered Holly.

"It's actually a wonderful idea. Your dad doesn't quite have the skills he used to, which is why he's never had the courage to initiate the band getting back together. But he practices on and off when no one is around but me. He says it reminds him of the good old days. Like I said, he's not as polished or quick with his instrument as before, but Holly, I'm telling you, he's still got the basics. And the look on his face when he plays is something to behold."

"I'm so glad to hear that."

They pulled up to St. Schäfer's and carried in the paint.

"While you and Mrs. Meyer duke it out over this, I'm going to go convince Pastor Meyer to join the ranks."

"Good luck!"

"Thanks." Holly squeezed her mom's hand.

After explaining the time-sensitive request, Pastor Meyer agreed.

"It's a busy time of year, but if your dad and the others guys are in, so am I. Better go practice my French horn. It's been awhile. We can host rehearsal at my place. Ingrid can go shopping if the noise bothers her. I'm sure she won't mind— shopping is her spiritual gift," chuckled the pastor.

"I can't thank you enough. Now I'm off to get Walt and Dad on board. See you tomorrow!"

Holly left her mom working at the church while she drove over to Walt's place. After several rings of the doorbell, there was no answer. Dad had a cell phone but wasn't swift to pick it up and was slow to talk, so she called Walt. He told her they were over at the soup kitchen serving dinner.

Holly headed that way, anxious to get things underway and hopefully send a successful report to Elaine and Lena. It felt like her big moment to shine under the floodlights that seemed to follow Lena wherever she went. Holly's solution could save the grant and help Chase and the other clients finish the album project in time.

Holly walked into the crowded soup kitchen and scanned the room for her dad and Walt. There in the middle of the action was Nik, laughing with an elderly couple as he wiped down the table next to them. Apparently Dad and Walt weren't the only ones volunteering that day.

Walt and Dad roped Holly into helping for the last few minutes of the meal. Afterwards they all grabbed a bowl of broccoli cheese soup and sat down for a quick bite before leaving. Partway through Holly's appeal to get the band back together, Nik walked up.

"Mind if I crash the party?" he asked.

"Not at all," said Walt. "Holly was just telling us about her plan to save the grant at Music Keys."

"Well, it looks like I'm right on time," he smiled.

Holly did her best to stay focused on laying out the plan in spite of handsome Nik, Lena's *boyfriend,* who was a captive audience member.

"I don't know, I'm not s-s-s-oo good at playing any-any-more," her Dad responded after hearing her grand scheme.

"Well, Mom said you've still got it. And you and I both know she wouldn't just say that if it weren't true."

"I think it's a great idea," added Walt.

"Me too," assured Nik. "In fact, I may have played trumpet in the jazz band at college. I'd be happy to help you brush up, Carl, if you'd like."

"Is there anything you don't do?" Holly asked, impressed by his breadth of skills and how he generously spent his time helping others.

Nik quirked a smile that made Holly feel like the only one in the room. She put a hand on the table to steady herself.

"Well, I'm lousy at euchre and terrible at drawing, if that counts for anything," Nik laughed.

"Not good at euchre? That's unacceptable, young man," scolded Walt.

"I'm not a fan of it either," whispered Holly. "But don't tell anyone…I don't want to be written out of the inheritance."

"I huh-huh-heard that."

"I think between us we can help you improve upon your weaknesses. I'll teach you to love euchre, and Holly can teach you how to draw the best stick people you've ever seen," reasoned Walt.

"I appreciate the offer, but I think I'll stick with what I'm good at. Now, when can we schedule that tune up, Carl? Lena's got an album to record."

"Yes she does." Holly jumped up from the table. "Are you sure you have time, though?"

Good gracious, she sounded like her mother scolding her for overcommitting. Nik studied Holly for a moment and she tried not to squirm under the examination.

Nik grinned and patted Carl's back. "I think I can make the time for this."

Holly breathed a sigh of relief. "If you guys can work that out, I'll text Elaine and Lena with the good news. I've gotta go pick up Mom before she lets Mrs. Meyer talk her out of the paint color for the fellowship hall."

"Run along now," instructed Walt. "I'll bring your dad back after dinner."

Holly headed out the double doors toward her car.

"Hey, can we talk for a second?" Nik ran up to her. His coat was unzipped and his white serving apron was still tied around his waist.

"Sure, what's up?"

"Remember how I told you I was trying to figure out my next steps and you said I was probably too busy for that because I was filling my days with all this volunteering?"

"Well, I don't remember saying it like that exactly, but I think that was the gist."

"Here's the thing. You were right to ask me if I had time to help your dad. Ever since we talked about it at the party, I've been thinking about what you said. I've been trying to do everything and be everything for other people. I so want things to work out here and not turn out like they did in Leavenworth…"

At the mention of that town, Nik smirked and Holly lifted her arms halfway in surrender.

"Don't worry, I know—the town, not the prison."

"Glad we got that cleared up. So like I was saying, I haven't taken the time to really sort things out after everything went down in Leavenworth. That's why I moved here—well, that and to help Aunt Claire and to be closer to Lena. But in the process of meeting new friends and helping out around town, there hasn't really been time. Don't get me wrong, it's fulfilling to help people, but if I'm honest, I feel stuck in this pattern of overextending myself without really knowing what I want and—I don't know, you just seemed like someone who would get it…not because you don't know what you want. You seem the opposite of that, but you've mentioned feeling stuck here, and in a different way, I do, too."

"Have you talked to Lena about this?" Holly asked.

Nik looked at his feet and shoved his hands into his coat pockets. After a brief pause he confessed, "Yeah, so, we're not a thing anymore."

Holly twitched as if she had been woken abruptly. She tried to put forth her best euchre face, but again, she wasn't any good at euchre.

Why does this feel like good news? Don't smile…empathize.

"I'm sorry to hear that." She laid a sympathetic hand on his arm. *That was an appropriate response. Right?*

"Thanks. Things have been tense for weeks, but I really care about her, and after hearing Santa's advice about lavish displays of love, I thought the surprise proposal would be a good idea and help Lena and I take the next step forward, since she's been so preoccupied with Music Keys. I realize now that wasn't the way to try and patch things up. I believe in what Lena's doing and I support her, and gosh, it's a blast working with those kids, but a relationship can't work if only one person is all in."

"That's really tough."

"Y'know, I hung in there. I picked up hobbies—like

volunteering at the shelter, dressing up as an elf, and attending concerts *alone*—to try and give Lena space as she worked, and worked, and worked some more. But it became evident that this was more than just a busy season. The bottom line is that Lena is more committed to her career than to a romantic relationship for now, or maybe forever…her words, not mine."

"Nik—"

"I was surprised when it hit me—what I thought was love for Lena was actually more care and admiration than it was commitment and affection."

Gulp.

"When did you realize that?" Holly managed, her voice wavering slightly.

The half grin again. *Lord, have mercy.*

"I'll have to tell you sometime, but I know you've gotta go. There's an album to record."

"Won't it be weird for you to keep helping Lena?"

"No—I mean, kind of, but I'm confident we will remain friends. In fact, we'll probably get along better this way. Besides, I'm not the type to leave someone hanging when they need help."

"Can I offer a piece of advice?" asked Holly carefully.

"Of course."

"If you spend all your time trying to be everything to other people, you'll never really discover who you really are, on your own. Don't get me wrong…it's noble to help people out, but I wonder if you're doing so much for everyone else in an effort to avoid finding out who you really are, apart from all that."

Nik stood in silence as the smile dropped from his face.

"It's like that Jana Bonparente song lyric that's helped me so much recently: *The way to freedom is not out of reach; turn the knob, let yourself be found.*"

Nik blew out sharply, his breath condensing an airy cloud between them.

"I think you might be right," he said softly, zipping up his jacket. "It feels strange, yet also kind of nice, to be on the receiving end of someone's help. It's usually the other way around."

"It's the least I can do, since you helped me see more clearly at the Christmas party." Holly fiddled with the zipper on her jacket.

"After this album project is done, I'm going to pull back a bit and try to figure things out. Hold me to it?"

"Sure thing," agreed Holly.

They stood there in silence for a few seconds. Nik rubbed his chin like he was debating something. Holly swallowed, not sure what she wanted to come next. She really did need to go, but—

"You know what I think?"

"What's that?" Holly curled her toes in her boots.

"I think what you offer this town, and the people in it, is pretty great. They're lucky to have you here—even if it's only temporary."

Holly felt the warmth of the compliment heat her cheeks. Other people had said similar things, but it meant something more coming from Nik.

"Thanks for that."

"Of course it's your decision, but I don't think you have to leave this town to be yourself after all. I think there's more here for you than you realize."

"What do you mean?"

"Well, take Frank, for starters. He's a great guy who's obviously a big fan of yours." Nik's eyes danced.

"We're just friends. He wanted it to be more than that, but his early onset clinginess was too much. It made me feel like he wanted me to be his everything, and that felt suffocating."

"Wait, what? But you said—"

"I wanted you to think I had a boyfriend. I don't know why…maybe because I get tired of people asking why I don't have one. I thought it'd be easier to pretend I did. Not that I need a guy to be complete or anything, I just didn't expect to be single this long. Or, more than likely it was because I thought you were a dangerous criminal roaming the streets of Bavarian Falls, and I thought I might need a guard."

Nik breathed out a laugh. "Do you still feel that way?"

"I mean, you proposed to me the last time we were alone together, so I'm not sure I've let down my guard completely."

Nik laughed full and free, and Holly couldn't help laughing with him.

Standing outside together, volleying their observations about one another back and forth felt like one of the most natural things in the world, like taking your next breath or putting one foot in front of the other. Holly felt more like herself than she had since moving back to Bavarian Falls.

"Hey, it's cold and I know you have to go. But thanks for hearing me out, and for helping me see how I've been using my good deeds as a distraction from figuring things out."

"That's what friends are for."

"I'm really glad we're friends, Holly," Nik said, placing

his hand on her shoulder and giving it a squeeze through her down coat.

Even through her coat's material, Holly felt a spark of exhilaration at his tenderness. Since he had stepped closer, she caught a faint whiff of his cedar and spice cologne.

He just broke up with Lena! Simmer down, girl. Don't be the rebound girl—although Nik hardly seems like the rebound type.

Nik put his exposed hand back in his coat pocket. Holly's shoulder still felt tingly from his touch.

"You better get going."

"Right! I'm headed to church now. See you later…unless you volunteer at St. Schäfer's, too," joked Holly as she turned with a wave. She resisted the urge to turn back and see if he was watching her from the snow-covered sidewalk.

Holly drove to retrieve her mother from church with a smile on her lips. It had been quite a day. She'd been on an emotional roller coaster, but as the day leveled out she couldn't help but feeling a sense of accomplishment—a breakthrough with the pain of the past, a pivotal conversation in the present, and now a promising way forward.

Holly was grateful that she was able to help Lena and her clients. In turn, she hoped this new development of the band assembling would fulfill the military personnel inclusion for the Music Keys grant and help her dad find his footing—discovering a purpose beyond occupying his recliner and watching sports on TV.

And she wasn't disappointed that she'd be seeing more of (now single) Nik in the coming days.

CHAPTER 17

The Yes of Christmas

WITH NIK'S HELP, HOLLY'S DAD GAINED A BIT OF CONFI-dence back with his trumpet playing. It wasn't enough to win any contests, but it was sufficient for the task at hand. Upon Carl's insistence, Nik joined him and the old band members—the mayor on trombone, Pastor Meyer on French horn, and Walt on the tuba—to create a new band. Nik played the more complex descant with his trumpet while Carl offered steady undertones.

Nik's kindness and patience toward her dad—not to mention his impressive musical talent—weren't making it easy for Holly to stay in the friend zone.

Holly and Elaine provided moral support and snacks for the band as they rehearsed each evening for almost a week straight, first at the parsonage—until Mrs. Meyer couldn't stand it anymore—then in the newly painted Ethereal White fellowship hall at St. Schäfer's. The two friends weren't sure they could take one more round of "Hark! The Herald Angels Sing." Elaine said it reminded her of her band camp days when she practiced the same sixteen measures all day long, then the beats plagued her mind while she tried to sleep.

The brass quartet was now a quintet, with the addition of Nik. His skilled playing transformed the sound from mediocre to majestic. But even more so, Nik's encouragement transformed Holly's dad, as he worked hard toward the common goal. What Carl Brigham lacked in skill he made up for in heart. And Holly thought her heart might burst with joy because of it.

At their last rehearsal, Pastor Meyer insisted they take advantage of the outstanding acoustics in the church sanctuary. While Elaine helped set up chairs and music stands on the platform at the front of the sanctuary, Holly made her way to the balcony with her phone camera. The sound of brass permeated the room. Holly marveled at how it had all come together in such a short time. She zoomed in on her dad, noting his concentration and newfound confidence.

It was there, midway through the song, that Holly remembered her prayer to the rafters over a month ago: *Help my dad experience freedom.*

And he was.

He would never be the same, but he was making the most of what he had, for the good of others.

It took strength—physically and emotionally—for her dad to play his trumpet again. He didn't know it, but this step of healing was initiated because his brave daughter let him go earlier that week. It cleared the path enough for her to see the man before her now. Her dad was broken. He wasn't perfect, he sometimes got angry, but he was her dad.

When the rehearsal ended, Nik offered to close up the church for Pastor Meyer, who was running late for a dinner party at the parsonage. Holly's dad slowly closed his trumpet case, then looked from Holly to Nik and said, "Th-th-thanks for this." His few words and grateful expression spoke volumes.

Then he added, "You two ma-make a good team."

It was a six-word sentence, but coming from her dad, it sounded like a blessing.

"I think you're right, Carl," Nik agreed.

Holly nodded her approval, hoping there would be more opportunities to team up with Nik.

"It's s-s-settled then." Carl tapped his cane as if adding a period to the end of his sentence.

Her dad might never be that pillar of support, whispering timely advice in her ear on her future wedding day. But he could still play the trumpet. And he loved his daughter in his own simple way. Somehow, that was enough.

Just as Holly and Carl were making their exit to the parking lot, Nik called out, "Hey Holly, do you know where the overhead light switch is for the dome? I can't find it anywhere."

The powerful domed light that illuminated St. Schäfer's altar area was the only light still on, besides the exit signs. Holly joined Nik behind the massive altar, searching for the hidden light switch.

"Found it!" she sang.

"Oh yeah?" Nik rounded the corner to investigate.

All of a sudden everything went dark.

"Nik?!"

"I'm here," he answered. His hand cupped her elbow. "Sorry, just making sure it was the right switch," he explained. "I'm going to turn it back on now."

"You are?" Holly whispered.

"Unless you don't want me to," Nik answered. His nearness in the dark sanctuary had her feeling all sorts of mixed up.

He gently rubbed the back of her upper arm. The electricity between them was evident, even though the light switch remained in the off position.

With every ounce of restraint Holly could muster, she bravely voiced her hesitation. "Here's the thing. I don't want to be someone's Plan B. I want to be someone's one and only."

Her offering of honesty hung in the air between them as they stood inches apart.

After a few seconds, Nik responded thoughtfully, "Believe me, I understand where you're coming from."

"H-h-holly? You okay?" her dad called out.

"Yes, Dad. Just a minute!"

Holly was so caught up in the moment with Nik that she had forgotten that her dad was waiting at the exit in the dark.

Just then Nik turned the domed light back on. Holly's eyes—and heart—tried to adjust to the jolt. She felt exposed by her admission to Nik, yet glad she had laid it out there. He would have to choose which direction he was headed.

"I promise you, this wasn't a setup. I didn't know where that switch was when I asked for your help. Thanks for helping me see the light." He offered a partial smile.

Holly couldn't help but smile back, wondering if he intended the double meaning.

Recording day arrived. Cars lined the street outside of Music Keys. Inside, jitters and a pipeline of energy coursed through the building. The singers, accompanied by their parents, filled the lobby. The military band had recorded their part of the album the day before, so the instrumental track was ready for the children to add their voices.

Holly, Shayla, and Nik were there for whatever Lena needed to help make the taxing process as smooth as possible. Elaine was sorry to miss it, but hadn't been able to find anyone to cover her shift at the Inn. Shayla was tasked with vocal warm-ups, Holly was on snack duty and client relations with the parents, and Nik was in charge of making sure the kids knew when it was their turn to record. Lena and the sound engineer would be stationed in the studio, overseeing the recording process.

Holly retrieved the morning refreshments from the kitchenette. When she was about to step into the hallway, she heard a set of voices talking in hushed tones.

"Thanks for being here today." It was Lena. "It know it's a bit uncomfortable for both of us, but you're so good with these kids and it means a lot to me that you would put our differences aside to be here on the big day. You're a good guy, Nik. I'm sorry I hurt you."

"I'll be okay."

"We need to get started, but I wanted you to know that I thought I could manage a relationship and Music Keys, but it made me feel divided. Maybe my mom was right. She always wanted me to focus on one thing growing up, but I often got bored when I didn't have variety. I guess my strict upbringing is bearing its fruit, and I'm finally pleasing my mother."

"Lena, you don't have to—"

"Although, a husband and kids were part of her five-year plan for me. But that's not what I want. I'm just sorry it was at your expense that I realized that focusing on this program and these kids is fulfilling enough for me. It goes against what people expect of me, but it's what I want."

"I know."

Holly felt conflicted as she eavesdropped. Part of her wanted to keep listening, and another part wanted to make sure the kids got their snacks before the recording started. And who was she kidding? She wanted to make sure Nik was okay as she passed by.

She cleared her throat as she walked out the door of the kitchenette.

Nik looked like he was just about to say something, but stopped when he saw her.

"Holly, thank you so much for your help today. Let's get things started, shall we?" announced Lena.

"We shall," agreed Nik as he headed down the hall between Lena and Holly. Once he reached the lobby, he walked over to Chase, offering a high five.

"It's go time!"

Chase responded, "Yup-uh."

After donuts and fruit had been devoured and the singers had been well hydrated, Lena gave the nervous bunch a pep talk:

"This is an exciting day! You get to be a part of a real live recording session. Remember last week when we practiced using the studio microphone and how you need to be careful to not overemphasize your S's and P's?"

One little boy gave a quick nod. A little girl gave a thumbs up. Two more children nodded their heads up and down, and Chase responded with a "yup-uh." Most of the other singers showed some sign of mild distress—fingers drummed, bodies rocked. Holly would have been concerned that the recording was doomed for failure, except she knew Lena wouldn't let it. In fact, she stood at the far end of the room with her hands clasped in front of her with a radiant smile on her face.

"You're going to do just fine. Why don't we all take a deep breath? The kind that goes in through our nose and out through our toes. Ready?"

Holly joined in on the calming exercise.

"Miss Shayla is going to warm us up. Everybody stand, please—and Julie, you sit tall. Good singing posture."

The clients stood to their feet with pride and anticipation. At Lena's instruction, they began singing the title song for the album, "The Yes of Christmas," written by a local songwriter Lena had commissioned.

He is the yes of Christmas
The long-awaited one
He came down to redeem us
God's begotten Son

Jesus, Emmanuel
Sent to die for sin
He came to redeem us
And make a way to Him

The Father said, "It's time, Son"
To start the rescue plan
So He left Heav'n and went down
Took on the form of man

Jesus, our Savior
He is the Good News
He came to forgive us
And restore me and you

He is the yes of Christmas
The long-awaited One
He came down to redeem us
God's begotten Son

Jesus, we love You
The Best Gift of All
Thank You for coming
And answering the call

J-E-S-U-S, He is the yes of Christmas
J-E-S-U-S, God's one and only Son

Will you say yes this Christmas
To the long-awaited One?
He came down to redeem us
God's begotten Son...Jesus.

Since Holly had been tasked with the military personnel inclusion on the grant, she hadn't yet heard the clients sing. They were each exceptional in their own way: Tony's crooner flair, Julie's gusto, Chase's angelic voice, and the others who worked in unison to fill in the sound. They were all in, sprinkled with talent and a whole lot of enthusiasm. It was a blueprint to enlarge any Grinch's heart.

Throughout the rest of the morning and into the afternoon, the team worked together to help the kids persevere through the long day of recording. Holly had never been part of a professional recording experience before, and she was amazed at all that happened behind-the-scenes to produce a quality product.

The kids were troopers, fighting their nerves and learning (and re-learning) how close they needed to be to the microphone. At one point little Julie cried out, "Oh no! I accidentally put my lips on the wind guard of the microphone. Does that mean I kissed it? I'm not supposed to kiss any boys yet. Daddy said so."

Thoroughly amused, Nik assured her that no, her lip smack on the wind guard had not counted as her first kiss, and that she had nothing to worry about. But in five years or so, she could learn karate, at least from the waist up, so she could ward off any unwanted kisses.

He's so great with kids. That is definitely an attractive quality in a guy. As if I need any more convincing that Nik is great...and attractive.

Once recording started, each of the adult volunteers had their updated assignments: Shayla helped the kids with their vocal preparedness and tone quality, Holly served as the liaison between the lobby and studio as the students cycled in and out as needed, and Nik was resident peacekeeper, doing whatever was necessary to help the students feel comfortable, cared for, and heard. One of the kids asked incessant questions, yet Nik ever-so-patiently answered, redirected, and even turned it into a game. Lena ran the show with a color-coded spreadsheet, fancy-dancy stainless steel water bottle, and phone in hand. She was all business yet not gruff. Holly wondered how Lena kept her emotions in check under the crunch and pressure of the album project.

Highly-capable Lena still brought out her insecurities, but not quite as much as before. In fact, Holly was glad she had said yes to helping out with Music Keys, even though it would have been easier to say no.

At the end of the day, Nik walked Holly to her car and offered to scrape the snow off her windshield.

He slipped in the passenger's seat afterwards while she warmed her car.

"You have a gift with kids," Holly said. "I was so impressed with the way you helped calm them, and made them laugh, too."

"Well, I enjoyed watching you mingle with the adults and steer them away from being stage parents. You're good at rallying people together for the greater good. I've seen you do it several times. First with the military band, then with the parents today…not to mention the patient way you deal with demanding customers at work."

"Thanks," Holly said, feeling a bit self-conscious.

"Like I said before, I think there's something here for you in Bavarian Falls. Not something you have to settle for, but something that you can't find anywhere else. And I think you have something to offer this town that they can't live without, either."

Are you referring to a future for us, Nik? Or are you strictly talking about work or volunteering?

"What do you mean?"

"Well, you're obviously a talented artist, but I think it goes beyond the page. You're an artist in other ways, too… in the way you care about others, and really see them. Gosh, I sound like a mushy greeting card. I should really stop catching parts of Aunt Claire's cheesy Christmas movies."

"Thank you," Holly laughed. "Sincerely."

"Well, I gotta go. See you around, Brigham," Nik said as he exited her vehicle.

The way he called her by her last name was equal parts sports teammate greeting and adorably playful.

Tired feet and a full heart accompanied Holly on her drive home. A rousing rendition of "It's Beginning to Look a Lot Like Christmas" played through the speakers, and she didn't change the station.

✳ ✳ ✳

Back at work on Monday, Holly prepared herself for a demanding day.

Upon Andy's arrival, she noticed something different about him. His furrowed brow from the last week had all but disappeared, and he was whistling while he worked.

"Christmas come early at your house?"

"Actually, it did."

"Did you and Oliver open presents this weekend?"

"Not yet, but something pretty amazing happened."

"What?"

He glanced around to make sure whatever he was going to say wasn't overheard by the employees and early shoppers that had started filling the store.

"She said yes."

"Yeah, you told me that Tammy accepted Bill's proposal. And it looks like you're feeling better about that?"

"Let me be more specific. The 'she' is Teresa, and she said yes to the house."

Something like a squeal and gasp escaped from Andy's coworker, crowned with air fist pumps.

"This is the best news!"

"Right?"

"Tell me more. How did it all go down?"

Andy explained how he had tried to keep his distance from Teresa so as not to scare her off more, but with it being prime gift-wrapping season and his two left thumbs getting in the way one too many times, he finally made his way over to her station.

"I told Teresa that I didn't want things to be weird between us and I didn't want to risk losing her friendship, but I just couldn't shake the house idea. Then she told me she's been thinking. She said my offer was incredibly kind and unexpected…so different from anything she'd experienced before. She didn't know what to do with it—with how she was feeling or what was being offered. She said it was like her prayers were being answered, like she and her kids could have some breathing room and not have to count every penny. She admitted to me that for the first time in a long time, it seemed like stability wasn't a far off land, but within reach."

"Wow, that's poetic," interjected Holly.

Andy cleared his throat and lowered his voice. "I feel like I'm at a girl's sleepover, dishing about the latest gossip. Not usually my style."

"Oh, come on. You're getting to the good part…don't stop now," encouraged Holly.

Andy recounted the rest of his conversation with Teresa. "She said she'd never been one for spontaneity and needed time to mull things over. She thought it seemed too good to be true. I assured her that I didn't have ulterior motives and didn't want to complicate things, and that my offer for her to have the house still stood, if she wanted it."

"What happened then?" pressed a captivated Holly.

"She said she'd thought about it, talked with her kids, and thought about it some more. And as crazy as it still seemed, she decided to accept my offer."

"Well, the price was definitely right," added Holly.

"So, there you have it. You should feel lucky—I just uttered more words in five minutes than I usually speak in a whole day," concluded Andy.

"I'm glad you did. Wait until Betty Jo hears about this! You're going to tell her, aren't you?" asked Holly.

"Oh, I suppose," he shrugged.

While on a late lunch break, Andy shared the news with Betty Jo. Her knee bends and arm flaps increased in speed throughout his account, ending with her arms overhead in the victory symbol and a few slight hip shakes. The manager embodied joy from head to toe, and this moment was no exception. Once she had gathered herself, she pointed her finger right to Andy's nose. "And that's what Christmas is all about, Charlie Brown."

After lunch, Andy and Holly hunkered down like Santa's elves on a tight deadline. While Holly's hands were busy adding her artistic finesse to each piece, she felt content. Hearing

Teresa's "yes" story was the gumdrop on top of the gingerbread house. Teresa still struggled with her health issues, Andy was still divorced, her Dad was still disabled, her start-up had still flopped, and she was still single in her thirties—but that didn't mean she had to live a life of "no."

As she personalized a Nativity ornament, one particular line from the Music Keys album was stuck on repeat in her mind. It didn't let up until she paid attention to its persistent question.

Will you say yes this Christmas?

There was something about Andy's lavish gift to Teresa that made the song lyric come to life. He had put himself out there, setting himself up for rejection, forgoing his pride, in order to sacrifice for the good of his friend. He didn't force her to accept his offer. It was her choice as to whether she would say yes or not. She could walk away, misunderstanding his intention, or discarding his grand display of care. Or she could willingly accept his offer to gift her a home, with no strings attached. She didn't have to repay him, she just had to accept that which had been freely offered.

Holly could walk away. Or she could say yes. Not yes to a house, but yes to finding home wherever her feet took her… whether back to Chicago or somewhere further away, or, like Nik said, even here in Bavarian Falls, where a little bit—or a whole bunch—of Christmas was present every day of the year.

For decades she had barely tolerated Christmas but not embraced it. It felt like the holiday season had robbed her of so much, so her recompense had been to keep its joy at arm's length.

Holly knew that—barring a miracle—Dad's condition

would not change, but there was a settled feeling that took up residence within her frame now that she had stopped trying to outrun grief.

She felt good about saying yes to counseling, letting go of an unrealistic version of her dad, going to the concert with Frank, helping out at Music Keys, encouraging Betty Jo, and helping Nik figure things out. Those weren't small things, but they weren't everything. She was still holding back in some ways. She wondered what it would look like—and what it would cost her—to say a wholehearted yes this Christmas. What would she lose if she did? What would she gain? It felt easier to keep her hopes low, anticipating disappointment, instead of raising her expectations.

After some deliberation, Holly decided she was willing to say yes this Christmas. She wasn't signing up to be the next Miss Christmas Queen. It wasn't a go-tell-it-on-the-mountain yes—at least, not yet. It was a quiet yes, like when Mary pondered the mystery and majesty of the first Christmas in her heart all those years ago. Holly accepted the dare to open up her heart and hands to what might come next. She didn't do this lightly or without trepidation. It felt a little bit like signing her name to a check but letting someone else fill out the amount with whatever they saw fit. It wasn't easy, but she knew it was right.

Saying yes didn't make everything better, but it did change her perspective for the better.

CHAPTER 18

The Homing Pigeon

"I'm afraid I have some bad news," said Ms. Claire. She stood in front of Holly and Leslie, who was filling in for Andy. He had taken the day off to spend time with Oliver while Tammy and Bill were in Kentucky.

"What's that?" asked Holly.

"I think what Holly meant to say was, 'I'm so sorry to hear that. How can I be of assistance to make things right?'" coached Leslie.

Thoroughly annoyed, Holly tried again, but in her own way, "Can you tell me more, please?"

"It's the ornament."

"The one for Nik and Lena?"

"That's the one. I know you worked diligently on it. But there's something wrong."

Leslie's disapproval felt like a magnifying glass burning a

hole through an oak leaf when the sun hit it just right.

"I'd be happy to make it right, Ms. Claire. Just tell me what went wrong," responded Holly.

"More than the ornament went wrong. Their whole relationships went *poof!* Up in smoke," gestured Claire.

"What happened?" Leslie pressed.

"Something about her career being more important than their couplehood, and something about him thinking he loved her but it was actually more care than romance."

"I see."

Holly acted like this was her first time hearing the news, so she wouldn't complicate the conversation.

"So, I'm not going to need the Nik & Lena ornament anymore. But I'm still paying for it, of course."

"You don't have to do that," Holly assured her.

"Well, I am. You worked so hard on it and we had no way of knowing they'd break up before Christmas. Such a shame."

"Since you have this under control, I'm going to run over to Customer Service and make sure they're not drowning without me." Leslie jogged over to check on things.

"I'll get the ornament, just a minute."

Holly returned with the work of art, holding its satin ribbon in one hand and cupping the air beneath it with the other.

"Ooh, would you look at that? Stunning. Just stunning. You have a supernatural gift with the paintbrush."

Holly spun the ornament around slowly, admiring the beauty of what she'd produced. She had spent extra time on this one.

"Teresa can wrap it for you if you'd like. You never know, maybe they'll get back together," said Holly, trying to look on the bright side.

Ms. Claire shook her head. "No, I don't think so. It seems final."

"What makes you say that?"

She lowered her voice, even though Leslie was well across the store. "Ever since Monday night, he's been different. He was out late, was supposed to be on a date with Lena. But he said she never showed."

"Really? What happened?" offered Holly, fishing to see if Nik had told his aunt about the proposal debacle.

"I'm not entirely sure, except he said there was a misunderstanding, and he was afraid that he'd hurt one of his friend's feelings because of it. He seemed worried about that, but not just in the usual way…like there was more to it than he was telling me."

Oh, there was more to it all right. Like the shiny ring he offered me in the dark movie theatre—just a stone's throw away from where we're standing now.

Holly didn't say this out loud, of course. Instead she offered, "That's interesting."

"Word travels fast in small towns like ours. So if he's not going to tell me, I'm sure someone will soon enough. Why don't you hold on to the ornament? Maybe you could use it as part of your art portfolio? I'd hate to see it thrown away, but I don't want it around the house for Nik to find."

"That's an idea," stalled Holly, not wanting to admit that while the ornament was beautiful, she didn't want to include it in her portfolio.

"Thank you for your labor of love on this. Truly. I guess things don't always turn out like we expect."

"I know that's true."

"Elaine tells me you have a birthday coming up tomorrow?"

"That's true, too."

"On Christmas Eve, how wonderful. Any big plans?"

"I have the day off, so that's something. Took a bit of finagling, but it worked out in the end."

"Oh good. I hope you do something special. I'd say come to the Inn, but it'll be a madhouse and that's not exactly out of the ordinary for a townie like you, is it?"

Holly cringed at the term "townie." After the holiday rush, she needed to come up with a more concrete plan of escape, or her hometown was going to become her permanent residence instead of just a temporary forwarding address. Yet Nik's observation about there being more here for her kept replaying in her mind, as much as she tried to downplay it.

"I might try to get out of town for a bit tomorrow. I think a change of scenery is just what the doctor ordered."

"Well, drive safe. There'll be a travel rush on the highway." Then she added, "And watch for deer!"

Ms. Claire headed to the checkout with the receipt for the ornament she was paying for but leaving behind.

Holly placed the hand-painted "Nik & Lena" ornament in a white gift box and set it on a shelf in the supply room.

Just then Frank strolled up. "Thirty-three tomorrow! You old lady."

"Watch it, ya whippersnapper, you," threatened Holly with her best old lady impersonation and pointing finger.

"I'm terrified," mocked Frank. "Any birthday plans?"

"Besides trying to compete with Christmas Eve services,

holiday parties, family gatherings, and panicked last-minute shoppers?"

"December birthdays are tricky, huh?"

"If you want people to forget how old you are or that it's even your birthday, it works out. If you want some extra attention and a healthy fuss over you, then you're pretty much sunk," admitted Holly.

"Aren't you a delight?"

"Just call me Turkish."

"What?

"Narnia. Edmund. White Witch."

"Are you feeling okay?" asked Frank.

"I'm fine," sighed Holly. "I was just hoping for a different ending to this year. Or at least an alternate ending of sorts."

"I'm tracking with ya…like those *Choose Your Own Adventure* books, where you control how things turn out—or at least change them?"

"Those are the ones."

"If only life were like that," mused Frank.

"We definitely can't control how it all turns out, can we? Lots of twists and turns, ups and downs. But I'm learning that I can choose how I respond to that which I cannot control."

"You in counseling or something?"

"That obvious, huh?"

"Hey, I'm a fan. It helped me through Great Grandad's passing and a few other heartbreaks along the way."

Holly wondered if she'd ever been the topic of conversation at Frank's appointments, with her firm boundaries in response to his playful advances.

"Well, Holly Noel. You know I think you're pretty great.

Someday—and I predict it won't be long—some guy is going to be the luckiest around, having you for his girlfriend."

Holly resisted the urge to blow off his compliment.

"And don't worry, you've made it clear," Frank continued, "it's not me. Just think of what you're missing out on. You could have been mine—my hobby, Holly. Or should I say my Holly Hobby." He laughed with a blast, cracking himself up.

"Um, Frank, for starters…aren't Holly Hobby dolls a little—or a lot—before your time? And no offense, but you really need to work on your pickup lines. Let's just say they're a little over the top."

"Why, that's my specialty," he said with an exaggerated bow.

Upon rising, he added, "But in all seriousness, on the eve of your birthday, I think you should know how special you are."

Holly didn't know what to say.

Frank didn't let her silence mute his running commentary.

"For you," he announced, pulling an envelope from behind his back. On it was her first and middle name in fancy lettering. A realistic wreath of holly, with perfectly shaded berries, encircled her name.

"Did you do that?" Holly gasped.

"Ha! Not a chance. Leslie did it for me. She's been taking a hand lettering class online and needed the practice. I think she's trying to take over your job. Better watch out!" Frank warned her.

"Should I open it now? Or wait until tomorrow?" asked Holly.

"Your call—which reminds me, I've got to hop on a conference call! Peace out, my friend." And with that, thoughtful Frank morphed back into goofy Frank, flashing the peace sign to the almost birthday girl as he darted off.

Holly was equal parts curious and apprehensive about the envelope's contents. She decided against opening it at work.

When her shift ended, Holly decided to walk over to the Stille Nacht Sanctuary before heading home. Feeling melancholy and contemplative on the eve of her birthday, she needed some breathing room, a little sacred space to reflect.

December's blanket of white crunched beneath her fur-lined boots. As she neared her destination, her gaze followed the steeple to the inky sky.

Any chance You're gonna send that homing pigeon to show me what to do next?

Snow-laden pine trees welcomed Holly as she walked under the archway that led to the Stille Nacht Sanctuary. She passed by the wooden signs that held the first few lines of the historical carol:

Silent night, holy night.
All is calm, all is bright.

Before entering the domed chapel, Holly paused at the snowy white Nativity display.

She studied it briefly, searching for answers in the faces and postures of the lead characters. Mary knelt before the crèche with open hands, but it was Joseph that drew her in. He stood, holding a lantern in one hand and a staff in the other. His attention was fixed on the child as he watched over Him with intention.

Holly felt her heart thaw in the night air. No longer counting reasons why she hated Christmas, she decided to start counting the positive aspects of the season. Following Joseph's gaze, she located what—or Who—deserved first place.

Reason #1: The Yes of Christmas.

She had some other thoughts about what to add to the list, like cocoa at Stocking Stuffers', the upcoming Christmas sing-along at Klingemann's, and her entertaining coworkers at the mile-long Christmas store.

Just then Holly realized she was no longer counting the pain of the past; she was focusing on the joys of the present.

She continued beyond the Nativity and walked up the short set of stairs which led to the serene chapel. She pushed open the heavy door, entered the hushed space, and sat down on a wooden pew. At almost thirty-three years of age, it was tempting to focus on all she didn't have or hadn't done. Instead, she decided to appreciate what she did have and had done.

She didn't have her notepad or charcoal pencils with her, but she started mentally sketching some ideas about where she'd like to head in the New Year. She dared to hope. It felt thrilling and risky at the same time.

The door to the chapel opened, and a draft and young family blew in. Two of the kids were shouting and their mom was shushing them. The dad held the youngest one cradled in his arms, doing his best to wrangle the rambunctious crew.

No more silent night. Instead, Holly felt a renewed sense of purpose and vigor.

Twenty-four hours later, Holly was dolled up and ready for some fun. She met Elaine and Shayla downtown for a last-minute birthday outing. Lena was supposed to be there too, but canceled at the last minute, apologizing profusely for the change of plans. Holly wondered if Lena's absence was work-related or relationship-related.

The mission of the evening, as brainstormed by Elaine and approved by Holly, was to pretend they were tourists in their hometown. Elaine had gotten the idea from a book she read, in which the author stopped focusing on all that was lacking in the place she lived and instead started noticing its lovely attributes. Holly especially liked this idea in light of her epiphany in the chapel the night before.

Arriving on Main Street with a hunger—literally and figuratively—the friends were armed with fully charged cell phones so they could take a bazillion pictures. They had decided to take on the crowds and get through as many of the most popular attractions in Bavarian Falls as they could until their money, time, or patience ran out: club sandwiches at Edelweiss, a selfie in front of the Glockenspiel Clock, tortes at the Engel Haus for dessert, a few stops for souvenirs, and a walk on the covered bridge.

The laughter was frequent and the lightheartedness real as the friends pretended they were experiencing the wonder of Bavarian Falls for the first time.

Holly selected a knickknack replica of the Glockenspiel Clock as her souvenir—only after she inspected it for evidence of rats. She picked up a second one for Gabe's stocking, as a tribute to his endless childhood teasing.

The friends made it through most of their tourist list before calling it a night. It was a birthday to remember. One that hadn't passed like a blip, but had been seen, felt, and celebrated to the last tock on the clock.

Back at home, a few minutes before her birthday ended and Christmas began, Holly decided it was as good a time as any to open the envelope from Frank. She unfolded the hand-written note inside, and two tickets fell into her lap.

> To Holly Noel:
>
> Don't freak out! These aren't for us. They're for you. I'm sure you and Elaine would have fun using these, and you totally can—I'm not the boss of you—but might I suggest you wait to use these carriage ride tickets for when that special guy comes around—the lucky one you'll say "yes" to without hesitation? But again, do whatever you want. It's your special day. Happy Birthday!
>
> Your Friend,
>
> Frank (from the Falls)
>
> P.S. These expire in a year.

Holly hoped that special guy was already in her life and it was just a matter of timing.

The big hand on her oversized wall clock advanced, re-minding her that she wasn't getting any younger.

CHAPTER 19

Ice Fest

FOR THE FIRST TIME IN TWENTY-FIVE YEARS, DECEMBER 25th didn't break Holly's heart. She entered into the imperfect reality before her, not the polished version she had tried for decades to replicate.

Watching her niece, Claudia, open the artwork Holly had painted for her was a Christmas morning highlight.

"Ooh, it's so pretty! I love it, I love it, I love it!" beamed Claudia, hugging the framed treasure.

If you looked carefully, you could see the artist's signature, "Holly Noel" in the right-hand corner.

"Is this one called 'Goldendoodle topped with a mono-grammed Santa hat in front of a massive fireplace?'" asked Gabe, boasting a mischievous expression.

"You could say that," said Holly, amused with herself for capturing her niece's fondness for the breed while tapping into some inspiration from Mrs. Rasmussen.

After Mom read the account of the first Christmas in the gospel of Luke, the all-day dinner prep started for the traditional German feast. Holly persuaded her mom to include Dad and Gabe in the meal prep. They were stationed at the kitchen table, peeling apples to go into the sausage stuffing.

Mom had gotten up early to get the turkey roasting, and took it out of the oven to baste it again. Monica and Holly worked side by side prepping the red cabbage and potato dumplings.

Ding dong.

"Santa?" asked Claudia, running to the door.

"Santa already came, Sweetie. I wonder who that could be?" asked Holly's mom, wiping her hands on her festive apron before reaching for the door.

"Hi, Anna. Merry Christmas!"

There stood Nik with a gift bag and a wide smile. He offered the gift to Anna.

"From Aunt Claire. It's her famous stollen. She sends her love. She was going to drop it off herself, but I insisted. After all, I was familiar with the street where you live."

Holly, who had been watching the scene unfold, couldn't help but notice Nik's second reference to the Harry Connick Jr. song, and that he had turned his attention from her mom to her as he delivered his last sentence.

Their gaze met.

Monica whispered into Holly's ear, "Is he still taken?"

"Nope," she whispered back.

"Do come in, Nik. We're prepping for our very Bavarian Christmas dinner, but we can take a break to visit."

"Thanks, but I need to finish my deliveries for Aunt Claire and then head over to the shelter. It's my last day volunteering there."

Again Nik's gaze shifted back to Holly, a quiet knowing between them, as he made good on his decision to pull back for a while in order to figure things out.

He lingered in the doorway.

"I'll walk you to your car," announced Holly spontaneously.

She imagined her family's eyes following her every move as she grabbed her coat and headed for the door. Once outside, she closed it behind her.

"Merry Christmas, Holly."

"Fröhliche Weihnachten, Nik."

"I hope it was okay I stopped by. I know you've got plans with your family, but I wanted to talk."

"You did?"

"Listen…." He paused, looking down Kühn's Way as if trying to make up his mind about what to say next. As he turned to face her, a gust of wind swept past them. Holly tucked her flyaway hair behind her ear. Nik took a step closer as if to shield her from the wind.

The intoxicating cedar and spice scent drew Holly closer.

She looked up at Nik. "What was it you wanted to talk about?"

"Remember when I said there was a defining moment when I realized I admired Lena more than I felt drawn to her romantically?"

Holly nodded.

"Well, this is kind of embarrassing to admit. But it was

when I saw you, shocked and angry, standing there in the dark theatre, on the other end of my unsuccessful proposal."

"Really?"

"You were quite endearing, with your hands on your hips, spewing your accusations about me being a prisoner and all."

Holly looked away sheepishly.

"But it was like I could see a glimpse of what could be, if only I slowed down to really think about it, instead of filling my days with so much."

"You realized all that through my tirade?"

"Well, not right then. But it was enough to cause me to second guess the direction I was heading."

"Where are you heading now?"

"Over to Walt's to drop off his stollen…but not before I ask you something first."

"What's that?"

"Do you want to go to Ice Fest with me next month? I hear it's pretty amazing, and well, by then I think I'll have some things sorted out and—"

"Like with a group of people, or just us?" Holly interrupted.

"Well, I hear over a hundred thousand people are expected to attend this year, so we won't be alone. But, yeah, I was meaning just us."

Holly's heart thumped in her ears as she contemplated his ask.

"Holly, I promise I'm not the type of guy who moves from girl to girl. And I don't want to complicate things. But there's something drawing us closer. Don't you feel it?"

100% Nik, but you just broke up with Lena. Are you going to decide one day that what you might be feeling for me is also more care than commitment, more admiration than affection?

She tried to downplay her response and failed. "I do."

I do?! That sounds like a response to a wedding vow, not a "there's some chemistry between us" response.

"It's settled, then? One month from now, you and me at Ice Fest."

"Is that the same night of the Karaoke Contest there?"

"Could be. Are you going to enter?"

"I don't think so...I'll leave that up to Frank and Elaine. But one day I want to try my hand at ice sculpting."

"You'd be amazing at that! I'd vote for you."

"Well, I mean, I don't really know how to use those tools, and I'd have to practice, and I'm not sure I—"

Mid-sentence, as she was backpedaling from his compliment, Nik leaned closer and slowly placed his lips on her forehead, kissing her gently.

It shut her right up in the best way.

Unlike Frank's clumsy temple kiss at the concert, Nik's tenderness melted Holly like a puddle on the driveway of her childhood home.

"Nik..." Holly whispered as she placed her hands on the chest of his ski jacket. He smiled at her, resting his gloved hands on hers.

"Was that okay?"

"Yes," she said with her whole heart that Christmas morning.

Andy convinced Holly to work at Neumann's for another month. Holly figured it wouldn't hurt to earn a bit more money since her bank account was not yet fully replenished after her failed start-up. It also bought her time to formulate a specific plan of action for whatever might come next. Nik's observation from the Christmas party kept replaying in her mind: "Whether in Bavarian Falls, Chicago, or somewhere else, you are an artist, Holly. That's all there is to it." For the first time, she considered that she might not have to leave her hometown to be herself.

True to his word, Nik stopped volunteering at so many places, except for checking in with Chase from time to time at Music Keys and playing trumpet at St. Schäfer's. Pastor Meyer and Holly's dad had convinced Nik to join them as their re-united quartet played occasionally on Sunday mornings.

Holly and Nik spent some time together in the weeks between Christmas and the end of January, but it was usually in a group setting like at Klingemann's or Music Keys. They had agreed in light of Nik and Lena's recent breakup and their individual needs to sort through some pretty major things that they would wait until their Ice Fest date to define their relationship.

Nik was determined to figure out who he was apart from what everyone else wanted or expected, and Holly was determined to outline her next steps with her art and upcoming move. After that, they'd see what happened.

After a month of resisting the urge to text Nik every day, check in on what he was discovering, or make arrangements for a pre-date, Ice Fest finally arrived.

Holly took the time to curl her hair and attempt the smoky eye technique that Elaine had sent her a tutorial on. She reached for her dewy lip gloss then decided against it, in case the forehead kiss became a lip kiss.

Holly had suppressed her attraction to Nik, first because he was taken and then because she thought he was a criminal—but now that those barriers were removed, she could be honest about the way her heart beat faster whenever he was near. The truth was, the night of the romantic scavenger hunt and subsequent proposal, she had wanted it to be for her—not just because she wanted to be proposed to one day, but because Nik seemed to see right through any façade she tried to put up.

Holly didn't feel claustrophobic around Nik like she had with Frank. With Nik, there was room to dream and be herself, and to be taken seriously.

Nik picked her up right on time, after what felt like the longest month of waiting.

Holly pretended not to notice her mom peering through the transparent living room curtains as she situated herself in the passenger seat and they pulled away.

"How are you, stranger? Haven't seen or heard from you in a week or so. That's not easy to do in this zip code. Did you go rogue?"

"You could say that, I guess," said Nik, not turning toward her.

"Why so mysterious?"

"Just trying to sort things out, like we talked about."

"So are we taking this as we go, or is there a plan?"

"For the Ice Fest?"

Yes, but also for us, Nik. What's your next move? Where do we go from here?

"Sure. Where are we headed when we get there?" Holly didn't voice the questions she really wanted to ask.

"Why don't you pick, since you've been here before?"

"Nice deflection. I'll play along. How about we head to the ice sculptures first, then the snow carving section?"

"Sounds good to me."

After they found a parking spot, they walked toward the sound of the festival in full swing. Holly linked her arm in Nik's. She tried to ignore the fact that he seemed distant; she had waited too long for this date for it to disappoint.

As they made their way to the ice exhibit area, Holly attempted some small talk, but she had always been lousy at it and soon she heard herself saying, "So, do you think it will be weird if Lena sees us here tonight?"

Nik stopped so he could face her. "I took her out for brunch the other day."

Mayday! Mayday! Nik must still have feelings for Lena. Are they getting back together? Why did you untether your heart, Holly? You knew it was too good to be true.

"You did?"

His serious face phased into a hint of a smile. "She got called into an emergency business meeting before brunch was over—something to do with the album and an interview in New York. But I wanted to make sure she was okay. And I told her about our date. She seemed happy for us and said, 'I think you and Holly make a lot of sense.'"

Nik's award-winning smile replaced the subtle one he had originally offered. Holly released the breath she had been holding, filling the space between them.

"And what do you think?" Nik asked, moving his hand

from his side to her elbow.

Holly searched his eyes, looking for clues as to what he was thinking.

"I think Lena's right."

"I'm glad to hear that. Now, how 'bout that ice?" He rotated, moving his arm so it was around her shoulder as they proceeded forward.

The couple took in the masterful ice carvings. Holly was mesmerized by the iridescent light that shone through the ice. Her favorite sculpture was a large eight-point reindeer. Its crystal nose pointed to the night sky and its front right leg was poised as if it were getting ready to take a confident step into the unknown. That's how she felt, too.

The date was going well until they started watching the karaoke contest in the heated tent.

Frank and Elaine had decided to collaborate, at Holly's insistence. They were up next, primed and ready to impress the crowd with a parody of "Ice Ice Baby," followed by a moving version of "Colder Weather" by Zac Brown Band.

Right before they took the stage, Holly asked, "So, what did you figure out this last month regarding your next steps?"

"About that…you sure you want me to answer that now?" He looked toward the stage as their two friends waved to the crowd.

Holly stopped to cheer and offer a shrill whistle. "That's my girl!"

Frank, hearing Holly, offered an Elvis-style hip thrust and finger guns in her direction.

"You got this, Frank!" Nik shouted, clapping above his head in approval.

Klaus started the iconic first beats of the song as Elaine and Frank bobbed to the music.

"Last week I flew out for a job interview in Leavenworth," Nik said quietly into Holly's ear.

Wide-eyed, Holly turned to him, their faces inches apart. "You what?"

"Sorry, bad timing. I'll tell you more after this." He nodded toward the stage.

Holly felt torn. She wanted to watch her friends perform, but the bomb Nik had just dropped demanded her attention.

"I think we need to talk now," she said loudly over the booming music. The crowd was eating up Frank and Elaine's antics and adjusted lyrics to coincide with the Ice Fest.

"Okay." Nik rose, leading her out of the tent and into the brisk night air.

"Leavenworth?" Holly asked, trying to shove down the intensity of her emotions as they threatened to explode like the upcoming fireworks show.

"I didn't want to tell you because I didn't know if anything would come of it. But over this last month, I realized that I needed to try again at a different company, instead of giving up on my goals. I'd been running from what's hard instead of facing it. And I didn't want to leave loose ends, ya know?"

"Oh, I know all about facing hard things." Holly proceeded to fill in Nik on everything about her dad—what she had lost and what she had found, the counseling experiment and everything.

"Wow, Holly. That had to be so hard, but I'm proud of you."

Supercharged by her feelings, she extinguished his pleasantry with an accusation. "Well, you know what? I find it ironic that you basically told me to stay here in Bavarian Falls and figure out a way to be an artist here—that I didn't have to leave to find myself—and now you're doing exactly that… what I wanted to do for months."

"You wanted to find a job in Leavenworth?"

"Well no, but you know what I mean. It's like you left me behind and blocked me out of whatever you're doing next. I mean, I'm not your boss—or even your girlfriend—but I thought we were close, Nik. Why wouldn't you tell me?"

"I didn't want to say anything in case the job didn't pan out."

"Well, did it?"

"I'm not sure yet—which is why I hadn't told you yet."

"And if it does? Then what?"

"Holly—"

She scowled, "I've never been good at masking my real feelings. They're written all over my face."

"It's a gorgeous face, by the way."

"There you go again, charming your way into my heart."

Whoops! I just said that out loud, didn't I? How will I back track out of this one?

She crossed her arms in defiance and leaned toward him for emphasis. As she did, she nearly slipped on the icy surface as he reached to catch her. She fell into him, his strong arms holding her close.

"Those guns again! Why do you have to have such nice, strong arms?" She half-laughed, half-cried.

They stood that way for a moment. The lyrics from "Colder Weather" surged from inside the karaoke tent.

Outside the tent, they held each other in silence.

"Holly," Nik whispered into her hair, "I don't want to hurt you. But if I don't give Leavenworth another try, I'll always wonder. I don't want to live with regrets. I need to figure things out so I don't make the same mistakes again."

Holly willed herself to speak calmly, embarrassed by her explosive reaction earlier. "This decision affects more than just your future."

"I know. It's so unlike me to do something like this. But I need to figure things out so I can be a man who knows who he is, so I can better help those I care about."

"Maybe you've taken my advice to heart a little too much. I didn't know that you finding out who you really are—apart from being everything to everyone—would hurt so much."

His eyes were filled with concern. "Holly, it's not a sure thing yet. I should hear in a week or so."

"Then what? Are you going to tell me whether you get the job or not? Or are you going to keep that from me, too?"

Applause erupted from under the tent as Frank and Elaine took a bow.

"Great, we missed it!" Holly said sarcastically, gesturing toward the crowd.

Nik kept his attention on Holly, studying her.

"Holly, we don't have to miss this."

He reached to cup her face. She let him for a moment before pulling his hand down.

She stared at the icy ground beneath them.

"I don't know, Nik. I guess we'll have to see what happens next."

Holly hadn't known that her encouragement to Nik to

figure things out might mean he'd move across the country. The possibility of Nik leaving mirrored the pain of her dad leaving all those years ago…and how things were completely different after he returned. She feared that things would not be the same if or when Nik came back. After all, they hadn't really even defined their relationship yet.

Nik brought Holly in close for a hug. She wrapped her arms around him, tears stinging her face.

CHAPTER 20

Love in Bavarian Falls

One year later

FOR HOLLY NOEL BRIGHAM, TURNING THIRTY-THREE had ushered in major change, although a few things remained the same. On the night of her thirty-fourth birthday, she found herself back in her childhood room, but this time as a passing visitor.

Above the bed was a framed picture of a painted horse. A gift from Chase. As she retrieved a pair of gold hoop earrings, she smiled at the snapshot she had placed under the glass top of her antique dresser—a photo of her standing outside the Music Keys building on her first day as a paid staff member.

After the successful release of the Christmas album the previous year, complete with "The Yes of Christmas" and "Hark the Herald" accompanied by the military band, Lena Albrecht was busier than ever. The story of Music Keys and the grant project had been picked up by a national morning television program. Lena, Shayla, Chase, and his mom had been flown out to New York City and interviewed. Afterwards the album flew off the shelves, and Lena had job offers from all over the country to start branches of Music Keys in various locations. Lena was gone most of the time, flying from place to place, serving as CEO and consultant as more programs were started.

Lena appointed her accompanist, Shayla Johnson, as the director of Music Keys in Bavarian Falls so the program would continue to thrive in her absence. Shayla was an excellent choice. She was in her element working with the clients. She also had a vision to expand the local nonprofit to reach clients that weren't as musically inclined. She had been impressed with Holly's commitment to the grant project and her innovation to include the military band, so she offered Holly a job.

Holly's seasonal job at Neumann's had ended, and even though she had grown to love the staff there, she was ready to use her art degree in a more challenging capacity—although hand-painting a zillion ornaments had definitely been challenging...and pretty fulfilling, too.

Holly was flattered when Shayla offered her a position. The only problem was that staying in Bavarian Falls had definitely not been on her vision board for the future. She wrestled over the decision, talked to her counselor about it, debated about it with Elaine, prayed about it, and ultimately decided to give it a chance for a year.

Saying yes to staying meant saying no to her dreams of trying the community art space again in the city, but no wealthy Mr. Darcy lookalike had yet shown up at her door offering to serve as benefactor.

Within a few months, Holly couldn't imagine not working at Music Keys. With Shayla's encouragement, she had designed a program called Heart Turn for young people and senior citizens to come together for basic art classes. Based on her own turn of heart through the sketches that helped her process her pain with her dad, the program turned the hearts of the old and young toward one another. Holly and her dad had been brought closer through working on the album project, and now she helped different generations find a common bond through creating with one another. The young and old painted to music—everything from classical to jazz. At the end of each semester, Holly helped the clients turn their art into stationery, prints, buttons, and shirts to sell on the nonprofit's website to help fund the program.

It was fulfilling work that incorporated her art degree, her unique history, and the transformation that had taken place within her when she started living a "yes" life. It wasn't all rainbows and unicorns. Researching grants and coming up with creative ways to keep the program going was no cake walk. The pay made things tight, too. But thankfully, she had been able to afford a small apartment downtown above one of the local businesses. It was humorous that the once anti-Christmas girl's window overlooked the holiday lights and decorations that the city of Bavarian Falls displayed 365 days a year.

Bzzzt. Bzzzt.

Are u almost ready, birthday girl?

> Trying to hurry thru dinner w/ fam. Bro + crew are here too.

Tell them hi. See you at 7?

C you then! ;-)

Per usual, Claudia kept the family entertained with her antics during the family dinner. Holly's mom held her dad's hand as the couple smiled wide, enjoying the few days with the whole family under one roof.

Her mom's determination to hold her husband's hand through all the difficulty and uncertainty they had faced over the years was quite the legacy.

Holly thought back to several conversations she and her mom had had over the past year, about how there can still be good found even when there are loose ends and tension. It was similar to what Holly had walked through in counseling regarding her dad. However, her mom had helped her realize that she could live a yes life with an open heart even when things were unknown and looked differently than expected (as her mom had modeled for years). Her mom encouraged her not to give up on what might be growing between her and a special guy, even though it might be harder than she envisioned. Holly was an adult, but her mom still had some things to teach her—not always with words, but by her example. They still had misfire conversations from time to time, but in the past year mother and daughter had grown in admiration and respect for one another.

After Holly's enormous homemade chocolate chip cookie cake had been devoured and the dishes cleared from the table, Gabe asked, "Anyone up for a round of euchre?"

"On my birthday?" whined Holly.

"Wait, you don't like it?"

"Not really."

The rest of the Brigham household gasped, amazed that their blood relative had concealed her secret for so long.

"I don't even know how to process this info, sis." Gabe shook his head in mock disbelief.

"Dinner was delicious. Thank you, Mom. And the company was delightful." Auntie Holly stroked Claudia's cheek. "But now, as a thirty-four-year-old, I'm headed out for a night with my friends."

"Will *you know who* be there?" inquired Monica.

"Perhaps," added Holly before exiting the room.

Holly rounded the corner to her former place of employment on 1225 Mistletoe Trail.

Neumann's closed early on Christmas Eve, but Frank had arranged to unlock the door—making sure *not* to ask Holly—so they could gather for an after-hours birthday celebration. No scavenger hunt this time, but hot cocoa, ornament decorating (Andy had insisted it would be fun), and a movie on the big screen.

She spotted the vehicles that belonged to Shayla, Frank, and Elaine out front, and a few she didn't recognize. She headed inside, anticipating a fun evening with friends.

Harry Connick Jr.'s Christmas album blasted from the sound system. Frank was sporting an ugly Christmas sweater, replete with gaudiness, googly eyes, and tinsel. He stood next to Elaine, who had created a Pinterest-worthy mobile hot cocoa bar for the special occasion. Little buckets of crushed up mints, dark chocolate shavings, and sprinkles were ready to doctor up the drinks.

Shayla was deep in conversation with Teresa, and Andy was talking with a party guest who had traveled a great distance to be there. After a hug from Frank and an enthusiastic greeting from Elaine, Holly grabbed a steaming cup of cocoa and made her way over to Andy.

As Holly approached, she heard Andy asking, "How's it going in Leavenworth?"

"You mean the village, not the slammer, right?" clarified Nik.

"Ha ha!" Holly responded dramatically.

"It's going well. Not what I thought I'd be doing, but more fulfilling in some ways."

"You and me both," said Holly.

"That's great, man. It takes courage to put yourself out there again. Especially after you've been hurt." Andy replied from a place of understanding.

"It's good to have you back for break," added the birthday girl.

"Thank you." Nik smiled at her.

"That cocoa looks great, Holly-girl. I'm gonna go get one." Andy walked away, leaving Holly and Nik alone.

"As I recall, this was around the time I accidentally proposed to you a year ago."

"Now that was a night to remember."

"Yes it was." His voice lowered.

Frank hollered over the music, "Who's ready to paint some ornaments?"

Teresa and Andy, with cocoa in hand, had Station 8 all set

up for the fun.

"Bring back memories?" Andy retrieved Holly's apron and name tag from behind his back.

"Where did you get those?"

"Leslie was going to toss them, but I hid them from her just in case you changed your mind and came back. I know it's going well with the art program thing, but I'm still holding onto hope that you'll return. Believe me, Leslie is not as fun to work with as you were."

Holly put on her apron and name tag for the ornament activity.

"I haven't seen Betty Jo around town in a while…how's she doing?" inquired Holly.

"Well, she hasn't had much free time with the holiday rush. You haven't forgotten what that's like, have you?"

"Oh, I remember all right. My feet are tired just thinking about it."

Teresa returned from the storeroom with several boxes of ornaments to choose from. She and her children had moved into Andy and Tammy's former house at the beginning of the year. Her younger child was in one of Holly's art classes so they interacted a bit, but Teresa wasn't one for many words. She seemed content, though. Holly was thankful for that.

The rest of the friends joined them at the counter, planning out how they were going to customize their individual ornaments.

"You have an unfair advantage, Holly," accused Shayla playfully.

"She has put her time in, that's for sure," added Elaine.

"Hey, Andy and Frank have experience, too."

"Well, I'm going to be the lone man out, because my artistic expressions resemble the work of a toddler with a blindfold on," admitted Nik.

"I've seen some of your creative work before," said Holly.

"Oh yeah? When?" challenged Nik.

"An elaborate scavenger hunt with clever clues and tiny Christmas lights decoratively hung to set the mood. And let's not forget the way you encouraged my dad to offer his limited trumpet skills for the album project. That took creativity."

"Maybe a few shots of creativity, but neither of those things involved artistic painting."

"I'm going to draw a microphone on mine to signify all the good times we've had at Klingemann's," announced Elaine.

"I'm either going to attempt to paint a frankfurter, for obvious reasons, or a piece of decadent torte from the Engel Haus. To remind you of our date—I mean double date—I mean the outing with you—*and Elaine*—to the Jana Bonparente concert," stammered Frank.

"If it's not clear, we're making these for you, birthday girl, to hang on your tree," clarified Andy. "That way you can feel our love each year on your birthday and throughout the Christmas season."

"You guys are the best."

"Uh-oh…this one is already painted on," said Teresa, holding it up to get a better look.

Shayla said loudly what the other guests read silently: "Nik & Lena?"

"Where'd that come from?" a flushed Nik asked, shoving his hands in his pockets.

Teresa quickly returned the ornament to the box, embarrassed that she had caused unintentional discomfort.

"You were never supposed to see that," explained Holly, reaching for Nik's forearm. "Well, not never…but after you and Lena broke up, it was no longer applicable." She went on to explain how his Aunt Claire had saved up for and commissioned the piece, and how Holly had meant to dispose of it but had forgotten.

"I'm sorry," added Holly.

"It's okay. That was another time. It just jolted me, that's all. It's all good. Now, what are you going to paint, Monet?"

"Hmm, I was thinking of a door with a knob that has a heart on it."

"Interesting choice. Tell me more."

"Well, last year I metaphorically turned the knob to open a door that had been closed. It was my way of saying yes to Christmas and a whole lot more."

"Like the song from the album?"

"Which one, Jana's or the Music Keys one?"

"Either?"

"Well, both, really."

"You are definitely the creative type."

"Why, thank you. What are you going to attempt?" she teased.

"You'll have to wait and see," Nik replied, shielding the red ornament in front of him.

As the ornaments were drying, the party of seven moved into the dimly lit theatre. Déjà vu hit Holly as she walked in and took her seat.

"Shall I stand behind the screen again, declaring my intentions?" whispered Nik from behind her, his breath on her neck.

"Well, Lena's not here, so…." diverted Holly.

"That's history." He fell back a few steps, looking defeated. "I'm sorry, I didn't mean to—"

A bellowing voice boomed from the projector booth: "Hey guys, keep it down, the movie's about to start." Frank and his timing again.

Once Frank started the film, he joined the rest of the group in the theatre seats.

"What are we watching?" asked Shayla as the lights went out.

"If I had my way it would have been *Pepper's Mint Twist* or some other rom com, but we let the birthday girl decide," explained Elaine.

"What did ya pick?" pressed Andy.

"The original Grinch," announced Holly with a wave of her hand.

"Well played." Shayla put her stamp of approval on her choice.

"He used to be my spirit animal, until my heart grew. But I still hold affection for the green guy," explained Holly.

"True story," added Elaine, smiling at her friend.

Frank nearly did the splits trying to walk over two sets of chairs to sit between Elaine and Shayla. Andy was a few seats down in the row in front of them, with several chairs between him and Teresa. Holly sat in the back row behind Elaine, not Frank.

"Can I sit here?" asked Nik, looking a little tentative.

"Sure," answered Holly, her pulse quickening.

Over the past year she and Nik had texted and video chatted once in a while, but they'd intentionally delayed defining their relationship beyond friendship until they had time to find their footing independently. It hadn't been easy, but they felt like it was the adult thing to do—to have their eyes wide open and get to know each other better before committing to more.

About the time that the Grinch was stealing the toys out of homes, Nik turned toward Holly and asked quietly, "Can we talk for a sec?"

"Here?" she asked.

"No, out there." He nodded toward the exit.

"Um, sure."

"Shh! I love this part," said Frank.

"We'll be right back," Holly whispered to Elaine as she followed Nik out of the theatre and into the showroom.

Once they were out in the shopping area, Nik, still facing away from her, reached out his hand behind his back, offering it for Holly to take if she wanted to.

She did.

He led her over near Station 8, where the mess of art supplies was strewn about.

He turned toward her, not letting go of her hand, just rotating his so they were still touching.

"I think it was right about here that you found clue #2 in the proposal gone wrong."

"I think you're right," Holly agreed.

"But here's what I'm wondering. Do you have a clue how I feel about you?" Nik's gaze moved from their hands to her wide brown eyes.

"I think I need some more information to answer your

question," Holly replied, trying to keep her tone even.

"Hang on." He let go of her hand to grab something off the table. Her hand almost ached to be empty of his.

What is happening?

She pinched her arm with her other hand to make sure it was real.

"For you." Nik returned with his hand under a freshly painted ornament.

The words *Nik & Holly* were written in glittery silver on the red ornament. The names looked like a toddler had painted them while wearing a blindfold.

"I don't know what to say…" laughed Holly. "It's a work of art for sure."

"Holly." The way Nik said her name felt like an embrace.

Her shy eyes met his.

"Say yes?"

Gulp.

"What am I saying yes to, exactly?" She volleyed the ball back into his court.

He paused before saying, "Yes to us figuring out what's next. Yes to more of this." He held up their intertwined fingers.

Holly swallowed hard.

He looked at her name tag before looking deep into her eyes. "Holly Noel, I can't be your everything. But I'd like to be your one and only."

A lump formed in Holly's throat. She swallowed again before answering, "I'd like that very much, Nik Beckenbauer."

"Really?"

"YES!"

"Well, that's the best news I've heard all year," he beamed, wrapping his arms around her and lifting her off the ground. He spun her around slowly as her feet dangled in the air.

"I know this long-distance thing won't be easy, but we'll figure it out—*together*."

"Together. I like the sound of that," smiled Holly as a stray tear escaped down her cheek.

"Happy 34th birthday to you," Nik said, wiping her cheek gently before moving his lips to her forehead. This time he held the kiss for a while.

As his lips retreated, Holly could still feel the warmth he had left behind.

He pulled her in for an all-encompassing hug. They stood there for a few moments as time seemed to stand still.

"What now?" he asked.

Holly leaned back so she could look at her one and only.

"I was hoping for a kiss on the lips and a carriage ride. But we have to hurry because they're about to expire."

"Your lips?"

"No, the carriage ride tickets."

Holly texted Elaine while Nik grabbed their coats.

> Changing my relationship status. I'll tell u more tomorrow. Let's just say I found love in Bavarian Falls, by way of Leavenworth. We'll be back after the movie is done.

Hand in hand, the new couple left Neumann's, stopping in front of Baby Jesus #1 where Chase had been found.

There was snow beneath their feet, but no snowflakes fell from the sky. There were, however, sparks present, as Nik placed one hand on the small of Holly's back and the other at the base of her neck. He drew her mouth to his as one of her hands slid around his waist and the other instinctively reached over his shoulder. Their lips met, locked...and lingered.

Holly's heart pounded as she and Nik eventually—reluctantly—parted from their gentle yet electrifying kiss.

With a wink, Nik offered his arm to the birthday girl as they hurried to his car.

"If you decide to paint some backdrop scenery for our love story, make it Bavarian—whether from across the country or in the same town, it seems to work for us, doesn't it?"

"Mind if I add some mistletoe into the scenery?"

"Only if Holly's there, too." Nik turned to kiss his one and only again, this time even longer than before, leaving them both breathless.

Cue the idyllic snowflakes.

When they reached his car, Nik opened the car door for Holly, executing the chivalrous gesture with care and respect. It did not annoy Holly in the slightest.

As she buckled and Nik walked around to the driver's side, she had a moment to collect her thoughts. She hoped their Bavarian backdrop wouldn't have to stretch 2,167.3 miles apart for very long (she had Googled the distance between Bavarian Falls and Leavenworth). But time would tell.

For now, she was determined to enjoy each moment with this man by her side.

Soon they were driving past the Stille Nacht Sanctuary and toward downtown Bavarian Falls for a Christmas Eve carriage ride.

Holly couldn't believe this was her actual life.

ABOUT THE AUTHOR

Katie M. Reid

KATIE M. REID is the author of *Made Like Martha,* podcast host of *The Martha + Mary Show*, a singer, and a songwriter. She has a Master's Degree in Secondary Education and is a fan of hot cocoa and Christmas lights. Katie, her husband, and five children live in Michigan, where the wonder of the holiday season is never far away. Connect with Katie at katiemreid.com.

Acknowledgments

Adam: Thanks for being my one and only, and for your help with "kiss research." I know it was quite a burden—ha! Thank you for being the kind of guy who holds the door open and also makes room for my dreams.

Brooke, Kale, Banner, Isaiah, and Lark: Thanks for waiting in line for *hours* at the Santa House and going with me on roads trips for research. Your enthusiasm, ideas, and patience during this project were greatly appreciated. You are five of my favorite gifts from God. I love you more than you know!

Dad and Mom: Thank you for introducing me to the charming town of Leavenworth and for your endless encouragement.

Brian: Thanks for modeling Chase's mannerisms and his heart of gold. I love yew!

Mary: Vielen Dank (many thanks!) for your willingness to proofread and for your German language insights.

Laura and Jake: Still laughing about our rom com movie brainstorming sesh.

Martha: Your vivid testimonies about God's work draw me closer to Him. Grateful for the inspiration you provided to help Holly heal.

Jody and Hailey: Thank you for your listening ears, excitement, and feedback.

Austin: Your line made it into the book. ;-)

Riley: Thank you for telling your mama about your vision, "This is going to be big!" May you always remain dependent and sensitive to the leading of the Holy Spirit.

Holly Noel: Where would this story be without you? Thanks for being my Christmas-loving friend. You're the real deal!

Janyre Tromp: You're an incredible developmental editor. Thank you for untangling the Christmas lights when it came to editing and improving this story and for the way you helped me bring on the sparks.

Jami Amerine: Your friendship inspires me. Thank you for collaborating on this project. Your cover art and illustrations are just right. Holly would be proud.

Melinda Martin: You put me at ease with your expertise and ninja-like formatting skills. A thousand thanks!

Kate Motaung: Thank goodness for a copy editor like you—kind, knowledgeable, and skilled.

Blythe Daniel: You're a wonderful literary agent and friend. Thank you for your blessing to go for it.

Harry Connick Jr.: Grateful that your music is part of this story's soundtrack.

Jen Bleakley: Forever grateful that you introduced me to the Santas, their school, and the "hair and chair" line. Still laughing!

Jenn Hand and Niki Homan: You live a yes life. Thank you for your examples.

Dawn Funnell: Thank you for your confirmation and encouragement to keep writing and show people how to love through this message.

Abby Banfield: Thank you for reading it all, and for your encouragement and honesty.

Lee Nienhuis: Please tell me it's better than the Christmas chick flick we saw :-) P.S. Thanks for reminding me not to skip a step!

Prayer Team, Mastermind Ladies, and Ministry to Business Guide Team: Thanks for your support and accountability to keep moving forward.

Mike, Kate, and Frannie: Your faithful example sings within these pages.

Jackie Scott: Thank you for the turkey delivery inspo!

Amy Durfee: Thanks for lending me your German skills.

Robin Jones Gunn: Your fiction books are part of the backdrop in my upbringing. So grateful you paved the way (Psalm 78:6-7).

Bethany Turner: Your amazing books gave me permission to try my hand at this whole rom com world. Can Hadley Beckett send her hot cocoa recipe for Stocking Stuffers' Eatery?

Annie F. Downs: Your enthusiasm for Hallmark movies is so fun. I'm still amused by your "Love Over the Flyover States" Instagram Stories.

Amber, Bethany, Crystal, Jenn, Kate, Lisa-Jo, Mary: You are dynamos! Deepest thanks for your investment of time and your gracious endorsements.

AVBC Launch Team: What a gift you are! Beyond grateful for your enthusiasm in spreading the word and making this season bright.

Early readers: My deepest thanks to those who purchased the early edition of this manuscript. You are the tinsel on the tree. I hope you enjoy the way we decked this version.

Cast of "The Yes of Christmas" musical (from Central Church): What a joy to watch you say "yes" to Christmas through your lines, movement, and singing as you invited others to do the same.

Jesus: Thank You for saying "yes" to Christmas so You could say "yes" to the Cross. Thank You for this story and the songs. Thank You for EVERYTHING!